Coven of the Soul Sisters

Laverne Stewart

Manor House

Library and Archives Canada Cataloguing in Publication

Stewart, Laverne, author

Coven of the Soul Sisters / Laverne Stewart.

ISBN: 978-1-988058-36-8 (softcover)

ISBN: 978-1-988058-37-5 (hardcover)

I. Title.

PS8637.T494635C68 2018   C813'.6   C2018-905564-2

Printed and bound in Canada / First Edition.
Cover Design-layout / Interior-edit-layout: Michael Davie
288 pages / 71,017 words / All rights reserved.

Published Oct. 15, 2018 Manor House Publishing Inc.
452 Cottingham Crescent, Ancaster, ON, L9G 3V6
www.manor-house-publishing.com (905) 648-2193

"This project has been made possible [in part] by the Government of Canada. « *Ce projet a été rendu possible [en partie] grâce au gouvernement du Canada.*"

Funded by the Government of Canada
Financé par le gouvernement du Canada

For women who are discovering the power and sanctity of their ancient and divine feminine selves as well as their connection to Mother Earth. My prayer is that women everywhere will rediscover the power of the Crone for she is the most misunderstood aspect of the triple Goddess: the wise woman, the healer and the midwife. Arise my soul sisters and know your power. Blessed be and namaste

- Laverne Stewart

Acknowledgements

Thanks to Fr. Sean O'Laoire, spiritual director of Companions on the Journey, for helping guide me through all things Celtic and Biblical, which are referenced within. Without his support this work may very well have not happened. Also, thanks to Manor House Publishing and Michael Davie for their efforts to bring this to my readers

Foreword

I imagine that Laverne's training and experience as an investigative journalist must be a great boon to her fiction writing also because her research skills are very obvious in her novels.

She really knows her topics. In Biblical research, scholars employ three main techniques in understanding the time-of-composition of various parts of the Bible.

Historical Analysis seeks to establish the 'intent' of each writer, so as to be able to translate accurately.

Materialist Analysis looks at the social, economic, and political environments at the time of composition.

And, *Structural Analysis*, especially using the 20th-century discipline of Semiotics, tries to determine internal consistencies and inconsistencies within the texts.

Semiotics is the science of understanding the grammar, not just of individual sentences (e.g., subject, predicate, object...), but of an entire text. Texts have a natural flow and when edits or redactions are done they leave footprints in the text.

They use these techniques to align as closely as possible to the veracity and intent of the original authors. That way they have been able to both detect anachronisms and adopt the mindset of both the writers and the characters about whom they write.

Laverne is flawless in this regard – even in her use of 'foreign' languages like Abenaki and Gaelic. So, her tales are the genuine article unsullied by sloppy research. Add to that her very fertile imagination and you get a storyline and a plot which appear, at times, to be 'channeled" material!

Her ability to develop the personalities of her protagonists is delightful and the story hums along at a cracking pace. I set aside, for two days, a book I, myself, am writing because I got engrossed in her manuscript.

Moreover, she treats of real issues that need to be aired, like the treatment of 'native' peoples and the near-slave status of pre-20th century women.

You're gonna love this book!

- Fr. Seán ÓLaoire Ph.D.

Praise for Coven of the Soul Sisters

"Eloquent, well written and researched... Stewart draws you in and holds you captive. As you turn the pages you cannot help but hold your breath knowing what may lie ahead. The fictionalized account of one of the darker periods in American history seems more real than dramatized. A stunning achievement. "
- **Tracy Riva**, Midwest Book Review

''Best-selling author Laverne Stewart (*Angels and the Afterlife; Healing After Homicide, Haunted Heart*) taps into popular subject matter with *Coven of the Soul Sisters.* Her novel follows those accused of witchcraft and sentenced to death in 1690s New England, then jumps forward to current times where reincarnated victims and persecutors of the past find themselves again locked in a deadly conflict.'' - **Michael Davie**, author, Great Advice

"While I read *Coven of the Soul Sisters* I thought 'This book was almost a memory of sorts. This could have been one of my past lives.' Laverne weaves a story that brings emotions to the surface and makes you feel that you are one of characters. You just need to keep reading to see what will happen next."
- **Patti LeBlanc** Intuitive medium.

"Being of Irish decent and living in Atlantic Canada, I dove into *Coven of the Soul Sisters* with anticipation of reading a story about my people from afar and the First Nations communities that welcomed us to this beautiful land. Author, Laverne Stewart was clever to keep me wondering the country origin of the Celtic couple that boarded the ship, in the 1600's, as they fled witch hunts to find peace with relatives in the New England states of America. Curiosity taunted me to the end... «
- **Julia Bannister**, Director, Ceili Kids of Canada, English Major, Social Worker, Irish Dance Teacher

Coven of the Soul Sisters / Laverne Stewart

8

1

Hessabah Parsons, a Celtic woman, came from a long line of healers. They were hounded. They were hunted. If captured, they were tortured and executed.

It wasn't always so. For many millennia tribe members sought their wisdom in times of sorrow, sickness and the sanctity of childbirth.

Their sacred rites and rituals, passed from grandmother to mother to daughter, continued long after Christianity arrived on their north Atlantic island home. Their faith was a melding of both the old and the new.

Throughout every aspect of their lives were woven the religious, the spiritual, the mystical and the ordinary.

Over time, churches were built on top of their pagan shrines and their gods and goddesses were adopted by the Christian church and called saints.

Despite their conversion to Christianity, Hessabah's tribe continued with many of the old ways. There was a reverence for Mother Earth and an understanding they belonged to the land rather than the land belonging to them.

From the rising of the sun, to moon glow, they performed hundreds of ceremonies in everything they did.

Hessabah started her days with a blessing at the hearth of her home. "Blessed be. I will raise the hearth-fire as Mary would, the incarnation of Bridgit and of Mary. On the fire and on the floor and on the household all"

And, at night, she and all who followed the ancient ways recited a blessing as they stoked the fire.

"I will build the hearth as Mary would build it; the encompassment of Bridgit and of Mary; guarding the hearth, guarding the floor. Guarding the household all."

She was a tribal leader; revered for her knowledge of healing herbs as well as powerful crystals and gemstones. The villagers looked to her and other female sages for help from birth to the time of death and even as their bodies were prepared for the grave.

All was well with these mystic healers until the church condemned them as devil worshipers. So the healers were forced to practice their craft in private. On pain of death, they continued to birth babies, heal the wounded and care for the sick and dying.

Hessabah was one of those healers who defied the church. She knew it was wrong in its condemnation of women who practiced the ancient healing ways. If helping and healing others made her a witch, then so be it. She was not in league with the devil. She was, however, in love with nature. She revered Mother Earth for all of her beauty and power.

The festival of Samhain, celebrated at the harvest, was a time to remember the ancestors. It was one of the four Gaelic seasonal festivals, once celebrated openly, but now was done in secret.

At the time of Imbolc, from January 31 to February 1, her people celebrated the beginning of spring. It was the time when ewes gave birth to lambs and the frozen earth thawed; giving way to early blooming flowers.

Hessabah and other women gathered straw, reeds or grasses from which they made Bridgit's crosses. Hung from their homes and barns they were seen as important protection from illness and evil. Young newlyweds would place them under their mattresses to encourage fertility.

She and her clanswomen placed bowls of salt water on their hearths in hopes that Bridgit would bless it. They tied ribbons and strips of cloth on the hearth for Bridgit's blessings. Both were used throughout the year for healing.

The night before Imbolc, Hessabah, her mother, sisters, and other women gathered to make Bridgit dolls and tiny beds, which they would decorate with ribbons and flowers. The night before Imbolc they would place the dolls in their little beds before the fire. In the morning they would look in the ashes to see if there were signs of Bridgit's blessing and sometimes to see whether there were omens of what was to come for the year ahead.

The rituals of Beltane, the celebration of the beginning summer when cattle were driven out to the summer pastures, included bonfires. The flames, smoke and ash held protective powers. Hessabah joined her sisterhood in the celebration that May 1. They walked around the flames. They danced around the flames. They jumped over the embers all in prayer for a good growing season.

Holding hands around the fires, blessings were recited. Hessabah's mother, the most senior of all the women in the tribe, led the prayers:

"Blessed be the longing that brought you here and quickens your heart and soul with wonder and merriment. May you have the courage to answer the call of the longing within you; May you seek and find the answers to the question 'Who am I?' May your soul be free and open to accept the calling of your gifts; May you have the courage to follow your path; May your outer dignity reflect your inner strength; May you see the miracle of each day as a gift; May the light of your soul guide you and may the spirit of the white light protect you from darkness. Blessed be."

"Blessed be," the circle of women replied.

Hessabah was next in the circle to speak.

"When the weight of your earthly journey causes you to trip and fall, may the earth rise up to catch you. When you see nothing but the darkness may the brilliant colors of nature fill your heart; When the storms cause your seas to become angry, may the winds be calmed to stillness and serenity to bring you safely home; May the light bathe you; May the earth nourish you and may the ancestors surround you, guide you, and protect you. Blessed be."

"Blessed be," the women of the coven replied.

These ceremonies were held at night. The Celts knew there was nothing to fear from the darkness for it happened before the dawn and the birth of a new day. When the persecutions and executions began, they met under cover of night in secluded forests where others would not carry gossip and falsehoods back to those who continued the effort to stamp out the old ways.

Church leaders spread fear among their congregations about these ancient ways and the women who kept to the time-honored rituals. "These witches are the brides of Satan. They perform evil acts of devil worship. They make human sacrifices, stealing babies and casting spells, making God-fearing men and women do their bidding," the clergy warned their congregations.

The once revered became the ridiculed and the reviled. So successful was the church's mission to stamp out women's place as spiritual guides and healers, that any woman who held an opinion or showed any inclination of independent thought or behavior was held in suspicion.

And, in the late 1600s, Hessabah Parsons and most other healers like her, kept their knowledge to themselves and only those they knew who would not betray them.

They understood anatomy; they birthed babies and held the dying in their arms.

The priests and doctors fumed that the villagers dared turn to these women for help. It further enraged them when the villagers showed their gratitude for the help and healing they were given.

The religious leaders decreed that nobody did more harm to the church than midwives. The pain of childbirth is punishment for the sin of Eve in the Garden of Eden, they explained. The church believed that birth pains must be endured by all women for Eve's original sin. The church condemned these women for interfering with God's will by the use of plants that would prevent or end pregnancies.

The law said any woman who practiced medicine was a witch and must die. Most of the evidence of witchcraft was provided by doctors and clergy who wanted to stamp out all forms of female power; the right to decide what happened in their lives and to their bodies including reproduction.

There was a suspicion among the clergy that if women gathered in groups they were plotting against men. Husbands were advised to beat their wives out of concern for their mortal souls. Those who dressed ornately were punished for their vanity. Those who were caught falling asleep in church were forced to wear a large and heavy iron rosary as penance.

So Hessabah, and those like her, continued to practice but in secret. They performed their ceremonies at night. They gathered in circles around bonfires. They sang the ancient songs of worship. If caught, they knew they would be hanged, drowned, burned or stoned to death.

Hessabah and her soul sisters had cause to be afraid. She, and they, had witnessed the brutality those women who were caught were forced to bear. Anyone accused of witchcraft was nearly always found guilty. The evidence was slight if there was any.

Hannah White, 16, was burned alive because her accusers said they'd seen her braiding her hair and singing songs to the devil while walking in her father's garden at midnight. Further evidence was provided after she was stripped of her clothing and a black mole, just under her left breast was discovered; surely it was the nipple upon which the devil's imps suckled, the witch trial judge agreed.

The beautiful young girl screamed as she was dragged to the village square where she was stripped of her clothing and tied to a ladder placed in the centre of a pile of tinder wood.

"Please, I beg you, do not do this! I am no witch. I am a good Christian girl," she cried.

"It is a trick of the devil. Do not listen to this wicked bride of Satan," the village priest said.

"If you love God then say the Lord's Prayer," someone in the crowd taunted.

She choked back tears. By now the terror she felt had overcome her ability to speak.

"The L-Lord is mmmy shhhepherd. I....."

"Burn her! Burn her. She cannot say the words," some of the villagers screamed.

They cheered as the fire was lit and the flames grew higher until they reached her skin. Her mother and father, crying from the sight of the execution of the eldest child, turned away in their grief.

Hannah cried out, begging God to save her from the torture. Her screams stopped as the heat from the flames seared her lungs and her body was then engulfed. The putrid odour of burning flesh filled the air. As the spectacle was over, the villagers returned to their homes and fields to work while Hessabah and others mourned the loss of one of their own.

At 18, Hessabah had married Samuel Parsons, a son of the village blacksmith, in 1680. They lived quietly in a cottage on the edge of the community for a decade. Samuel knew Hessabah was a healer. He shared her belief that the church was wrong to condemn those wise women who only wished to help ease suffering.

When suspicious eyes focused on her and gossips started spreading lies about his beloved Hessie, he knew it was time to flee before she too was subjected to the horrors so many women faced for crimes that didn't exist.

Samuel Parsons formulated a plan. His cousin, George Burroughs, a minister in New England, had told him of the many opportunities there were for a man with his blacksmithing skills. It would be a new life in a new world where they could start fresh. Surely they would be safer there than here. Staying would likely mean her downfall and death. Yet, going meant leaving all they knew behind. Also, there were dangers at sea and, after, as they made a new life in New England.

A feeling of trepidation was normal for anyone about to make the dangerous sea voyage from England to the New World but for Hessabah Parsons, the deep sense of foreboding left her afraid to the point of nausea.

Deep in her soul she felt that life would never be the same and none of it was going to be for the good. In fact, she'd been having nightmares so vivid she'd awoken in a cold sweat and screaming twice over the past month.

15

"All will be well my love," Samuel tried to reassure her.

"Have we not planned for this and saved all of our money to be able to pay for our passage aboard the Nonesuch? This is a new start and surely we shall reap the rewards of the bounty New England is providing to those we know who are already there," he said.

He sat on a wooden bench in front of the fire while she stirred the iron pot that contained the venison stew she'd prepared for their evening meal.

"Yes, Samuel 'tis true there are many who have made it to the new land and are doing well but it's a trip fraught with peril. We could be killed at sea in a storm or die of ship fever. It's true many go to God and a watery grave on the voyage. And what if this happens to us?"

Samuel arose from the bench and wrapped his arms around his lovely wife. "My love, have no fear. God, in his mercy, will see us safely over the sea and we shall build a home and be happy there as we have been here."

The blacksmith was certain all would be well. How could it not? They were both still fairly young and in good health. And, should they fall ill while aboard, he knew his beautiful wife had a box containing all of the herbs and tinctures necessary to revive the body from fevers and all sorts of ailments.

His Hessabah, whom he'd always called Hessie, was a gifted healer whom many in their island home came to for medical help. She was also the local mid-wife who'd birthed more babies than she could count since she was a girl helping her mother and grandmother.

Making preparations to emigrate was no small task. For weeks Samuel and Hessie planned down to the last detail what they would bring with them to start their new lives. In 1690, Maine was a wilderness frontier like many tiny coastal communities dotted on the Atlantic coastline of New England.

They were only permitted a certain number of wooden trunks aboard His Majesty's Ship Nonesuch. Necessities came before frivolities; not that she had many things. They'd been told rations were meagre at best on board, so Hessabah prepared salted beef and fermented vegetables. They packed herbal teas and all of her remedies and tinctures.

Her most treasured possessions were given to her from her mother; including her leather medicine pouches. A large wooden chest, with wrought iron hinges and lock, contained several linen dresses; a wedding gift from Samuel.

They would be leaving port on May 12, 1690. God willing, and with favourable winds, it was expected they should arrive just as the colorful leaves were turning hues of red, orange and yellow.

Hessie and Samuel were greeted by their relatives at the dock. She and her mother cried. They knew it was unlikely they would see one another again. Although a few returned, most would never see their loved ones or homes again.

"Goodbye Mother," she said as she hugged the grey-haired tiny woman tightly for what she knew was the last time.

"I will pray to Bridgit and Mary for your protection my child. Blessed be," her mother said.

"Blessed be," Hessabah replied.

Like her daughter, she too had a bad feeling about their future but kept it to herself. She wished them a safe journey and a good life in their new home.

"I will write to you often," Hessabah said before she turned to board the ship.

As she walked up the gangway, a cold shiver ran down her spine. Her fears of the voyage had only augmented since her nightmares began. She should have taken them as a sign they were not to go, but Samuel insisted they were doing the right thing. Staying was dangerous now that her secret as a healer was becoming more widely known.

The first few days of the trip there was fine weather. A strong easterly wind helped the Nonesuch make good time. Many of the passengers aboard took advantage of the warm spring air on deck, which was a relief from the cramped quarters below. Strangers quickly grew to know one another with the lack of privacy.

The smell of flatulence and vomit from indigestion and seasickness putrefied the air so nobody wanted to spend any more time below deck than necessary. After a week, the trip seemed like an eternity. At night, Hessabah lay awake in a narrow bunk beside her husband. It was almost impossible to sleep with the sound of crying babies and snoring men. But the worst was yet to come.

On the tenth day at sea the Nonesuch sailed directly into a summer storm that left all but the crew in the dank, dark hell that was below deck.

She tried not to panic as the ship was tossed up and down on the 20-foot waves. Although it was a sea-worthy vessel, the wooden ship was known to take on a slight amount of water in rough weather.

The stench of vomit and un-emptied chamber pots was overwhelming. Constant jousting about from weather and waves made even standing difficult and many had to strap themselves to their bunks to keep from injury, which was possible as one was tossed to and fro as the waves continued to assault the ship.

After a long 12 hours, the storm was over and everyone praised God for bringing them through it safely. The days and nights passed slowly. Mealtime helped to break the monotony. However the food provided did not afford a great deal of variety.

There was salt cod and biscuits, oatmeal, rice, tea, sugar, and molasses. Each person aboard was allotted three quarts of water daily. Hessabah and the other wives aboard supplemented the meagre rations with the foods they'd brought aboard including coffee.

"Coffee is much preferable to tea, the water being so bad, as to render the tea rather insipid and tasteless," Samuel was warned by a cousin, a sailor, who'd made many voyages to and from New England aboard trade ships.

Like other passengers, Hessabah and Samuel found eating difficult. They used her large trunk as a table. In rough waters it slid across the wooden deck. While the young couple were able to withstand the ship's movement without much queasiness, seasickness was a constant companion for many of their travelers.

She felt most sorry for one young woman who'd been ill from the time they'd left port. Rowena Williams, daughter of Peter and Rachel Williams, was a beautiful girl with bright blue eyes and straw-colored hair. After nearly two weeks at sea, and constant stomach sickness, she was a pitiful sight.

Hessabah made peppermint and ginger teas offering it to the girl and others to soothe their stomachs. Some people had adjusted but many others spent days bedridden with nausea.

Worse sickness struck the Nonesuch on June 1. In the cramped conditions there was no way to prevent the spread of ship fever.

19

Hessabah immediately recognised the symptoms of severe headache, a sustained high fever, cough, rash, muscle pain, chills, and sensitivity to light, before there was delirium and finally, death.

She did all she could to ease the suffering of the sick, which was precious little in the unsanitary conditions. Passengers prayed God would spare them and their loved ones.

The prayers of Rowena went unanswered as she watched her parents die horrific deaths. On June 10 their bodies, along with two babies and a 10-year-old boy, were carried to the ship's top deck where they were sent into the sea with prayers for their departed spirits. Rowena sobbed as she watched her parents' bodies, slip beneath the cold, dark ocean water.

Hessabah, who'd become friendly with Rowena's mother over the past two weeks, nursed both her parents as they lay dying in their bunk, was overcome with the sadness and fear which held nearly everyone aboard in its grip. It was certain more would fall ill.

Panic set in aboard the Nonesuch as one-by-one nearly half of the passengers aboard fell ill. Somehow Hessabah and Samuel were spared.

"I told you God would see us safely to our new home, Hessie." Samuel spoke too soon. For two weeks later he took to his bunk with a severe headache and high fever.

Hessabah placed cool cloths on his forehead and encouraged him to drink the broth she'd made for those who were ill. By morning he had all of the symptoms of the dreaded disease. A weakened Samuel whispered "I love you Hessie Parsons. God keep you safe my dearest one."

"You will not die Samuel Parsons. I will not allow it."

"I am afraid, my love, you do not have the final say on this matter. Our dear Lord will decide whether I am to stay with you or be called home."

As she continued to nurse him she prayed God would not take him from her. "Lord. I beg thy mercy. I pray you will see fit to spare his life and allow him to stay with me."

Somehow, as others succumbed to the dreaded illness, Samuel was spared. While weakened from the fever, he rallied around. It appeared God had heard her prayers. Samuel gave her a weak smile and said: "Good wife, it appears you will have to put up with me for a while longer."

For the rest of the journey she did what she could for others aboard who fell ill. Despite her hands-on care of the ill, the dying and the dead, the fever didn't touch her. By the time the Nonesuch made port on September 5, 1690, 50 souls had not survived the voyage.

Hessabah spent many nights trying to imagine how those left alone would survive in this new land. It would be impossible, she thought, especially for the Williams girl.

"How will Rowena get along without her parents my dearest?" she asked Samuel.

"How indeed? Rowena is now vulnerable to be certain," he replied.

Hessabah, now 28, and 30-year-old Samuel, were childless. She had five pregnancies and two births since their marriage began but neither infant had survived their first few weeks.

She found solace in helping other women bring healthy babies into the world as a mid-wife and she comforted the sick and dying with her skills as a healer.

In the weeks since Rowena's parents died, the 14-year-old girl became like her shadow offering to help her in her tending to the sick.

On the night before the ship made port Hessabah overheard the girl whispering prayers in her bunk. "Oh God help me to find my way. Protect me and keep me, Lord."

Hessabah knew the girl would be easy prey and was totally unprepared to deal with life in this new land. She could not allow Rowena to walk off the ship on her own so she and Samuel agreed the girl should come to live with them.

The morning they made port was sunny and warm; a sign from God Samuel said, as they walked toward the gangway.

"My dearest, let us thank God for all he has seen us through and his protective hand upon us now and into the future."

"Yes, thank you Lord for thy mercy and protection," she said in a whisper as she placed her feet on the dock.

George Burroughs, the village minister, was cousin to Samuel. He'd convinced the couple to come to this new land to start a new life. It would be an adventure and a means of prosperity for a man such as Samuel whose blacksmithing skills would be sought after.

While related, George and Samuel had never met in person for George had always lived in New England. Educated at Harvard University, he worked as a lay minister having never been officially ordained. An outspoken man, who held firm in his opinions and convictions, he did at times overstep his authority and offended some in the community.

Ministers and judges were ready to believe the worst of a man who moved freely between the wilderness frontier and settled areas, and who somehow escaped Indian attacks on more than one occasion.

George was a handsome man who was popular with the ladies in his congregations, but there were many who were suspicious of his dark hair and complexion with some even thinking that he might have non-Puritan connections, either spiritual or social.

This was, like most English settlements, located along the Atlantic coast. The King of England had granted land holdings to those who contracted with the Crown to reap the resources of the sea and land to be shipped back to England. The frontier settlements forced New Englanders to confront their two great fears; native attacks and the Devil.

George came to Maine in the mid-1670s after receiving a 200-acre land grant in Falmouth. The Abenaki people in the area became frustrated by the newcomers because they took without asking and gave nothing back except disease. In response they attacked the settlement. Somehow George managed to survive while others didn't.

The Puritan leaders of the church used the repeated aboriginal attacks of frontier settlements in Maine to instil fear in their congregations that the non-faithful had brought this kind divine retribution. Outbreak of illnesses was further proof God punished the settlers for their sins, they preached.

George had alternated his years as a minister in Falmouth, Black Point and Salem Massachusetts. In 1690 he was happily living in the New England frontier with his third wife. His previous two wives had died of illnesses. Excited to have family from England join him in the fishing village, he closely watched for people who matched the description in Samuel's letters. He waved as he recognized the couple he thought were Samuel and Hessabah.

"Welcome to New England! I am sure you are well and truly glad to be on land after those long and difficult weeks at sea." Samuel shook George's hand and then introduced Hessabah.

"Ah, yes, I understand you are knowledgeable in healing and midwifery. It will be a blessing to have someone here who can help in this way for there are no physicians to be found within miles."

"It is a relief to finally step foot on land Mr. Burroughs," Hessabah said before introducing him to Rowena. "Her parents, God rest their souls, were among those who succumbed to ship fever. She is now in our care."

"My dear, I am sorry for your loss. Orphaned in a new land is very sad indeed but there are many here who know the pain of losing loved ones to illness and to the attacks from raids that happen up and down the coast by the French and their allies the Abenaki people. Why it was only a year ago that my dear wife and I, along with many others, had to flee from Falmouth, north and up the coast to here, after the village was attacked. But it is far safer here. So far we have had no troubles with the natives and we are safe in our fortified village."

George led the way toward his horse and wagon and ordered their trunks be loaded on the back as Samuel assisted Hessabah and Rowena to climb aboard.

A rough ride on heavily potholed and washboard roads jostled Hessabah to the point where she was sure her backside would be bruised. Finally, the wagon stopped in front of a cottage and George said "Welcome home!"

By October, the days were getting colder and there was frost in the air. Samuel and Hessabah volunteered to work in the fields of other settlers in exchange for some of the harvest.

For the next several months Samuel, Hessabah and Rowena lived with George and his wife as their own cottage was under construction. While she was grateful for the shelter, she was also anxious to move. It was a hard but satisfying life. Seven months passed with the occasional skirmish with the Abenaki but nothing that caused great alarm.

As a house warming, many of the couples gave them salted fish and venison along with enough root vegetables to see them through the winter months. And, in kind, Samuel helped the men by making shoes for their horses while she, with Rowena serving as her apprentice, was busy tending to wounds or birthing babies

For the most part, life was good for Hessabah and Samuel. He opened a blacksmithing business and she tended to the sick and wounded. As always there were many women who needed help come time to give birth.

The supplies of herbs and tinctures she'd brought with her soon depleted and Hessabah took Rowena in search of bark, leaves, roots and berries from which many of her medicines were made.

On some of those excursions Hessabah and Rowena encountered Abenaki women who, like her, were gathering what Mother Earth had provided. Neither spoke the same language but they understood that both were healers in search of medicines.

As the days and weeks passed, Hessabah and the Abenaki's medicine woman came to respect one another. They shared things they'd gathered while on their outings, such as a fragrant, flowering plant called yarrow that was used to stop excess bleeding. Yarrow juice mixed with water helped an upset stomach or ease intestinal disorders. A tea made from the leaves and stems was an astringent.

Sumac served many uses including eye problems, sore throats and diarrhea. The leaves and berries were combined in tea to reduce fever or made into a poultice to soothe poison ivy.

Hessabah and the Abenaki medicine woman, who she learned mostly through a form of sign language they'd created, was a widow with children and named Wôbigen Nolka (White Deer).

She showed Hessabah the local plants not common to northern England, Scotland and Ireland.

The roots, when mixed with honey, or Hessabah's favorite and newly discovered maple syrup, produced soothing medicine that helped ease bleeding gums and strengthened the immune system.

Rosemary, she was taught, was as a sacred plant for White Deer's people. It was an herb greatly valued for its ability to improve memory, relieve muscle pain and spasms and improve the immune system and digestion.

Because there were tensions between the English and the Abenaki, neither Hessabah nor White Deer invited the other to their homes. Instead, they met one another in the forest where, over time, a respect was established and a friendship was beginning to form. When they met each would have small presents for the other.

And they shared their language with one another too. Soon they could have rudimentary conversations.

"Kway"

"Hello"

"How are you?"

"Doni gedowiozin?"

"Newowlowzi"

"I'm Fine."

The women would gather leaves, bark, roots and berries in amicable silence. Sometimes they would sit by a stream and share some food they both brought. And, as always, when they parted, they would wish one another well.

"Good-bye, take care of yourself."

"Adio, wli nanawalmezi."

Despite their differences there were many similarities. They shared the same reverence for Mother Earth. They celebrated the seasons. They prayed for a good harvest and they thanked the Creator for the bounty.

They came to understand they were walking the same spiritual path and shared many of the same understandings of the divine.

White Deer saw in Hessabah a kindred spirit and a wise woman that was pure of heart. Hessabah recognized a soul sister even on their first meeting.

While they still were unable to have in-depth conversations, these women understood there was much they had in common as medicine women who were called to heal their tribes. Both were keen to learn from one another. Both knew it could be possible to bring this good will to their villages and ease the troubles between the English and the Abenaki peoples.

The Abenaki were peace-loving people who'd been gracious in welcoming the newcomers when they first arrived decades ago. They realized quickly the European settlers took without asking and gave little in return except diseases that the first peoples had no immunity to protect themselves from.

Early in the century an epidemic called The Great Dying had an extremely high mortality rate. Symptoms included severe headache, nosebleeds, and muscle pain along with cramping, yellowing of the skin, lung congestion, haemorrhaging and lingering pockmarks.

Their numbers were more than 40,000 before the sickness and disease the newcomers brought with them. Influenza, smallpox and diphtheria ravaged communities to the point where entire tribes were wiped out. And, as always, those who remained sang the songs and prayed the prayers to honor those who'd gone before them.

With we who visit ghosts from the sun star of our birth and in our infancy that is from the land of the rising star as long as the deer and moose shall run free and the grass shall grow and the rivers run swiftly the Abenaki shall survive the white man's wickedness. Again our grandfathers' spirits have given us guidance and wisdom to rise and come together to dance. We have been taught to love Mother Earth and to respect her. We are the children of the dawn, the people of the east. May the Great Spirit and the Great Creator bless us and smile upon us.

Along with her friendship with White Deer, Hessabah was also becoming friendly with many of the women in her new home including Thea Slade. She was, like Hessabah, in her mid to late 20s and the mother of six children. While she loved all of her children she didn't wish to go through another pregnancy or delivery. The last time she nearly died.

"Can you give me something," she asked in hopes there was some potion she could take that would keep her from becoming with child once more.

Thea Slade's husband, Dougall, was like a rutting bull that was forever climbing on top of her to satisfy his lustful urges. And, early in their marriage, she learned never to refuse him in this or any other matter. When crossed, Dougall Slade became a monster with a raging temper that beat her until the fire within him was extinguished. By the time that happened, Thea was black and blue.

Nobody intervened. It was expected that a husband should beat his wife to keep her good and Godly.

Hessabah had seen her bruises. While it wasn't her place to interfere in a marriage, she did take it upon herself to supply Thea and other women with disagreeable and ill-tempered husbands some ingredients to calm tempers and ensure wives could expect their monthly flux.

Thea Slade needed both a sedative for Dougall and a contraceptive concoction. To soothe her husband's temper she was advised to place a blend of valerian root, wild cherry and skullcap power in his food.

"It helps to calm jagged nerves which can often lead to fits of rage," Hessabah explained. "Also pay attention to your cycle. There is a time each month when you are most fertile. You should avoid your husband's attentions if possible at this time. However, if this is unavoidable ensure you take this."

It was a tincture of celery, fenugreek, Motherwort and Shepherd's purse and was known to bring on the monthly flux.

"Thank you Mistress Parsons," a grateful Thea said with a smile.

"You are most welcome," Hessabah said. She wished Thea well and said goodbye to the pretty but pale woman who looked as though she carried a heavy burden on her shoulders.

Indeed, she did.

For the most part all was well in the small English settlement until April 30, 1692. That was the day that George Burroughs was arrested on charges of witchcraft.

2

George Burroughs was eating his supper at his kitchen table when he was seized by police on charges of witchcraft.

"This is nonsense! Are you insane? I am a man of faith. I have been a minister for some 20 years both here and in Salem. Who is bringing these false charges against me?" George demanded.

"You will hear details of the charges and see your accusers when you reach the court and attend your hearing," the man in charge of the arrest grunted.

Hessabah and Samuel stood in disbelief along with other villagers as George was placed in leg irons. They were aware of his ministry in Salem for several years until dispute with his parishioners over his pay brought him to Falmouth in 1683.

"Sir, you are mistaken. These charges are false. For each person here will testify George Burroughs is a Godly man who would never engage in anything other than worshiping our Lord God," Samuel said in his cousin's defence.

"Anyone who wishes to appear before the court as a defence witness can come to Salem and petition the court for an opportunity to speak," the man said as George was loaded on the cart by three other men.

Samuel insisted on travelling to Salem to support his cousin along with many other villagers. He promised Hessabah he would return to her and he assured her George would be with him.

"It is absurd to think anyone could accuse such a Godly man of being in league with the devil," he said.

"Please, Samuel, be careful. I fear for your safety," she said as he mounted a horse and followed after the wagon headed south to Salem.

"Have no fear my dearest. This is insanity. George will be found innocent. Of that I am certain."

A sense of foreboding held her in its grip as she watched George, his captors, her husband, and fellow villagers fade into the distance.

The charge of witchcraft was based on the accusations of some of George's former congregation who'd sued him for debt of money he'd borrowed from a family to help pay for his late wife's funeral expenses.

Many in Salem believed he was a satanic ringleader. For how could he have survived in the wilds for nearly a decade where so many had been killed in raids? He moved freely and unscathed while others had been slaughtered.

George Burroughs had moved to Salem in 1680, where a year later, his second wife died. He ministered there for only two years. In that time he made some bitter enemies over a salary dispute. And John Putnam, who'd loaned him money to pay for his wife's funeral, was angered it had not been paid back.

George's trial was held on August 5. Some of his accusers said they had witnessed his powers of extraordinary feats of strength.

"I saw him lift a musket by inserting his finger into the barrel," one man testified.

"That would be impossible without diabolical assistance," the judge pronounced.

He was said to have carried a whole barrel of molasses or cider a great distance.

"Did he indeed?" the judge said in disgust.

One of his main accusers was the Reverend Ezra Ward. The puritan preacher saw evidence of witchcraft at every turn.

In his defence, George explained neither impossible.

"A native man did the same thing before me," he told the court.

"That's merely evidence that the savage was actually the devil in disguise. I have been told that there have been times when you have been seen running faster than a horse and have gone from one location to another in a shorter time than is possible for a mere mortal," the prosecutor said.

"You're in league with the devil," Reverend Ward said cutting George off before he could respond.

There was no shortage of testimony that not only was he a witch, but also the coven leader.

One of his accusers testified that a specter told her that 'He was more than a mere witch'. In fact, she said, the spirit told her that George Burroughs was a conjurer who could bring the spirits of the dead back to life.

During his examination, afflicted girls became so agitated at the magistrates that they ordered them removed from the courthouse for their own safety.

Abigail Hobbs confessed that magical dolls had been given to her by Burroughs. "He told me that they have powers," she claimed.

Mercy Lewis, 19, was next.

"He carried me up to an exceeding high mountain and showed me all the kingdoms of the earth and told me that he would give them all to me if I would write in his book,"

Some of the most damaging testimony against him was by several confessed witches who identified him as Satan's personal representative at Salem Sabbaths.

"All the meetings were personally organized and presided over by Sorcerer Burroughs," the girls said.

The court magistrates were convinced they had finally located one of the central figures in the current diabolical satanic operations.

Ann Putnam claimed to have been visited by George's two deceased wives who told her of the mistreatment they suffered at the hands of their husband.

In his defence, many of the people who'd travelled to Salem said he was "self-denying, generous, and public-spirited, laboring with humility and with zeal."

"He is an able, intelligent, true-minded man; a sincere man, humble in his spirit, faithful and devoted as a minister, active and generous. These are hardly the characteristics one would expect to find in a close companion of Satan," Samuel said in George's defence.

Letters of support from the new frontier said he was highly regarded both as a friend and counselor.

And there were even some in Salem who, so believing of his innocence and despite the danger to themselves, signed a petition on behalf of Burroughs' innocence.

Even before his execution, one of his accusers recanted her accusation.

"I wasn't telling the truth. I spun a story of lies because I was afraid," she said.

It was no use. George Burroughs was sentenced to death by hanging on August 19 along with three other men and one woman, whom had all been found guilty of witchcraft.

Samuel stood at the back of the court as the sentence was passed upon his cousin who was found guilty of conspiring with the devil and of performing witchcraft.

There were some who knew George well who refused to believe this was true.

Still, there were more who either said nothing for fear of being accused themselves or, like the Putnam family who'd accused him, were praising God that the devil's servant had been caught and would die.

Nobody was permitted to speak to George or the others convicted of witchcraft.

Samuel knew that he would likely end up accused of the same crime if he tried to have the guilty verdict overturned. Samuel stood at the back of the large crowd that had gathered at Proctor's Ledge as his cousin was led toward the site of his execution.

"How can this be happening? There was little, if any, evidence against him. No tell-tale signs such as witches' marks on his body," Samuel thought as he watched his cousin standing on a ladder before the crowd, waiting to be hanged.

As he stood on the gallows awaiting the noose, George stunned the crowd by loudly proclaiming his innocence.

"I am a man who has always held dear the teachings of our Lord and saviour Jesus Christ. Now I shall prove it to you."

With one last attempt to convince the crowd of his innocence, George perfectly recited the Lord's Prayer.

"Our Father who art in heaven, hallowed be thy name. Thy kingdom come, thy will be done, on earth as it is in heaven. Give us this day our daily bread, and forgive us our debts, as we also have forgiven our debtors. And lead us not into temptation, but deliver us from evil."

Surely this was enough to secure his release Samuel thought. For the court considered this to be impossible for a witch to do.

The spectators, deeply impressed, called for his pardon.

"Release him. He is telling the truth. He is no wizard!"

While some people, like Samuel, were convinced of his innocence and called for his release, there were others, encouraged by the Reverend Ezra Ward, who continued to shout for his death.

"It's a trick of the devil. Hang him!"

So moved by George's speech many were in tears.

The call for his release continued to grow to a fevered pitch and it seemed to some that the spectators would hinder his execution. However, Reverend Ezra Ward, and others overseeing the execution, refused to pardon him.

George was hanged before the protesting spectators could organize their opposition. He continued to pray aloud even as the noose was placed around his neck.

As the floor beneath his feet gave way, his body dropped and his neck snapped while his feet kicked in a grisly death dance.

After the hanging, his body was cut down, dragged by the halter, which tore the clothing from his body which was then thrown in a hole between the rocks, partially buried with two others who had also been hanged that day.

As soon as George was dead, Reverend Ward spoke to the angry crowd.

"The prisoner was no ordained minister and the devil has often been transformed into an angel of light."

News of the trials reached Hessabah who cried when she learned George had been executed.

She didn't know the others but she wondered whether they, like the kind and generous George, were wrongfully convicted and killed.

She had witnessed many witch trials and the executions before coming to New England; like the one that had killed her friend Hannah White. She knew they were brutal and wrong. It was such a horrific death that she didn't wish it upon anyone.

Samuel, heartbroken by the sight of his cousin's remains dangling from the end of the rope at the bottom of the gallows, quickly made his departure. He needed to get back to his sweet Hessie.

He wanted to spare no extra time in this strange place with these people who were seeing evidence of witchcraft everywhere.

As the weeks passed, while Samuel and the other villagers had been in Salem, Hessabah and Rowena had remained busy.

They worked in the garden growing herbs and vegetables. They foraged for wild edibles including strawberries, raspberries and mushrooms in the nearby woods. Armed escorts attended them in case there were hostiles nearby.

Hessabah preferred to be alone so she might encounter White Deer but the opportunities were precious few.

One afternoon she slipped through the village gates as the man on guard duty slept on the hot August day. She'd told Rowena she was running an errand and asked her to continue with her work in the garden.

"Yes, mistress."

Hessabah longed to take off her shoes and walk on the cool forest floor or lay on the moss under the shade of the aspen trees. And there was a stream nearby which would be heavenly to bathe in on this hot summer's day, she thought.

Uncertain that she wouldn't be caught, she opted to take off her shoes and stockings and dip her feet into the stream.

The cold water sent a shiver up her spine. Or was it her sense of knowing she wasn't alone that caused the reaction?

Hessabah knew she was being watched. Fear caused her to leap from the ground gathering her stockings and shoes. She ran barefoot as fast as she could but fell and struck her head upon a tree root.

Unconscious, Hessabah was unaware that she was gathered into the arms of the one who'd watched her for longer than she realized. She lay still for some time and when she awoke the pain in her head left her sick to her stomach.

She touched her temple. It was sticky. She knew she had a head wound and blood had coagulated on her face.

She was lying on reed mats in a darkened place she didn't recognize. She lay frozen with fear. Where was she? Who was with her and what would they do to her?

She moaned from the throbbing in her head. She lifted her head slightly. Although dimly lit, she could recognize that she was among the Abenaki peoples in a wigwam.

Just then, she recognized a familiar face. It was White Deer who'd brought her a cup, which contained a hot liquid.

"N'dakwamadamen n'dep" (I have a headache), Hessabah said.

White Deer motioned for Hessabah to drink.

"Yo gagwi. Gadosmida." (Here is something … drink)."

As she placed it to her lips, immediately Hessabah recognized it as aspen bark tea.

She knew its anti-inflammatory properties would help ease her pain and cure any fever she might develop from the head wound.

She drank the tea nodding to the woman, trying to let her know she appreciated the help. Still, she was unsure of what was happening. Her last memory was running from the stream.

With the last sip of the aspen tea swallowed, she lay her head down and sleep overtook her once more.

Daylight steamed through the opening of the shelter where she lay. The pain in her head was gone but she had an urge to relieve herself. How would she explain this to the women who now watched her?

White Deer now motioned for her to stand. She took one of Hessabah's arms while another woman took the other and together they helped her to her feet. They slowly walked her to the wigwam's entrance and then outside.

Then they walked to an area that was sheltered with bushes and one squatted down to pee. Hessabah wasted no time debating whether to urinate in front of her hosts. Instantly she felt relief as she squatted and emptied her bladder.

"Ahhh," she sighed.

White Deer and the other woman laughed and so did Hessabah. They had found another patch of common ground with the most basic of human functions.

Hessabah dried herself with a nearby leaf and then stood on still wobbly legs. They then took her by the arms once more and returned her to the shelter.

One of the women motioned for her to sit while another wiped the dried blood from her temple and applied a salve to the wound.

Next she was offered a broth made from fish and vegetables. It was delicious.

She could tell hours had passed since she'd left the village. She needed to return before a search party was formed to look for her.

"N'gadi moji n'wigomnok." (I want to go home)

"Oho Alosa" (Yes, go walk).

White Deer went with Hessabah back through the forest close to the settler's village. Together they walked in silence. When they came to the forest edge, Hessabah turned and smiled. She touched White Deer's arm.

"Oliwn." (Thank you), she said

White Deer smiled and then slipped back into the forest.

Hessabah wished others could come to know the Abenaki people, as she had come to respect and like White Deer.

But there were many who would not understand their ways which, while they were very similar to her Celtic ancestors and their traditions, there were many who believed that the devil walked among the natives and any who were friends with them were also Satan's disciples.

In the four months since George's arrest and execution, the village had been without a faith leader. It would have been far better to have none than the man who arrived to take over the church leadership.

It was none other than Reverend Ezra Ward.

Immediately Hessabah was on alert. Ward, a religious zealot, was sent to flush out any hint of witchcraft and followers of Satan.

Ward was a brutal man with a hell and brimstone message. He was convinced anyone who didn't follow the strict teachings of Puritan doctrine was hell-bound unless they were reformed.

With Ward arrived his friend and physician Dr. Eli White who immediately took a dislike to Hessabah when he learned the villagers looked to her for medical help.

For several days Samuel rode only stopping to rest and to feed and water his mount. Soon he returned. But the village he'd returned to was unlike the one he'd left several months before.

On a rainy day near the first of September Samuel returned to her.

Hessabah welcomed him with open arms, relieved no hardship had come to him. Well into the evening they whispered about the horrors poor George and the others faced.

Samuel had more bad news to share. Soon another minister would be coming to their village.

"It's Reverend Ezra Ward. He is also bringing Dr. Eli white."

"Why is this bad news, my love?"

"They were part of the witch hunt which sent poor George to the gallows."

.

3

A week later the minister and the doctor arrived in the small community where they were welcomed by most but feared by others including Samuel, Hessabah and Rowena.

On a Tuesday afternoon there was a knock on their cottage door.

Hessabah was hesitant to allow them in but knew, if she didn't, it would cause suspicion. There was no avoiding the meeting. She steeled herself for the encounter and knew she would have to make them believe she welcomed them.

"Good sirs, do come in. Please make yourselves comfortable. I'll go fetch my husband. I believe you will have seen him in Salem recently."

"Ah, yes. We saw him there. He was a cousin to the late George Burroughs," the Reverend Ward pronounced in an accusatory tone

"I expect you and your husband will attend my first church service this coming Sunday. I have prepared a special message to help all keep fast to the Lord and pray for protection from evil and the wicked ways of sin and the devil."

"Indeed," she said feigning deference to these pompous men.

Just then, Samuel walked in the cottage.

"Samuel, there you are. Reverend Ward and Dr. White are here to introduce themselves."

"Welcome good sirs."

The men sat beside the fire. It was obvious these men were looking for signs of witchcraft in this cottage. Samuel knew it.

"My wife and I are looking forward to attending your first church service, Reverend Ward. It will be good to have a Godly man leading us, ensuring the protection of our souls."

Reverend Ward was a proud, vain man who liked praise.

"I do what I can to help lead my flock down the hard and narrow path to salvation and away from the road to hell."

After about an hour the men bid Samuel and Hessabah a good day and departed.

Hessabah quickly shut the door and sighed. These men were trouble she thought as a shiver ran down her spine.

"Bridgit and holy Mother Mary protect us all," she prayed.

As it was Saturday night, they knew they would face both men again during the morning church service.

Samuel, Hessabah and Rowena walked to the church, which was in the centre of the village, and arrived several minutes before the service began. They sat on the wooden benches as others filled the pews around them. Everyone in the village came to hear Reverend Ward's service.

The sombre man stared intently at the parishioners as he began a sermon that left no doubt he was fervent in his desire to rid the world of anyone who strayed from the narrow, hard path to God.

"Let me remind you of what the Bible has to say about those who conspire with the devil. In the book of Isaiah chapter eight verse nine it says "Someone may say to you, 'Let's ask the mediums and those who consult the spirits of the dead. With their whisperings and mutterings, they will tell us what to do.'

I tell you all that we should only look to God for guidance. Should the living seek guidance from the dead? No! This is an abomination and witchcraft! And what is it that God directs us to do with those who practice witchcraft? The book of Leviticus chapter 20 verses 26 and 27 says 'You must be holy because I, the Lord, am holy. I have set you apart from all other people to be my very own. Men and women among you who act as mediums or who consult the spirits of the dead must be put to death by stoning. They are guilty of a capital offense.'

And further, we see in the book of Chronicles chapter 10 verses 13 and 14 'So Saul died because he was unfaithful to the Lord. He failed to obey the Lord's command, and he even consulted a medium instead of asking the Lord for guidance. So the Lord killed him and turned the kingdom over to David son of Jesse.'

I tell you, brothers and sisters, that we must be vigilant in watching for the devil's trickery and stay far away from sin.

In 1st John five verses 18 to 19 it says 'We know that whosoever is born of God sinneth not; but he that is begotten of God keepeth himself, and that wicked one toucheth him not. And we know that we are of God, and the whole world lieth in wickedness.'

And 1st John four verse four says, 'Ye are of God, little children, and have overcome them: because greater is he that is in you, than he that is in the world. On pain of death of your physical bodies and your mortal souls I tell you to take no part in evil but rather seek it out and expose it. Even if it is your husband, your wife or your own children, I tell you to expose the devil wherever he may be. Even if those whom you love have been corrupted by Satan you must speak out, for in doing so you would be saving their souls from eternal damnation!

We are instructed in the book of Ephesians chapter five verse 11, 'Take no part in the worthless deeds of evil and darkness; instead, expose them. And again, in the book of John we are told in chapter one verse eleven 'Dear friend, do not imitate what is evil but what is good. Anyone who does what is good is from God. Anyone who does what is evil has not seen God.'

And in First Corinthians chapter 10 verse 21 it says, 'You cannot drink the cup of the Lord and the cup of demons. You cannot partake of the table of the Lord and the table of demons!'

Brothers and sisters I know recently Satan walked among you. The evil-one can oft take the form of an angel of light. You were fooled. I know the evil that was here has been cast out. I promise you that I am firm in my resolve to help keep all of you on the path of righteousness. There is no place here for the devil. Should I see any evidence of it, there will be no mercy. Together we will ensure that this remains a Godly place."

The service, which lasted nearly two hours, came to an end and one-by-one the parishioners stopped at the church door to greet Reverend Ward.

The doctor, always ready to promote his friend, said: "A powerful service. Don't you agree Mr. and Mistress Parsons?"

"Indeed it was that," Samuel said as he shook Reverend Ward's hand. While he was still mourning the loss of George, he did not want to start off on the wrong foot with either the doctor or the new church leader.

Hessabah nodded to the reverend and then turned her eyes from him. He unnerved her. She knew he saw trouble where none existed.

Rowena, who followed behind, had caught the attention of Dr. White.

"And who is this young lady?"

"This is Rowena. Her parents died on the crossing and we are now her guardians," Samuel explained.

"How old are you my child?"

"I turned 15 this summer doctor," Rowena said quietly and with her eyes downcast.

Hessabah noticed the attention the doctor was paying to the girl. She sensed this was more than polite conversation. Indeed the doctor, who was a widower, may be looking for a new bride. But Rowena wasn't ready for marriage and wouldn't be for at least a couple more years. And, even when she was ready to become someone's wife, it certainly shouldn't be to a man who was surely old enough to be her grandfather.

She would speak with Samuel about her concerns. He would have to ensure Rowena's protection.

Hessabah knew there was little else she could do. The doctor and the new minister were of the mind that women were far inferior to men and had no place other than in the home.

Women did not participate in town meetings and were excluded from decision making in the church or anywhere else for that matter.

Unlike her former island home, where women's opinions and knowledge were valued, here they were seen as instruments of Satan.

There were nearly twice as many men as women in this new frontier so there was a strong pressure for women to marry. Those who did not were ostracized and held in suspicion. Hessabah thought that unless she was willing, Rowena could not be forced into an arranged marriage. Still, without the protection of Samuel, she was vulnerable.

She knew the new minister would be of little help in this matter. For the church said Eve's role in original sin exemplified a woman's moral weakness. It taught parishioners women were much more susceptible to temptations and they possessed qualities that could be exploited and become sinful.

Hessabah's marriage to Samuel was a rarity. He saw her as equal and, together, they made decisions. Most marriages were far different. A woman was to love, obey and further the interests and will of her husband. If she was a good mate, she had fulfilled her God-given duty.

"Samuel"

"Yes, my dearest."

"Did you see how the doctor was looking at Rowena?"

"No, I did not. How was he looking at her?"

"Like a hungry cat eyes a bowl of cream"

"Him, interested in her? She's 15 and he is already an old man."

"Promise me you will discourage the doctor. I will speak to Rowena and ensure she keeps her distance."

"I promise, my dearest."

Women in Hessabah's clan were the matriarchs and leaders of their communities but here women here were subordinate to men.

In the new colonies, as in most of Europe, married women were not allowed to own property, sign contracts, or conduct business. Their husbands owned everything, including the couple's children. Only widows who did not remarry were permitted to live more independent lives and could own property and run businesses.

With the church service over, there was little to do on the Sabbath. It was a day of rest and sombre reflection.

Hessabah longed to escape the confines of the faith that often bound her with its restrictions. She preferred to walk in the woods and spend quiet time; nearly impossible in this strict community.

Hessabah thought of the days and weeks ahead. There was much to do to prepare for the harsh winter months. The vegetables in the garden would have to be harvested and stored in the root cellar. She needed to gather more bark, leaves and berries from which she would prepare medicines.

As she thought of the work ahead there was a knock on the door. She looked out. It was the doctor.

She opened the door. "Welcome, Dr. White."

The tall man stepped over the threshold and removed his tricorn hat. The man was bald with a deeply creased forehead.

"He is 40 if a day," she thought.

Samuel got up from the chair by the hearth and shook the doctor's hand.

"Come in, come in! Make yourself comfortable."

"Why thank you, Mr. Parsons. I hope this isn't am imposition. I am sure you want to rest after that stirring message this morning."

"We were just about to dine. Would you care to join us?"

Samuel knew the doctor was living alone and likely not able to cook a decent meal. He noticed the doctor staring at Rowena.

"Hessabah is right. He is here for more than a meal to be sure," Samuel thought.

Hessabah and Rowena remained quiet. They moved about the kitchen stirring the venison stew, and setting the wooden table with pewter plates and spoons.

The evening meal was ready and Samuel invited the doctor to sit. Hessabah served him a large helping of stew and then ladled up portions for Samuel, Rowena and herself.

They sat in an awkward silence until Samuel invited the doctor to give the blessing.

"I would be honored. 'Dear Lord. We thank thee for this food for which we are about to receive. Bless it to the use of our bodies so that we may be faithful to thy service. Amen."

"Amen," everyone said in unison and then started to eat.

"This is a fine stew, Mistress Parsons. You are indeed a lucky man, Mr. Parsons. I pray that God will see fit to bless me with such a wife who can make such a happy home with such good food," he said, as his eyes moved to Rowena.

Indeed, it would be a delight to have this beauty serve him supper and service a marriage bed, he thought. He would get to know and befriend Samuel and convince him she should become his bride.

Who wouldn't want an orphaned girl to have the advantages of marrying a respected gentleman and doctor, he thought as he took another mouthful of the steaming stew.

When the meal was finished the men got up from the table and retired to sit by the fire while Hessabah and Rowena cleared the table and washed the dishes.

Hessabah pretended to be preoccupied in her work but her ears were tuned into everything said by the doctor and her husband.

"I understand your wife has been serving the people of the village in the absence of a doctor."

"Yes, 'tis true. She has helped many people with illnesses and has helped deliver babies," Samuel agreed.

"You will be relieved to know with my established medical practice your wife will be relieved of that burden. She will be able to concentrate only on caring for hearth and home. Perhaps, should she look to her wifely duties fully, God will bless your marriage with children."

Hessabah's back went rigid and her hands gripped tightly to the cloth she'd used to wash the dishes.

"So the doctor is here not only to get a free meal and seek a wife but he is also making it clear he is in control of all things medical," she thought.

She wasn't surprised. Most people would prefer the treatment of a physician. The medical community had done a fine job of discrediting women healers and their methods.

Medical practices were more often hindrance than help to the ill and injured. Most doctors still thought there were four bodily fluids including blood, phlegm, yellow bile and black bile. Illness was believed to be the result of an excess of one or more of those humors.

Some doctors had become more enlightened and questioned these traditional ideas. Some turned to the healing methods of the Abenaki and discovered that malaria could be cured with bark from the bark of certain trees.

Dr. White was, unfortunately, not one of those enlightened physicians who were willing to admit they could learn things from traditional healing methods.

In his surgery, the good doctor kept a supply of leeches to bleed the bad humors from the body and bring about balance. Those with rotting flesh had maggots placed upon their bodies which would eat away the dead skin.

Dead mice were used to cure problems such as gout, earache and even to clean teeth. Ferrets and woodlice were included in the treatment of whooping cough; while spiders' webs were the preferred method to stop nosebleeds, heal wounds and draw out poisons.

Dr. White also advised his patients to swallow spiders to cure fevers. He'd never tried herbal remedies and wouldn't consider it. For the potions and tinctures concocted by those who weren't trained in medical schools were viewed to be useless, at best, and evil sorcery at worst.

The doctor looked about the Parsons cottage and noted the hanging herbs and earthenware jars.

"Indeed this woman is trouble," he thought.

As dusk was fast approaching, the doctor rose from his chair.

"It is getting late. I must get home before dark. One cannot be too careful in these wilds. Either the savages or the devil could snatch one up in the blink of an eye. Thank you again for your hospitality and for a lovely meal Mistress Parsons."

He tipped his hat to Rowena and then shook Samuel's hand. Samuel saw him to the door and said goodbye.

"It was our pleasure doctor. Take care on your way home."

Samuel shut the door and watched as the doctor made his way from their cottage down the road toward his residence.

Hessabah was shaken by the man who'd just told her husband she was dismissed from all things medical and midwifery.

Unlike most who now resided in the new world, Hessabah and her Celtic ancestors believed there was nothing to fear from the night for it was of the feminine which gave birth to the day.

"Samuel, I know there are many who believe the doctor is the best one to see to their medical needs but there are others, especially women, who look to me to help them. Do you really expect me to stop what I have been called to do?"

"No, my dearest, I do not. I do, however, believe Dr. White isn't someone to make an enemy of. Perhaps it would be best if you went about your business quietly. Do nothing to draw his ire."

"What of Rowena? Did you see how he was looking at her? A hungry wolf if ever there was one staring down its prey."

"I noticed. If he comes to me to inquire about her I shall put him off. He cannot argue with me if I tell him she is not ready for marriage."

"Let's hope so," she said as the sick feeling she'd felt since the doctor's arrival continued long into the night.

Hessabah knew her world was about to change once again and not for the better.

4

One morning Samuel was in his blacksmith's shop. There was a large order of horseshoes to fill. He placed iron in the fire and, when it was red-hot, he hammered it into the perfect U-shape before it was plunged into a wooden bucket of water. Steam rose into the air, which was cool for mid-September. He placed the shoe on a rack and then picked up another piece of iron.

A noise in the street drew Samuel's attention. Rather than picking up a cold piece of metal, his hand clasped the still hot shoe he'd just made. He howled in pain and released the shoe but not before the skin was seared red-raw and immediately started to blister.

He backed away from the fire and anvil not seeing what was behind him and tripped over a pile of iron. One of the pieces punctured his left thigh. The pain in his hand was quickly forgotten as Samuel knew he now had a serious bleeding wound.

His screams were heard by many who were working in their gardens and tending to other morning chores. Many rushed to the shop to see what was wrong.

By now Samuel had passed out from the pain. A pool of blood had formed on the dirt floor.

"Someone go fetch Mistress Parsons!

Another yelled, "No, Dr. White should attend him."

Carefully Samuel was loaded on a wagon and brought to the cottage where, by now, Hessabah was running as fast as she could to meet her injured husband and the ones that had brought him home.

"Bring him inside. Lay him on the bed in the back room," she ordered.

She needed to remove his britches to more closely examine the bleeding wound.

"I must stop the flow of blood. Rowena please fetch my box of herbs."

Quickly the girl returned with the box from which Hessabah pulled an earthenware bottled filled with yarrow powder. She poured the powder on the cut and then applied fresh; wet yarrow leaves and flowers on it before wrapping it in long strips of linen to apply pressure to the wound.

Next she treated the burns on his hand. The blisters were oozing. It was bad. Carefully she applied a salve concocted from calendula and comfrey. She knew these leaves would promote the repair of new skin.

She brewed a tea from white willow bark and allowed it to cool before she encouraged Samuel to take it.

"Drink this, my dearest. It will help with the pain in your leg and your hand."

Samuel sipped the brew and, in a little while, was asleep.

Hessabah knew she needed something to stop his wounds from festering. She'd applied honey for she knew it could inhibit infection.

"Stay with him. I am going in search of something that will help him. If he wakes, give him more willow bark tea for the pain."

"Yes, Hessabah," Rowena promised.

She ran from the cottage and, as soon as she was sure nobody was watching, she slipped through the fortified village gates, across the grassy field and into the woods.

She had only been at the Abenaki village once. She hoped she remembered the way.

She'd only gotten part way when she was met by several Abenaki men. Since the English were their enemy, and because they didn't recognize her as a friend of White Deer, they were not happy to see her.

Kway. (Hello)

Kadgwi achiwaldaman? (What do you want?)

Wôbigen Nolka (White Deer). Nidoba agema. (She is my friend)

The Abenaki men now understood this must be the white medicine woman that White Deer spoke of. Despite her being English, White Deer said she believed she was a woman of honor who was on the same journey as they; loving Mother Earth and always thinking of others with her kind, healing hands.

"Alsoda" (Let's go), the leader of the group of men said and motioned for Hessabah to follow them.

After walking for nearly an hour they'd arrived at the village. The men took her directly to a long house where they motioned for her to enter.

Several families were inside. White Deer was saying something, which was making everyone gathered around the fire laugh.

Immediately the laughter stopped when the people saw Hessabah.

"Oligen nidoba agema." (It is good. She is my friend), White Deer reassured everyone.

"Wôbigen Nolka N'sagzi nizwia wkod nolidbamalsiw" (White Deer I fear my husband's leg is sick).

How could she make her understand?

"Mena ni ida." (Say that again). White Deer was trying to determine whether it was a broken leg or a wound.

"Sanoba wkod nolidbamalsi." (Husband leg sick)

She picked up a stick and snapped it in two.

"Oho?" (Yes?)

"Nda." (No)

Next, White Deer picked up a knife and made a cutting motion next to her leg.

"Oho! Mili gagwi". (Yes! Give me something!)

White Deer ran from the long house and Hessabah followed. They entered her wigwam and White Deer searched through several pouches. She handed Hessabah a small root.

"Gagwi yo?" (What is this?)

"It is a powerful thing that can help to strengthen his blood and heal his wounds," White deer wanted to tell her but she didn't have the words to explain it in English so Hessabah might fully understand. Instead she simply said:"Kadosmo" (He drinks).

Hessabah knew that White Deer had given her a root that she had never seen before but she understood that it was meant to help with his severe leg wound.

"Wliwni ni! n'pedgi nizwia." (Thank you. I am returning to my spouse).

"Adio Wôbigen Nolka."(Goodbye White Deer)

"Adio Hessabah." (Goodbye Hessabah)

Hessabah hugged her friend and ran out of the wigwam and toward the woods that lead back to her village.

She had already been gone more than three hours. When she returned she found Dr. White in the cottage.

"Where were you Mistress Parsons?

She couldn't tell him she'd been at the Abenaki village looking for medicine from White Deer so she lied.

"I was searching for you."

"We must have missed one another because I came as soon as I was told of his injuries. I was told he was in severe pain but when I arrived I found him asleep."

"Yes, he is injured. A burn to his hand and a leg puncture from a piece of iron. I applied yarrow powder and yarrow leaves to his leg and then bound it with clean linen strips. His hand is covered in comfrey and calendula salve. His pain has eased from the willow bark tea I gave him to drink."

Dr. Ward's face turned red.

"Mistress Parsons, you are not a physician. You have no training in the medical arts. You shall refrain from any further interference with my patient. Have I made myself clear?"

"Dr. White, this is my husband. I have had favorable results with such injuries using these herbs and salves for many years. Have you not considered them in your practice?"

"I shall not discuss my profession or anything to do with medicine with a woman. You are interfering in things you don't understand. This is the last time I shall warn you Hessabah Parsons. Have I made myself clear? Good day to you Mistress."

The still sputtering doctor grumbled to himself as he slammed the door shut and stomped down the street.

Hessabah knew she had just made an enemy of the doctor. She knew it would come back to bite her but what was not clear was exactly when or how. It didn't take long before she had her answer.

Two days later Hessabah heard a knock at the door. It was Reverend Ward.

She opened the door to a grim-faced man who was intent on two things. Firstly, to check on Samuel's health, and secondly, to admonish Hessabah for interfering where she didn't belong.

"Good day to you Mistress. I have come to see your husband."

Hessabah showed the reverend to the room where Samuel lay.

"Samuel, the good Reverend Ward has come to call on you. Isn't that kind?"

"Indeed it is," Samuel said.

He insisted on sitting up in his chair by the fire despite her protests of him getting up.

"My dear man, it's a terrible thing that has happened to you. Are you in great pain?"

"It stings a bit, I must confess," Samuel said.

"We shall pray God sees fit to heal you of these injuries. 'Lord, I come to thee to humbly beseech thee to bind the wounds that our brother Samuel has suffered. I ask that, should thee see fit, ease his pain and suffering and help him to recover quickly from his wounds. Amen'."

"Amen," Samuel said.

"And now let us discuss some news I have been given about your wife."

"What is it you have heard Reverend?"

"She is practicing medicine. This was tolerated in the absence of a physician but now Dr. White is here. There is no need for this to continue. Indeed, some are whispering that she is walking a dangerous path. Brother Parsons, you realize that it is necessary to always keep watch for any sign your wife and your ward, being women and weak, are vulnerable to the wicked ways of the devil who can easily trick them into unknowingly engaging in acts of sin?

It is your duty, as her husband, and Rowena's benefactor, to teach and guide them. Perhaps a beating to bring your wife to submission is in order," the Reverend said as he folded his arms across his chest.

Samuel had hoped not to draw the ire of either the doctor or the reverend but it seemed to him his good wife's efforts to help him had seriously damaged her reputation. He knew he needed to reassure the reverend he would correct his wife and ensure she behaved herself.

"Good. See to it that you do. Good day brother Parsons."

As soon as the reverend had departed Hessabah went to Samuel.

"What did he say?"

"He warned me I needed to beat you into submission and I was to ensure you will no longer interfere in Dr. White's work."

"I am not interfering. I am answering the call that every woman in my family for generations has answered as healers and midwives. You know I am not doing anything wrong Samuel."

"I know this my love, but it seems necessary we stop this before it leads to more trouble."

"Are you actually going to beat me?"

"No, my dearest, I am not. However it will be necessary to give the appearance you have been beaten so the reverend and the doctor believe they have won."

"How do you propose to give the appearance of a beating?"

"I shall tell Rowena to leave the cottage and make a show of being angry with you for disobedience. I shall tell you that you must cut a switch from a willow tree that's to be used to beat you."

"You wouldn't dare!"

"No, my dearest, I would rather die than see one mark upon your beautiful body."

"Then how shall we convince people you have beaten me?"

"We shall make a great show of it. I shall yell loudly enough for those nearby to hear. You shall scream and beg me to stop as I apply the switch not to your backside but to the table instead."

Just then, Rowena, who'd been gathering the last of the season's blackberries from the bushes next to the forest, came in with her basket overflowing.

"See how well I have done finding so many berries," Rowena said.

The smile on her face vanished as she saw what she'd not seen before. Samuel was clearly angry and Hessabah was the cause of his upset.

"You will go now into the garden and cut a switch from the willow tree. You will bring it to me and receive your punishment Hessabah. Rowena, leave now."

The girl had never seen the couple in a disagreement let alone Samuel ready to administer corporal punishment to his wife. Quickly she ran from the cottage and remained in the garden. She watched as Hessabah cut a switch from the tree and then went back inside.

From the yelling and screaming coming from inside the cottage Rowena, and many of the villagers, were sure she was being thrashed violently.

The sounds of the corporal punishment continued for several minutes. Then Samuel put his finger to his lips as a signal for Hessabah to stop her play-acting.

"You shall have to appear as if to have a sore backside for the next week I'd say. The beating, had it been real, would have left your bottom red and full of welts," he said with a grin.

The act of whacking the table with the willow branch had exhausted him. He needed to lie down. In fact, he wasn't feeling well at all and asked Hessabah to look at his leg.

They went to the bedroom where he lay down while she removed the strips of linen and the yarrow leaves. The wound had begun to fester. Red streaky lines were forming and crawling from his thigh to his knee. He started to shiver and yet he was very hot. He was in extreme pain and his skin was ghostly white.

"I am suddenly feeling very tired, my dearest. I think the beating I gave you has played me out entirely."

By nightfall Hessabah was having difficulty getting Samuel to wake and, when he did, he was confused.

"Dearest one, I have a frightening sense that I am slipping away," he said struggling to breathe.

Hessabah had seen this sickness before but she was unsure of what was the best method of treatment. She was panicked. Nobody, in all of her experience with medicine, with these red streaks on their skin survived.

Out of desperation she called for Rowena.

"Rowena, prepare a tea to help bring his fever down and add some of the root that White Deer gave me. I am going to her to ask for anything that might help calm those red streaks which are a very grave sign indeed."

As Hessabah ran through the woods she prayed.

"Blessed, holy Mother Mary and Saint Bridgit I pray you intercede and restore my beloved back to health. Samuel, my dearest one, don't leave me. I love you my darling. Please stay."

In the hour it took her to reach the Abenaki village the doctor had arrived at the Parsons' cottage to check on Samuel.

"He is gravely ill. I must bleed him to restore balance to his humors," the doctor told Rowena and ordered her to find a bowl in which to collect the blood.

Like most physicians of the day, he believed that tension in blood vessels was at the root of disease. He used bloodletting to treat most of his patients for a variety of illnesses.

"Where is Mistress Parsons?"

Rowena was unsure of what to tell the doctor. He couldn't know Hessabah had gone to the Abenaki village.

"Of that I cannot tell you sir."

"Never mind. I shall drain off a quart of blood several times over the next several days to balance the bodily fluids."

Rowena knew Hessabah wasn't in favor of blood-letting and that she didn't see much point in it. However, Rowena was intimidated by the doctor and remained silent as the procedure began.

By the time Hessabah had arrived back at the cottage Rowena was taking the blood-filled bowl from the doctor.

"What do you think you are doing?"

"I am treating your husband, of course."

"I do not wish that you should do this sir. He has already lost quite a bit of blood from his wound. This bleeding will only make him weaker!"

"No, it will balance his humors. I will not discuss what you lack in intelligence to understand. If you do not remain silent, I shall have you removed while I try to save your husband's life."

"Save his life?! I believe you will kill him if you keep this up!"

"Do you indeed Mistress Parsons?"

The doctor gathered his coat and stared coldly at Hessabah.

"You will soon regret your words. I will be back."

True to his word, in about an hour, the doctor returned with Reverend Ward and Dougall Slade.

"What do you think you are doing here?"

Reverend Ward and the other men ignored Hessabah. The minister went to Samuel and prayed. Then both he and Dougall then grabbed Hessabah's arms and pulled her from the cottage.

"Take your hands off me? Who do you think you are? You cannot remove me from my own home!"

"On the contrary, Mistress Parsons. The doctor tells me you are interfering with his treatment of your husband. You will come with us and remain out of the way while the doctor tries to save your husband's life," the minister admonished.

Hessabah kicked at the men's' legs trying to get free of their grip. Dougall Slade, a rather large and brutish man, picked her up and threw her over his shoulder not flinching as she beat on his back with her firsts.

"Keep her confined until I tell you she is to be freed," the minister said.

"No! No! Samuel!! Please don't take me from my husband," she screamed as she was being carried like a sack of potatoes down the road toward the Slade's cottage.

After they arrived he placed Hessabah in the root cellar and locked the doors so that she remained alone in the dark, damp, musty space below the Slade's home.

She screamed until she was hoarse but no one came to her rescue. Instead, she was given a jug of water, some food and a chamber pot.

Over the next three days the doctor had taken more than three quarts of blood from Samuel's arm. He didn't rally. He got worse. Five days after his accident in the blacksmith shop Samuel Parsons was nearly dead.

Only when it became apparent that he was near death, Reverend Ward told Dougall Slade to allow Hessabah up from the root cellar so that she might say goodbye to her husband.

Hessabah was in shock when she saw Samuel. He was a shade of whitish grey. She knew that her beloved, who was once so strong, so healthy and so much a part of her, soon would leave her. An hour later he was dead.

A sorrow, unlike she'd felt before, overtook her. She screamed like a wounded creature. She stared at the doctor and then the minister.

"You did this to him! You killed him," she screamed.

"Mistress Parsons! You will control yourself immediately or you will soon find yourself back in the Slade's cellar," Reverend Ward warned.

Hessabah, who didn't wish to be forced from her husband, somehow found the strength to stop crying and say no more. The doctor and reverend told Rowena she was to help her mistress prepare Samuel's body for burial, which would happen the next day.

"You may stay with him for the night but we will be back to collect the body tomorrow morning before it starts to rot," the doctor said.

Long into the night Hessabah remained with Samuel's body, which she cleaned and then wrapped in clean white linen. Then she prayed over his body.

"I pray you will have the blessing of being consoled and sure about your own death. May you know in your soul there is no need to be afraid; May you be given every blessing and shelter you need. May there be a beautiful welcome for you in the home you are going to. You are not going somewhere strange. You are going back to the home you never left. May your going be sheltered. May your welcome assured; May your soul smile in the embrace of the Divine. May you rest this day in the peace and love of your eternal home; May you be as free as the wind, as soft as sheep's wool; as straight as an arrow that you may journey into the heart of God," Hessabah said in a whisper to her husband's spirit.

She knew the time would quickly come when the villagers would come to take him from her. These last few hours she spent alone with the only man she would ever love.

Hessabah sat in the church with Rowena by her side. All of the villagers attended the service. Samuel Parsons was well liked and respected.

As Reverend Ward spoke, the funeral service for Samuel became another opportunity to lecture those in attendance about the wages of sin and the damnation that lay in wait for those who refused to follow a Godly life.

Hessabah bristled at the message. Her Samuel was the kindest, most giving and purest of souls she had ever known.

"If anyone is singing with the angels in heaven it is he. Reverend Ward knows nothing of my husband," she thought.

As she walked from the church toward the cemetery with Rowena, Hessabah knew life in this new land was about to get a lot harder for the two of them without the love and protection of her dear Samuel.

And as his body, contained in a pine casket, was lowered into the ground, the doctor and the reverend both looked at Hessabah and Rowena.

Indeed changes were coming and none of it was what Samuel would have wished for his beloved Hessabah or Rowena.

5

"What is to be done about Mistress Parsons and Miss Rowena? Surely we cannot allow those two women to remain on their own. Why it is simply not safe. They both need a guiding and firm hand," the doctor said as his reverend friend was seated in front of the fire in the doctor's cottage.

"Indeed, it is an issue that must be dealt with. Mistress Parsons can hardly care for herself let alone a ward now that her husband is gone, God rest his soul."

"May I make a proposal, my dear friend?"

"Certainly."

"Miss Rowena and Mistress Hessabah will both need to marry as quickly as possible."

"Tis true."

"Might I suggest that we do the honorable thing and wed these women? For both you and I are two lonely widowers and they available. I must tell you, the young Rowena has caught my particular admiration. I have prayed on it and I believe, in my heart, God is leading me to take up the responsibility of being her husband. And you, my friend, are also in need of a helpmate. You could use someone here to cook and clean for you," the doctor looked around the minister's parsonage and saw how unkempt it was.

The reverend placed a finger on his lips. Tis true, he thought, I need a woman here to keep the place clean. It had been more than a year since his wife had passed.

He was, like most men who'd know the warmth of a woman in his bed, desiring once more to enjoy the carnal pleasures marriage allowed.

"It is a good idea."

For Hessabah, while older than he would have liked, was still a pretty woman with a lean body, piercing green eyes and flaming red hair that he could see when a stray lock had once slipped out from beneath the white stiff cap which all women were required to wear.

"We shall allow the women a fortnight to grieve for Samuel Parsons and then we shall pay a call on the widow and her ward. It shall be made plain that they are to marry or suffer the consequences of being alone and without means in what can sometimes be a cold and cruel world and a fiery hell in the afterlife when one disobeys the will of God."

The two men smiled at one another. Both were thinking of the delights that awaited them once they had secured their new brides.

Hessabah was in a fog of mourning. She hardly wanted to get out of bed.

Rowena was struggling to know what to do for her. A week after the funeral she convinced Hessabah to go for a walk with her. They ended up in the woods just outside the village gates. Hessabah thought of her friend White Deer. She started walking in the direction of the Abenaki village.

Rowena, unsure of what was happening, asked: "Where are we going?"

"You remember my friend who is the medicine woman in the Abenaki tribe?"

"Yes, I believe so."

"I need to go there."

"Why?"

"I am not sure. I just need to find something to ease this pain in my heart. Perhaps White Deer has something that can help me with this crushing sadness."

Hessabah and Rowena were met on the outskirts of the village by several young Abenaki men.

"Kway. Nd'achwaldam klozimek Wôbigen Nolka. Hello. I want to speak to White Deer."

The men, as all of the people, now knew of Hessabah and White Deer's friendship. They motioned for her and Rowena to follow them to the heart of the community where White Deer was preparing a meal for her family.

There were no words needed. For one look at Hessabah told White Deer all she needed to know. Hessabah's husband was gone and she was in deep mourning. She understood that excruciating grief. Her husband had died three years earlier on a hunting expedition.

White Deer took Hessabah's arm and led her into her wigwam. She hugged her and offered her a place at the fire and then passed both her and Rowena a hot drink that tasted of camomile and St. John's wart.

It was a tea to help with stress and depression, she realized. But there was nothing to ease the ache in Hessabah's heart except for time, White Deer knew.

Long into the afternoon they stayed with White Deer and her family. To honor the spirit of Hessabah's husband, White Deer placed sweet grass, cedar, mushroom, sweet fern, and tobacco into a large shell, which she then lit. She then took an eagle feather to move the smoke from the smudge over Hessabah's body.

White Deer said a prayer to thank the ancestors for welcoming Hessabah's husband back to the spirit world.

"Great spirit watch over me and, when I am old and weak, give me guidance as I leave the earth."

Next, she sang a beautiful, yet mournful, death song to thank the ancestors and the Great Spirit.

When White Deer had finished singing she could see Hessabah was exhausted and needed rest. Rowena had already fallen asleep and Hessabah's eyes were growing heavy.

"K'kadgominogwzi. You look sleepy," White Deer said.

"Yes. Oho," Hessabah said and then yawned.

White Deer motioned for Hessabah to lie on the reed mats. She then covered them with blankets.

"Gawi Oligawi. Go to sleep and sleep well."

"Oliwni. Thanks," Hessabah said as she smiled at White Deer and then lay her head down and closed her eyes.

Both women slept for hours. When they awoke it was already evening. White Deer had prepared a meal of vegetables and venison, which she offered them.

Since Samuel's death Hessabah hadn't felt like she could eat. Out of respect for their host both she and Rowena thanked White Deer for the meal, which they shared with her and the rest of her family including Wibguigen Wiboz (Grey Eagle), Hessabah guessed, was about 16.

What there was no misunderstanding, were the looks both Rowena and Grey Eagle were stealing when they thought the other wasn't looking. Clearly they were drawn to one another and why wouldn't they be? They were young. He was as handsome as she was beautiful.

Now the sun was setting and it would soon be too late to see to walk back through the dense forest. White Deer invited them to stay the night.

"Oliwn. Thank you."

The rest of the evening passed quietly.

Grey Eagle asked his mother if he would be allowed to take Rowena to the nearby lake to watch the sun set.

White Deer smiled at her son. She too could see the mutual attraction forming between the two teens.

"Grey Eagle would like to take Kakasakw Wsizgowal for a walk. Yes?"

"Who is Kakasakw Wsizgowal?"

"It is the name the people are calling Rowena. It means Blue Sky Eyes."

"Oho," Hessabah said to Grey Eagle and smiled.

"Lossada tak., Let's go there," Grey Eagle said to Rowena who didn't understand much of what the boy was saying but knew she wanted to spend time with him.

Together they walked to the nearby lake. The setting sun lit the sky up with hues of pink, red and orange. It was breathtaking.

When Rowena turned to look at him she noticed it was her face and not the sunset he was staring at. He reached out and touched her cheek. She did not move.

He had never seen anything like this girl. She took his breath away. Rowena too was finding it hard to breathe and the sound of the blood pumping through her heart was all she could hear.

He leaned toward her and kissed her tentatively.

He then looked at her and she smiled shyly at him. Taking this as a good sign he leaned in once more for another, deeper kiss.

Rowena responded with a blush and a giggle.

Grey Eagle smiled and then jumped to his feet before stretching out his muscular arm to help her up.

Once standing he wrapped his arms around her waist and pulled her close to him. He looked deep into her eyes. Rowena thought she might faint.

"Kakasakw Wsizgowal Wajemi! Blue Sky Eyes kiss me."

They stood closee until the last of the sun slipped below the horizon.

They smiled at one another and held hands until they came back to the village. Then they separated as they walked the distance back to his mother's home.

He knew she was an orphan. He knew he wanted to be with her. He needed to speak to his mother about this.

For the rest of the evening there was conversation and games. Grey Eagle and Rowena mostly used a made up sign language to speak to one another with some help with first words in one another's language from Hessabah and his mother.

Finally, it was well into the night when everyone wished one another a good sleep.

In the morning, Hessabah helped White Deer prepare breakfast.

She desperately missed Samuel but being here was soothing to her soul. She felt a connection to White Deer that was difficult to understand. It was as if she'd known her forever and for many lifetimes before this one.

Like the Abenaki people, the Celtic tribes understood the soul could experience many lifetimes to learn the lessons only learned when spirit came to earth in human form.

Hessabah and White Deer quickly were learning one another's language but it would be a while longer before they would be able to have these kinds of deep spiritual conversations.

Still, they both knew beyond a doubt, that they were spirit sisters and had been together many lifetimes before now.

The morning meal was over and Hessabah knew it was time to return to the settlement before it was noticed she and Rowena were missing.

"We must return to the village," Hessabah said and thanked White Deer for her family's hospitality.

Many people in the village smiled and waved at Hessabah and Rowena as they said so long and promised to return as soon as possible.

Grey Eagle volunteered to walk them through the woods to the edge of the field that lead to the English Settlement.

Hessabah walked a couple of paces ahead of them knowing the boy had offered to escort them so he could have more time with Rowena. He reached out his hand and took hers as they walked in silence each looking at the other and smiling as they went.

When they arrived at the clearing Hessabah said goodbye to Grey Eagle.

"Adio."

"Adio Hessabah."

She kept her back turned so the two young people could say goodbye.

"Adio Niben," he said. Although he would have liked to have kissed her he didn't dare in front of Hessabah.

"Adio Wibguigen Megeso. Goodbye Grey Eagle," Rowena said.

Hessabah and Rowena gathered wildflowers on their way back to the village. She wanted to place them on Samuel's grave.

They'd arrived back at the village gates and, thinking they were unseen, slipped back into the village and quickly to their cottage.

But they had been seen on their return by the sentry on duty who wasted no time informing Reverend Ward the women had been outside the village without an escort.

The minister knew these women were far too independent and, for their own good, he would insist that they both take husbands immediately.

He was not prepared for the reception he received when he arrived to lecture them on the need to accept both he and the good doctor as their future husbands.

6

Hessabah and Rowena had just returned home after they placed the flowers on Samuel's grave when they heard a loud knock at the door.

She looked out the window. It was the minister. What could he want now?

She opened the door and he walked in without being asked. Next he took his place in the large chair beside the fireplace. Samuel's chair.

He never asked permission to enter her home. He never asked how she was feeling or whether she needed anything from anyone. This boar pushed his way in and was acting as though he were lord and master.

Hessabah could feel her cheeks burning. Her jaw was clenched.

"What a pleasant surprise Reverend Ward," she lied. "Have some tea? I have the kettle hot. It won't be but a minute."

Hessabah made a blend of rhubarb, vervain, senna and buckthorn and sweetened the brew with honey. These herbs were known by healers for their laxative qualities and could cause severe intestinal cramps. She handed him the tea and, as he drank, she knew in about an hour he would clutch his stomach from the pain and run to the outhouse every 30 minutes until tomorrow.

"See if the good doctor can fix that with his precious blood-letting," she thought.

"Mistress Parsons I will come right to the point."

"Yes?"

"The sentry saw you and the young Miss Rowena walking in the field outside the village walls. You know perfectly well this is a most irresponsible and dangerous thing to do without an armed escort. What were you doing in the field early in the morning?"

"It's my fault Reverend. I asked Hessabah if we could gather flowers for Samuel's grave. Soon there will be frost and all of the field flowers will be gone. I wouldn't stop pestering her until she agreed to go with me."

"We are sorry Reverend," Hessabah added. "I must confess the grief I am feeling over the loss of my husband has me addled to the point of not thinking clearly. Of course you are right. It is most dangerous to be outside the walls unescorted. We women, as you know, are ruled by our hearts and need more intelligent, level-headed men to guide us," she lied once more.

"Indeed, Mistress Parsons. That is exactly right. And, since you have raised the subject, I will tell you that this is precisely why I have come today!"

"What subject?"

"That you and Miss Rowena are not equipped. You are in need of protection and guidance that only two mature men, who are leaders in the community, can offer."

"How kind of you sir. It would be most appreciated if you could make sure we are secure as we continue to live here. Perhaps you and some of the other gentlemen in the village would be willing to help out with some of the heavy lifting jobs that Samuel did, bless his soul."

"Oh, my dear, but you misunderstand me. I don't mean that you and the girl should continue to live here on your own. No, not at all. I mean you both must to take husbands immediately."

Hessabah and Rowena were shocked into silence. Finally Hessabah managed to choke out: "Husbands?"

"Yes. It is the best solution to two problems," he said with a satisfied smile.

"You need husbands to keep you safe and on the straight and narrow path to God and two men in the village are willing to marry you."

"And who, pray tell, are these men?"

"My dear friend Dr. White has expressed his great admiration for Rowena and I am willing to provide you with a home, as my wife."

Rowena, who was normally demure in the presence of men, was unable to contain her disgust of the idea. She had found the start of what she hoped would be love with Grey Eagle and she couldn't bear the idea of being married to the balding and wrinkled doctor.

"No! I will not," she protested.

Hessabah went from shock to anger.

"Get out of this house sir!"

"What did you say?"

The reverend was scarlet with embarrassment.

"Why I have never been so poorly treated. You, Mistress Parsons, have forgotten yourself. I can only think that you are being so ill-mannered because you are still grieving. I will forgive you my dear but there will not be a next time. When you are married to me you shall be taught to understand that obeying one's husband is of God and that being contrary will be beaten out of you for your own good!"

The tea had taken affect quicker than she'd expected. The reverend doubled over in pain and moaned. Then he passed a large amount of gas. Embarrassed, he wasted no time to say goodbye as he opened the door and ran down the road toward the church rectory.

"He won't make it before he's soiled himself," Hessabah explained to Rowena as they watched him go.

Sure enough, he stopped in the middle of the street and placed his hands on the back of his britches. Hessabah couldn't be exactly sure from this distance but she thought she saw a large brown stain on his backside.

"Oh dear, I must be more careful with the measurements of the tea the next time. Perhaps I added too much rhubarb or vervain," she said with a wink and a nod to Rowena.

They laughed for the first time since before Samuel's death.

Reverend Ward could not be sure of the cause of his gut pains, flatulence and explosive diarrhea now tormenting him.

Perhaps it was the meat he'd eaten earlier that day. He'd suspected it might have started to turn but ate it anyway. But then he thought of the tea he'd had at Mistress Parsons' cottage.

Perhaps she'd placed something in it to cause the terrible affliction he now suffered from.

With each trip to the outhouse he was enraged thinking of the possibility that the woman had done such a grievous harm to him. If he could prove she was to blame he would have her placed in the stocks and whipped. He fantasized of the beating he would give that woman as soon as his backside was not raw from shitting liquid fire.

Hessabah and Rowena were left alone over the next few days. They talked of their return to the Abenaki village. Hessabah wanted to see White Deer again and bring her a gift to thank her for her kindness and Rowena was giddy with the thought of seeing Grey Eagle once more.

"Hessabah could the reverend and the doctor force us to marry them?"

"No, Rowena they cannot. And we shall not. I will never allow that to happen. We will figure out a way to live as we are now. I had one love, one husband and I shall not take another. You, my dearest Rowena, will marry for love."

"What if I love someone who most might say isn't acceptable?"

"Would that someone be Grey Eagle?"

"I like him. He is kind and so handsome."

"You would not be the first Celtic woman to be attracted to a native man. I would not object to such a union if you learn the people's language and understand their customs, which are in many ways, like our own. And, of course, his family would have to approve. However, you hardly know Grey Eagle."

"I wish to know him better."

Rowena would not have to wait too long for her wish was about to come true. For the next day it became clear that they would have to soon run for their lives or die trying.

Hessabah and Rowena were harvesting the last of the root vegetables the next day when the Reverend Ward and Dr. White arrived in the garden demanding an immediate meeting.

Hessabah sighed and calmly stood up wiping the soil from her hands on an apron she wore to keep her dresses clean.

"Hello good sirs. Come inside."

The men sat themselves at the kitchen table as Hessabah stoked the fire and filled the iron kettle with water and put it near the coals to boil.

"Tea, Reverend?"

"Erm, no. I think not."

Reverend Ward, embarrassed by of his recent intestinal issues, which had caused his bowels to let go violently, had said nothing to the doctor about the suspected cause.

"And you, Doctor?"

"No!" Reverend Ward declined loudly on his friend's behalf.

"That is to say, we do not have time to take tea with you ladies today. We are here to discuss the details of your quitting of this cottage as soon as the marriage ceremonies can be arranged. I shall, of course, perform the ceremony for Dr. White and Rowena. I have written to a colleague of mine in Salem who's agreed to perform our wedding ceremony, my dear," Reverend Ward smiled but there was nothing warm in it.

Hessabah knew she needed to think of something fast or both she and Rowena would be caught in a trap she had no intention of becoming ensnared in.

It seemed she needed to outfox these two old dogs. Let them think they were about to get their way and then, when the opportunity arose, she and Rowena would silently slip away from the village unseen under cover of darkness.

Hessabah followed the cycles of the moon as the women in her tribe always had. She knew in three days the moon would be full and would cast enough light that she and Rowena would be able to see well enough to make their way through the woods to the Abenaki village.

The doctor and the reverend wouldn't dare leave the safety of the village walls to go in search of them. She knew the men were terrified of the dark for the evil they perceived that abound in the night.

They would not dare face the devil and his imps that they believed in the woods beyond the safety of the settlement's fortified log fencing. And then there was the danger of

78

encountering the Abenaki who they knew were hostile to the English settlers.

"I have spoken with Rowena about your offer and we will need some time to pray on this. We realize that it could be a solution for the predicament we now find ourselves in. You are right, we cannot possibly cope here on our own," she said demurely.

"Now, there's the first sensible thing I have heard you say," the doctor said as he looked at Rowena as if she were a pudding he could hardly wait to gobble up.

"However, we must pray on it so we may seek guidance from God," Hessabah said gambling that the Reverend would consent to a request to pray on something as serious as taking marriage vows.

"Very well then; you shall have from now until Sunday next to pray on it. And then, we shall announce the reading of the banns for both marriages," Reverend Ward said.

The banns of marriage were a proclamation of an impending marriage. It allowed time for anyone with concerns that would prevent invalid marriages. Hessabah knew what these impediments were. A pre-existing marriage neither dissolved nor annulled, a vow of celibacy, the couple's being related, or lack of consent would stop both marriages from going ahead.

Hessabah needed no time to pray about it. The thought of marriage to the horrid Reverend Ward and the union of Rowena to the aging doctor disgusted both women.

The doctor, who could hardly wait to bed the young Rowena, would have to endure another month of celibacy. He would have to be content in continuing to pleasure himself as he fanaticised about driving himself into her sweet virginal body. The very thought of Rowena in his bed to warm the sheets and satisfy his urges was making him hard. The evidence of his erection would have been plain for everyone to see if he hadn't kept his tricorn hat on his lap.

"Very well then, it is settled. By All Saints Day we shall be wed," the Reverend Ward said looking at Hessabah and thinking of the pleasure he would have in giving her a sound beating as all women needed to keep them closer to God.

"Indeed, we shall," the doctor said looking at Rowena who was so nervous she was visibly shaking.

"Ah, I see you are aquiver at the thought of becoming my wife, my dear."

Rowena flinched as his wrinkled hand touched her arm.

"Have no fear my dear. It is only natural that you should be nervous as most brides are in the days leading up to their weddings and what follows."

Rowena kept her eyes downcast.

"Submissive. Good, I shall not have to break her of an independent spirit," the doctor thought.

Ward and the doctor stood knowing there was nothing more to be said.

"Good day gentlemen."

"Good day Mistress Parsons," the men said in unison and bowed before they turned and opened the door to the bright, sunny fall day.

Despite the warmth in the air, a cold chill swept through Hessabah. Fear of a future she knew she would do everything in her power to prevent.

Once again she knew help for both she and Rowena would be found through White Deer and the Abenaki people. As soon as possible, she would make her way to the village and consult with her dear friend.

7

Hessabah and Rowena devised a plan that would make it possible to go without others knowing her whereabouts. Hessabah would leave on the night of the full moon so she could see her way through the woods on the long walk to White Deer's village.

Should any of the ladies in the village question where Hessabah was, Rowena was to say she was in bed with the pains from the flux. It was common enough for women to confine themselves at home so neither the reverend nor the doctor would suspect anything should they enquire about her.

The next night, when she was sure everyone except the sentry was asleep, she made her way to the gates. She waited until his back was turned as he walked the length of the fence wall and made her escape.

Despite the moonlight, which partially lit the way, Hessabah knew she would have to be careful not to trip on roots and rocks as she walked toward the Abenaki village. It was 5:30 a.m. and she estimated that she would make it by sunrise as White Deer and the others were preparing to start the day.

Her unexpected arrival sparked fear among some in the village who still were unsure they could trust her. But, looking to White Deer, and knowing she trusted this newcomer, they said nothing.

White Deer welcomed Hessabah warmly with a hug. She'd been expecting Hessabah's arrival. For the past several nights she'd been dreaming of her and understood that her friend was deeply grieving her late husband and in need of protection from two who would seek to do her and the young girl, Rowena, harm.

"Doni gedowiozin? How are you?"

Hessabah, unable to think of the right words in Abenaki to express her feelings and to explain what was happening, started to shake and cry.

White Deer took her friend by the arm and lead her to her home where she offered her food and suggested she rest after her long walk.

When Hessabah was feeling somewhat rested and refreshed from her meal she told White Deer that their holy man and the medicine man in their village were making it impossible for them to remain living on their own now that Samuel was gone. Hessabah then told her that the men were pressuring both she and Rowena to marry them.

"Nda k'dachwi ni llalokawen. You should not do that."

Hessabah nodded. For a long while that morning the women talked about the problem and a possible solution. They agreed the answer was to be found here with the Abenaki people.

White Deer said she would go to the council and seek their approval to have both Hessabah and Rowena come to stay with them. It would work well. For these women needed protection and she could use the help of two who, like her, knew much about medicine.

For the first time since Samuel's accident she felt a sense of peace. White Deer asked Hessabah to wait as she went to the tribal leaders to seek their approval. After an hour Hessabah was asked to join them in the long house where the meeting was being held.

"Chief and council say they know Niboiwi Agakidozik is a pure heart and is on the same journey as the people."

"Niboiwi Agakidozik?"

"It means Night Spirit. It is what you are called by the people."

"Why?"

"Because for many moons some of the people have watched as you pray to the Creator and the ancestors at night in the woods near the English settlement. They see your heart. They know it is on a good journey. They know you are a medicine woman, like me, and they ask that you and Blue Sky Eyes come to stay with our people."

Hessabah's eyes filled with tears of gratitude. She wanted to express herself properly and yet there was still so much of the Abenaki language that prevented her from finding the right words to use. She smiled and simply said:

"Kamoji, pita ni wligen. Oho, wliwni ni. Well, that is very good. Yes, thank you."

It was decided among the people that Hessabah and Rowena should come to live with them as soon as they could leave the English settlement.

She would wait until nightfall to return. The full moon once again would provide enough light for her to find her way back.

Grey Eagle offered to walk with Hessabah back to the edge of the forest that night.

"Adio, wli nanawalmezi. Goodbye. Take care of yourself," White Deer said as she hugged Hessabah.

"Wliwni ni. Thank you."

Together Grey Eagle and Hessabah walked in amicable silence. They were both deep in thought.

Hessabah was carefully planning the escape from the settlement while he was thinking about Blue Sky Eyes.

He was excited for her arrival. It would allow him to spend more time with the beautiful girl with the long golden hair that shone like the sun.

After the long walk through the woods they arrived at the clearing. Grey Eagle smiled and nodded to Hessabah that he felt it was safe for her to cross the field to the settlement without being seen.

Taking no chances she decided to crawl on her hands and knees so the tall grasses would hide her from view.

She waited a long time before she felt it would be safe to re-enter the village unseen. Carefully and quickly she ran to her cottage and was safely inside before 1 a.m.

She found Rowena in her bed and asleep.

Hessabah, exhausted from the long walk and her grief, removed her now soiled dress and slipped into her bed. She slept fitfully for there was great risk in what she and Rowena were about to do.

Reverend Ward and the doctor would be livid if they discovered their plans to escape to the Abenaki village.

As the sun rose Rowena awoke. She noticed Hessabah's shoes by the door. She was relieved to have her home. She had been worried about her and fearful it would be discovered by someone that Hessabah wasn't in bed as she'd said to those who'd come calling yesterday.

Rowena stoked the embers in the fire and added a couple of logs to it before she heated some water for tea.

Soon Hessabah was awake and told the girl about her visit with White Deer and everyone in the village. They decided it would be too risky to try and carry many possessions with them. A knife for protection and some water to drink along the way with an extra set of clothing, which they would wear to help keep them warm as they travelled.

"When shall we leave Hessabah?"

"The sooner we leave here the better I think. Are you afraid Rowena?"

"A little," she confessed.

"There is more to be feared if we stay here than if we go to live among the Abenaki people. I have seen more kindness among them in a short time than I have since we first stepped foot off the Nonesuch. The Abenaki people are more like us. They understand our ways. Their beliefs are much like ours. They respect women and appreciate the gifts that are given by the Creator to tribal healers. There is no kindness or compassion in this settlement. The men consider women to be chattel and no different than the chicken that provides the eggs or the cow that gives the cream. There, among the Abenaki people, we shall find kindness and safety, I am sure."

Rowena smiled. She was relieved to escape the future that was waiting for her if she stayed in the settlement.

Only yesterday, as she was working in the garden, Dr. White arrived and she realized she had much to fear from him. She was disgusted by the very sight of him. His hands, cold and clammy, touched her arm and his breath was foul. For as much as the thought of bedding her excited him, it made her cringe.

Grey Eagle, however, was the stuff a young woman dreamed of; tall, muscular, a handsome face, expressive eyes and strength of character.

Hessabah and Rowena went about their day thinking of their escape but acted as though there was nothing out of the ordinary happening.

By mid-morning there came a knock on the cottage door. It was Thea Slade.

"Good morning Mistress Slade," Rowena said.

"Is Mistress Parsons in?"

"Yes. I shall fetch her for you."

Hessabah was in the next room organizing her herbal kit, which she knew she would need in their new home.

"Mistress Slade is here."

Hessabah wondered why the woman, whom hadn't come to see her since the doctor's arrival in the village, would be at her door.

Indeed most of the villagers had stopped seeking her medical help for they knew that it would be seen as an affront to the doctor and, more importantly, against what Reverend Ward said was a sin in the eyes of God.

Women, who concocted powders and potions were suspect and should be avoided for fear of having a spell placed upon them by some form of black magic.

Despite the warning Thea Slade was in the cottage and looking desperate.

"Oh, Mistress Parsons," Thea said and broke down in tears.

"Whatever is the matter? Come now, it can't be as bad as all that."

"I tried to follow your advice but I forgot to take the potion and I fear I am with child. I cannot go through another delivery. I know it shall be the end of me. Please, do you have something I can take that will stop this?"

Hessabah carefully weighed Thea Slade's situation. Already with six children and twice close to death from the last two deliveries, she would surely die if this pregnancy continued.

"How long has it been since your last flux?"

"A month," she said as she wiped her eyes with the hem of her apron.

She also noted the many bruises on the woman's skin. The marks of the latest beating she'd suffered from her boorish husband.

Hessabah produced a small pouch. "This powder will cause you to feel contractions and, should you be expecting, it will cause you to miscarry. Take it three times over three days."

"I shall, thank you. Good day Mistress Parsons." Thea said as she opened the door and looked both ways to ensure nobody would notice her leaving Hessabah's house.

The rest of the day was quiet enough. Hessabah and Rowena packed only what they could carry in leather satchels.

In late September sundown happened just after 7 p.m. Hessabah had told White Deer they would wait until the sky was fully dark before they made their way from the settlement.

White Deer and the other council elders assured her a group of scouts would be watching for them and, should trouble arise, they would be prepared to intervene to bring Hessabah and Rowena safely to the village.

Hessabah wanted to take no chances on being seen by the watchmen on sentry duty leaving the settlement after dark. It would be better if they could leave without notice.

She decided to increase their odds by preparing a drink that would cause the men to slip off to sleep while at their post.

A tea brewed from celery, passionflower, valerian, wild cherry and yarrow sweetened with honey would work. With the setting sun she and Rowena walked to the sentry post with the brew.

"Good evening good sirs!"

"Good evening Mistress Parsons. Miss Rowena."

"There's a chill in the air this evening. We thought you could use something to warm your bones. Would you care for some tea?"

Both men, who knew how cold it would soon get, accepted the offering with gratitude.

"That's very kind of you Mistress Parsons."

"It is our pleasure good sirs. You are doing a fine job of protecting everyone. We wanted to show our appreciation," Hessabah said with a smile.

"Thank you both," the older of the two men said and then took a drink.

"Have a good night ladies. Sleep well," the younger man added before he too took a drink.

Hessabah winked at Rowena after they'd turned back toward the cottage.

"We shall not, but they shall sleep like babes in their mother's arms."

She estimated that within two hours they could safely make their way from the settlement as the effects of the brew would have taken hold leaving the men fully sedated for the remainder of the night.

They made their final preparations to leave and, by 9 p.m., all was ready for their departure. Hessabah looked around the cottage that she'd built and shared with her beloved Samuel.

Since his passing it no longer felt like home. It was a reminder of how much she missed him. She would regret nothing about leaving it or the settlement.

In truth, there was nobody she would miss here. Rowena, who was like a younger sister, was coming with her. Her friend White Deer and the Abenaki people were welcoming them into their community. There was nothing to regret.

Quietly the women left the cottage. They wondered what the settlers would think when it was discovered they'd vanished. Maybe they'd been kidnapped by natives. Maybe they'd wandered off and were eaten by animals. Maybe it was a trick of the devil. Maybe they were witches who'd cast a spell making it appear as though they were invisible.

Hessabah smiled. "Let them wonder. Let them worry," she thought.

They carefully slipped through the settlement gate and crawled through the field's tall grass until they came to the edge of the forest where, as promised, the Abenaki scouts had been watching and waiting since just after sunset.

Grey Eagle was among them. He and Rowena looked at one another and smiled.

Hessabah knew a relationship between them would come with challenges as they learned one another's language and navigated through the complexities of their cultural similarities and differences.

She noticed that they looked at one another the way she and Samuel looked at one another in the early days of their courtship.

A heady feeling to be sure, young love was. There was no better feeling in the world than discovering the one who made you giddy as your pulse raced and your heart feel so full it could nearly burst.

Grey Eagle reached out and took Rowena's hand and then started the long walk through the woods that would lead them home.

He would do everything to protect her and make her happy Grey Eagle thought as the group walked silently making their way over the many miles that separated the English settlement from the Abenaki community.

By 10:30 p.m. they arrived much to the relief of White Deer and many others who'd been waiting to welcome them.

"Kway. Doni gedowiozin? Hello. How are you?"

"Newowlowzi. Ni doni gia? I'm fine. And how are you?"

"Nia atsinowlowzi bitta. I too am very well."

"Golibamkanni? Did you have a good trip?"

"Oho. Nolibamkanni. Yes. I had a good trip."

White Deer and several of the other mothers of the scouts had prepared a light meal for everyone.

As they all sat around the fire in the long house, Hessabah tried her best to explain how they managed to escape after drugging the guards. With body language she acted out the scene of the men drinking the tea and then slipping off into a drugged sleep, slumped over and snoring.

It was a funny sight to behold and caused laughter to erupt around the fire.

"Oligen. It is good!"

They sat around the fire for several hours talking, sharing stories and getting to know one another. It was clear the people liked Hessabah and Rowena who would take some time to get used to being called by their new names; Night Spirit and Blue Sky Eyes.

The fire was now little more than glowing embers and people made their way back to their homes to sleep.

White Deer invited Hessabah and Rowena to stay with her family until a home could be erected for them.

As they were preparing for bed an exhausted Hessabah looked at her friend and smiled.

"Oligawi Niboiwi Agakidozik. Sleep well Night Spirit."

Soon an exhausted Hessabah and Rowena drifted into a deep and relaxed slumber. Both knew they would be safe among these people.

Hessabah would have time and space to grieve for Samuel and Rowena would come to know and love Grey Eagle and his family.

As happy and content as they were in their new home, Reverend Ward and Doctor White were as equally baffled, frustrated and angry when they learned of the disappearance of the women they'd believed would soon be theirs to have, to hold and to control.

A search party was formed. Every inch of the settlement was scoured. There was no sign of either Hessabah or Rowena. They'd vanished.

As the reverend and the doctor searched her cottage they discovered a telltale sign of witchcraft.

It was a small, hand-carved stone that contained an ancient alphabet letter beneath Hessabah's bed.

He knew that witches used the runes for magical purposes according to their needs. Through his time spent interrogating witches both in England and Scotland as well as here in the New World, he knew that even a single rune could be used to cast love spells or place hexes on unsuspecting souls.

As news of the disappearance of Hessabah and Rowena spread throughout the settlement and the discovery of the rune beneath her bed, the rumors and falsehoods about them intensified and spread like a wildfire.

By the end of the week everyone in the village was convinced these women were indeed witches.

Then Dougall Slade found the potion Hessabah had given his wife.

"Woman, what is this?"

"It's n-n-nothing," she stammered.

"I know when you are not being truthful you filthy bitch. You shall tell me now or I shall beat it from you," he threatened.

She would take the beating rather than confess to having taken herbs to stop a seventh pregnancy.

Dougall Slade grabbed her by the hair and dragged her to the center of the village. He then tied her to the stocks used for public humiliation for those who broke the law.

A crowd gathered as he then produced a horsewhip and lashed her back causing her to scream as the cloth of her dress was shredded along with her skin.

She cried. She begged for the whipping to stop. It did when Reverend Ward arrived.

"What is the meaning of this?"

"I found some kind of a potion in our cottage. No doubt it was given to my wife by the witches."

For taking the potion, the Reverend Ward agreed that the flogging was an appropriate punishment, as well as a lesson for others not to have anything to do with witches and their evil ways. The sight of the screaming woman whose back was flayed open and the rivulets of blood which trickled down her back was a reminder to all that witchcraft was to be avoided at all costs or suffer this and worse.

"Untie her. We shall take this up in a less public manner." Reverend Ward said.

He would extract the information he needed about the witches' whereabouts from Thea Slade in time and given the right interrogation tactics. So far, the woman wasn't talking, further proof, he believed, that she'd become one of their converted coven members.

Reverend Ward and Dr. White were relentless in the torture of Thea Slade. She screamed and begged for mercy when she was conscious which, as the day wore on, was less and less.

"I will extract a confession from her even if it kills her," the reverend said.

"You're a witch. Say it! You are a bride of Satan and you have given your soul to the devil. Say it!"

With a slight nod of her head and through swollen bloody lips she croaked: "I confess."

"Hessabah Parsons and Rowena Williams are members of your coven aren't they! Say it."

"Yes," she said as the life gave way to death and she breathed her last breath.

"She's dead," the doctor pronounced.

"But we haven't discovered where those other two witches are," the reverend fumed.

"Don't worry. We shall find them and we shall bring them to trial," the doctor assured his friend.

Both men felt a great sense of satisfaction knowing the witches would suffer during their interrogations and after their convictions at the time of their executions.

But where were these women? They would stop at nothing to find them and give them what was coming to them.

Coven of the Soul Sisters / Laverne Stewart

8

As the days turned into weeks, with still no sign of Hessabah and Rowen, the doctor and the reverend spent many evenings discussing how they would deal with them once they were caught.

Since finding proof of witchcraft was no ordinary task, it would take all of their strength and cunning to outsmart the devil and breakdown these devil's brides. They would put them through the tests that were known to get the evidence needed to convict even the craftiest of witches.

Perhaps they would apply the swimming test, Reverend Ward suggested. Both Hessabah and Rowena would be dragged to the ocean, stripped naked before their hands and feet were bound. Then, they would be tossed into the water to see if they would sink or float.

"Witches are known to have spurned the sacrament of baptism; surely the water will reject their bodies and prevent them from sinking under the water," he said.

Dr. White preferred the method of looking for telltale physical signs. He considered himself an expert at identifying devil's marks on witches' bodies.

He fantasized about stripping Rowena and Hessabah and then shaving all of the hair from their bodies to uncover unsightly blemishes that witches receive upon making their pact with Satan.

"If we do find the devil's marks on their bodies we shall carry out the prick test. If they do not scream in pain when these marks on

95

their skin are pricked we shall have further evidence of their crimes."

And likely, he was sure, that he would find on both women witches teats. A mole, a scar, an extra nipple; all were proof that these women suckled the devil's imps.

These misogynistic men, who were repressed sexually, were brought to arousal at the idea of the extreme violence they anticipated carrying out on Hessabah and Rowena.

Long celibate, after the deaths of their wives, they were obsessed with the idea that these sirens of Satan were insatiable in their carnal lust.

"It is a well-known fact that these witches collect male organs in great numbers, as many as twenty or thirty members together, and put them in a bird's nest," Dr. White said.

"I have seen one or two of these poor men who lost their manhood. Why one told me he went to a witch to have his lost member restored: She told the afflicted man to climb a certain tree, and that he might take whichever one he liked out of the nest. And when he tried to take a big one, the witch said: You must not take that one because it belonged to a parson and I want to keep it."

Reverend Ward, blanched and his hands moved to his lap where he covered his groin.

"Indeed women are impediments to true spirituality and union with God. This is why I am diligent in my work to constantly remind husbands and fathers to exact corporal punishment on their daughters and wives. Their vulnerability to sexual urges and their weak minds are the very reasons they cannot hold any position of authority or responsibility. God reserves this exclusively for men."

Returning their attention to how they would extract confessions from Rowena and Hessabah, they turned to their experiences in past inquisitions.

"I have found the use of red-hot tongs to be very useful. When applied to women's breasts and genitalia, a witch will not be long in making her confession," the doctor said.

"Indeed, I have seen many men to become aroused by these witches even in the midst of these acts of carrying out the work of extracting confessions. These evil women were projecting their carnal lust on their victims," the reverend agreed.

Satan knows that women are weak and uses them to carry out his will. After all, we only need look to the book of Genesis where we read of Eve's temptation by the devil.

When we find Mistress Parsons and the young Rowena we shall carry out this trial quickly. Once convicted all of her possessions, including her cottage, shall be turned over to the church.

"Which is your preferred method of killing a witch?" the doctor asked.

"For me the punishment must fit the crime. I believe hanging is too quick. Drowning causes its victims to struggle but then, I am told, it is a peaceful end as one drifts into a sleep-state before death. I believe death by fire is the only way to rid a community of such evil."

The doctor nodded.

"Indeed, I agree that burning at the stake is the preferred method. However, the fire must not be large for the smoke will cause the witch to choke to death long before they feel the pain of the fire. However, if the fire is small it can take a good while before the witch succumbs. In this method their blood and other humors will flow from their bodies before their flesh peels away from their bones."

While the doctor and the reverend made their plans to find and interrogate the witches and then force a confession from them, Hessabah and Rowena were getting to know the people in their new community.

By the end of October they moved into their own wigwam. Hessabah and Rowena were kept busy helping White Deer tend to the sick and wounded. There were young women who were expecting that needed pre-natal care and the services of mid-wives when their due dates drew near and at the time of their deliveries. Night Spirit and Blue Sky Eyes in a very short time had become well-liked and respected community members.

Samhain is a celebration of the end of the harvest and the start of the coldest half of the year. It was, for Hessabah's people, a time considered to be the spiritual New Year.

The fire festival and feast of the dead, which honored the Celtic ancestors, had always been guarded and celebrated privately for many generations in fear of church persecution.

This year, like all of the years since Hessabah could recall her first Samahin, she planned to celebrate quietly with Rowena. Then, because she knew it would not seem strange to the people who they now lived with, Hessabah decided to invite everyone in the village to join them in their celebrations.

She prepared a feast for her guests including the village elders, White Deer and Grey Eagle. She set a place for their ancestors, Samuel, White Deer's late husband and Rowena's parents. They then shared stories of their family history including their happiest memories of their loved ones.

They danced in a circle around the sacred fire; all understanding the traditions that were familiar to both the Abenaki peoples and their Celtic residents.

For the first time in their lives, Hessabah and Rowena felt safe in the knowledge that they no longer had to fear being caught for carrying out the rites and rituals of their people. For here they found an acceptance.

To nearly all of the newcomers to New England, the ways of the Abenaki were strange and so too was the mistrust of the old pagan beliefs and customs, but both were familiar to the other with the following of their similar shamanic faiths.

Long into the night the celebrations continued. It was a time of friendship and of thanking the ancestors and the Creator for the good harvest that would see them through the long winter months that lay before them.

Hessabah smiled at White Deer who she was coming to feel a deep connection. Family was not always formed of blood and bone.

In White Deer she had found a sister. In Grey Eagle a nephew. Among the tribe she found a kinship she had not felt among anyone since her husband's death and the family she'd left behind when they'd made the journey from their former island home in the north Atlantic.

As the months passed and the snow lay heavy on the ground, there was much time spent around the fires of the families she came to know and respect. They shared generously whatever they had with her and Rowena.

In turn, Night Spirit and Blue Sky Eyes did everything they could using their gifts as healers to make the lives of the people better.

One young mother and father were so grateful for the help Hessabah and Rowena provided during the delivery they named their first born, a girl, in their honor. She was to be called Sky Spirit.

As the days and weeks passed, the sleeping earth was tucked safely and snugly beneath a heavy blanket of snow.

The people spent many days and long nights by the fires enjoying the company of family and friends.

Grey Eagle was now openly courting Blue Sky Eyes. With his desire to marry he knew he needed her family's blessing, his mother's permission and the community elders' blessings.

They saw that although there were many differences between the two, it was clear they had much in common.

She was quickly learning the language and the ways of the people. Under the teachings of White Deer and Night Spirit she was becoming a gifted medicine woman in her own right.

Mostly, they saw how in love the two young people were. With Night Spirit's consent, they agreed there could be a marriage between the two before spring.

It was decided that the ceremony would take place after the snow melted and the first flowers started to bloom. In the tradition of the people, White Deer and Grey Eagle presented a cedar box to Blue Sky Eyes and Night Spirit. They in turn gave a similar gift to White Deer and Grey Eagle.

With the wedding day drawing near, clans from neighboring villages began to arrive to meet the bride and to participate in the celebration.

Assembled in a circle, all of the people surrounded the young couple and their wedding party. A marriage pole was placed at the eastern entrance of the circle.

Anyone who didn't approve of the marriage was expected to strike the pole with a club, tomahawk, or stick. Nobody came forward and it was understood that Grey Eagle and Blue Sky Eyes had the blessing of all of the assembled clans.

Gifts for the couple were placed on a blanket beneath the pole. Tribal elders then performed a purification smudge with sweet grass. It was followed by a pipe ceremony before prayers were said and songs were sung.

The Creator was called upon to witness and bless the joining of Blue Sky Eyes and Grey Eagle.

"Marriage was established by the Creator, who created us male and female for each other. With the Creator's presence and power we have been given the example of the love of husband and wife," a tribal elder said as the wedding ceremony continued.

"Woman's role is to control the lodge, food, family, spirit, culture, and medicine. A husband's duty is to protect the family, lodge, and food - to hunt and to provide meat and game.

Both are to love and honor all of their relations, Blue Sky Eyes and Grey Eagle now give themselves to one another in this sacred bond. I ask you now, in the presence of the Creator, and all of your relations, to declare your intention to enter into the sacred union with one another."

"Blue Sky Eyes, you stand before the people and the Creator now. Is it your desire that you should be joined together with Grey Eagle and that you live together in a sacred marriage?"

"It is."

"Will you love him, comfort him, honor and keep him, in sickness and in health, and be faithful to him as long as you both shall live?"

"I will."

"Grey Eagle, will you have Blue Sky Eyes to be your wife, to live together in sacred marriage?"

"I will."

"Will you love her, comfort her, honor and keep her, in sickness and in health, and be faithful to her as long as you both shall live?"

"I will."

"The marriage of Grey Eagle and Blue Sky Eyes unites their families and creates a new one. They ask for your blessing," the elder said to all of those assembled in the circle.

"We are pleased by your marriage and pray for the Creator's blessing upon you," both White Deer and Night Spirit responded.

"Will all of you uphold and care for these two persons in their marriage?"

"We will," all of the people said.

"Creator, giver of all life, bless with your goodness Blue Sky Eyes and Grey Eagle, who come now to join in marriage. Grant that they give their sacred words to each other in the strength of your love. Enable them to grow in love and peace with you and with one another all their days."

Next Grey Eagle was asked to give his vow of marriage to Blue Sky Eyes.

"I, Grey Eagle, take you, Blue Sky Eyes, to be my wife, to have and to hold from this day forward, for better, for worse, in sickness, and in health, to love and to cherish, until we are parted by death. These are my sacred words," he said as he looked deeply into Rowena's eyes.

"I, Blue Sky Eyes, take you, Grey Eagle, to be my husband, to have and to hold from this day forward, for better, for worse, in sickness, and in health, to love and to cherish, until we are parted by death. These are my sacred words," she said looking up at her love.

Grey Eagle and Blue Sky Eyes held hands as a ring of sweet grass was placed over the young couples' hands.

"With this scared ring of sweet grass, which symbolizes the unbroken circle of life, we unite them as one."

Colored ribbons representing both families were then tied around their hands.

"You have declared your consent and sacred words before the Creator and this gathering of family and friends. May the Creator confirm your sacred words and union and bless you both.

Now that Blue Sky Eyes and Grey Eagle have given themselves to each other by their sacred words and with the joining of hands, I announce that they are husband and wife. Those whom the Creator has joined together, let no one break apart. Creator, you have heard their sacred words of marriage. We ask for your blessing upon Blue Sky Eyes and Grey Eagle that they keep their marriage union, and grow in love and goodness together that their lodge may be filled with your blessing and peace forever. May the peace of the Creator be with you always."

The marriage song was then sung to the beat of a large drum as Blue Sky Eyes and Grey Eagle then danced four times around the circle of those assembled.

For many days leading up to the wedding day White Deer and Hessabah, together with the help of other women in the village, prepared a large wedding feast for all who were there. At midnight, after the dancing, a supper was served.

With the celebrations finally at an end, it was time for Blue Sky Eyes to be escorted by White Deer and Night Spirit and a number of other elder women to her husband's wigwam, carrying with them her bedclothes. It was understood that this was the final ceremony that joined the couple in their marriage bed. She hugged Hessabah and White Deer before turning and entering her new home with her husband.

As they kissed one another they could hear all of the people cheering and laughing as the celebrations continued well into the night by the wedding guests. Soon everyone else was forgotten as their attention was solely focused on one another.

As happy and content as they were, miles away, an angry doctor and reverend had decided that there was enough evidence against Hessabah and Rowena that arrest warrants were issued for their capture and trial on charges of witchcraft.

They contented themselves throughout the fall and winter that as soon as they could they would assemble another search party and find these evil brides of Satan and return them to the settlement where they would be given speedy trials. Now, with the spring's arrival, there was nothing stopping their plans.

9

Every day a search group went out from the English Settlement. For more than a month they combed the area of the forests and fields looking for any sign of Hessabah and Rowena.

Just when they believed there was no hope of finding them, the searchers saw a group of Abenaki women gathering berries in the distance. Among the group two women stood out from the others. One had hair the colour of straw while the other's was a fiery red.

The searchers had been instructed to bring news of the sighting of Hessabah and Rowena immediately back to the reverend and the doctor. They had waited so long for this moment; they wanted the pleasure of capturing these women who had made fools of them by running away to avoid marrying them.

Together, the doctor and reverend, along with a group of other men, decided to lay in wait for Hessabah and Rowena the next day. They hid among the berry bushes waiting for their chance to capture these devil's brides.

By mid-morning their opportunity presented itself as Hessabah, Rowena and White Deer along with a few other women made their way to the area where they'd been picking berries the day before.

The women screamed as the English settlers jumped from the bushes with black power guns pointed at them.

Doctor White stepped forward with a look of cold rage on his face.

"Rowena Williams and Hessabah Parsons I have here a warrant for your arrests. You are both charged with witchcraft. You are to be brought immediately back to the village where you will stand trial."

Reverend Ward held Hessabah as another in the group from the settlement pointed a gun at her head.

The doctor, wishing to humiliate Rowena before they made their way back to the settlement, insisted on examining her. He pushed her to the ground and crouched over her. He then lifted her deer skin dress.

"If this woman is in league with the devil there will be the telltale marks of Satan. There. You see! There it is; a red mark on her thigh. It is further evidence that she is a witch," he said as he looked to the men who were part of the search party.

His satisfaction was short lived. As he was explaining how what was actually a birthmark was an imprint of Satan, Rowena made her move. From her deer skin legging she pulled a knife that Grey Eagle had given to her as a wedding gift.

She didn't hesitate as she plunged the blade deep into his lower back, which found its way to the doctor's liver. He screamed in pain and rage at the attack but was silenced as White Deer, who took the opportunity to make her move, sliced the doctor's jugular.

He choked on the blood as it filled his mouth and poured from his throat and seeped from his back.

So unprepared were the men for the attack, those who were holding the black powder guns failed to fire. They had no time to spare to escape when they saw dozens of Abenaki men and women in the distance who were running in their direction and were ready to fight the intruders.

The men, who'd hidden their horses in a nearby stand of trees, ran as fast as they could to get to their mounts before they were captured. It was a close call but they managed to ride off with Hessabah as their prisoner.

Grey Eagle rushed forward and gathered Rowena in his arms and held her as she cried.

He assured her that the settlers would be followed and they wouldn't stop until they managed to free Hessabah. A rescue group of 30 men assembled their weapons and were ready to depart the village within the hour.

They knew they had no time to spare for, with the death of the doctor, they knew English settlers would want revenge and would kill Hessabah without a trial and conviction.

As soon as the reverend and the other men arrived with Hessabah, now bound and tied to a pole. She was carried to a pyre, which would soon be set ablaze.

She screamed and begged for mercy looking out at the faces of the dozens of people she had treated for illnesses and to the mothers of the many babies she had helped to deliver since her arrival in the community.

"Will no one speak for me? You know this is wrong. For the love of God please listen to me. I have done none of you any harm. You know this!"

"Silence you witch bitch. Light the fire now," Reverend Ward ordered. Today you shall burn in body and soon your soul shall burn in hell for all eternity!"

Torches were thrown on the pyre, which quickly ignited.

Just then the sound of a man screaming could be heard from the sentry post.

Abenaki warriors had managed to climb the walls of the settlement. Grey Eagle plunged a tomahawk into the sentry's chest as the others breached the settlement's defences and ran toward the settlers. They were intent on killing those who were assembled to watch Hessabah die. Women and children rushed to their homes as many of the men tried to load their black power rifles.

Choking on the smoke, Hessabah was unable to cry out for help. Grey Eagle knew there was no time to waste if he was going to be able to cut her down from the pole in the centre of the pyre before it was engulfed in flames and they both burned to death.

He jumped on the logs at the back of the pyre, which had not yet started to burn and cut Hessabah free and then carried her from the execution spot. She was unconscious and her legs were badly burned. He could not be sure she would not die.

Reverend Ward screamed at the men to fight.

"God is with us men. Do not allow the devil to have his way. Fight the heathen."

An arrow, fired at the reverend, narrowly missed him but went into the windpipe of Dougall Slade and he dropped like a stone on the ground.

By now the fire had spread to nearby cottages and the settlement's wooden fencing.

The smoke-filled air made it nearly impossible for anyone to see. Reverend Ward knew his only chance for survival was to run blindly through the smoke and pray he made it to the safety of the forest without being followed and killed. In the ensuing chaos and confusion more settlers ran for their lives into the forest.

Now that Hessabah had been rescued and cradled in Grey Eagle's arms, the warriors left the settlement knowing it would be destroyed by the fire and the few who remained alive would likely perish without food or shelter.

Slowly and carefully the rescuers made their way back home. Hessabah was still unconscious when they arrived.

Grey Eagle carried her to his mother's wigwam where White Deer and Rowena were waiting. Tears filled their eyes as they saw her injuries.

There were blisters from the third degree burns on her legs. Some of her skin had charred.

The heat of the fire seared her arms and singed her hair. She was a pitiful sight and looked nothing like the beautiful woman she had been.

Carefully White Deer and Rowena removed what remained of Hessabah's dress. With the exception of her legs, the burns on the rest of her body were superficial and White Deer was sure they would heal.

The severity of the damage to Hessabah's legs, however, caused her great concern. Rowena sobbed as she saw what had been done to the woman who had cared for her like she was her own these past several years.

They would need strong medicine to save her.

White Deer had treated many burns over the years. Rowena, who'd never seen any as severe as those on Hessabah's legs, felt nauseated but summoned all of her strength and courage to help her mother-in-law and the woman she adored like her own mother.

First, it was important to cool the skin and clean the wounds. While painful, it was necessary to place Hessabah's legs in cool water.

After about 10 minutes, White Deer and Rowena removed her legs from water and carefully patted them dry before applying juice from the plantain plant to help prevent the wounds from festering and stimulate the growth of new skin cells. Comfrey and calendula ointment was applied too as an antiseptic.

To help stop the skin from further blistering and prevent scar tissue, White Deer placed compresses of calendula to the burn areas.

When Hessabah regained consciousness she cried out from the pain of the severe burns. She was still hoarse from the smoke inhalation and was unable to speak, but was able to swallow which was a good indication that she had not suffered any real damage to her lungs from the smoke and fire.

She needed something to reduce the pain and help her sleep.

White Deer made a tea from wild lettuce which she steeped and then cooled. Rowena cradled Hessabah's head as White Deer assisted her to take small sips of the medicine, which eased the pain somewhat and caused her to slip off to sleep.

It was important that the burns were kept clean and covered. Carefully White Deer and Rowena wrapped her legs with plantain leaves to keep dirt from entering the wounds.

All of the people in the community asked what they could do to help. "Pray," White Deer told the people. They did long into the night.

Hessabah was never left alone as White Deer and Rowena took turns caring for her. On the third day she developed a fever and became delirious.

Hessabah was speaking now in Abenaki. White Deer knew her spirit sister was battling for her life. She prayed the prayer she had come to know during her time among the people.

"Oh Great Spirit, whose voice I hear in the winds and whose breath gives life to the world hear me; I come before you one of your many children. I am small and weak. I need your strength and wisdom. Let me walk in beauty and make my eyes ever behold the red and purple sunset. Make my hands respect the things you have made. My ears sharp to hear your voice. Make me wise so that I may know things that you have taught my people, the lessons you have hidden in every leaf and rock. I seek strength not to be superior to my brother, but to be able to fight my greatest enemy; myself. Make me ever ready to come to you with clean hands and straight eyes, so when life fades as a fading sunset, my spirit may come to you without shame."

Then, in a language White Deer knew was one her friend spoke in her far away homeland across the seas, Hessabah spoke to the goddess Bridgit.

"Bridgit of the flame that burns away all ill; Bridgit of the words that grant comfort and might; Bridgit of the anvil and the fiery forge, I pray to you for healing and for life. Ease my pain, strengthen my spirit, help me to become hale and whole and in all ways sound. Good and gentle Bridgit, kindest of goddesses, grant me your blessing and your gift of renewal I pray."

White Deer knew that the injuries were bad enough that only the Creator would decide whether Night Spirit would live or die.

After several more days it became clear that Hessabah wasn't ready to give up her fight to live.

While still in pain, she was now awake. The trauma of being captured and nearly burned to death was causing her vividly violent nightmares. Each time she would fall asleep she would wake screaming from the emotional and physical pain.

White Deer knew that she would be left with many scars both on her skin and deep inside her mind. The most she could do was to keep her sedated with herbal teas and, should she be willing to talk about it, White Deer and many others in the community would be there to listen.

The two had formed a sisterhood that was a rare thing. They were from different worlds and yet they discovered that, despite their differences, they had so much in common. For many months they sat and talked about their lives and the things that mattered most.

Slowly, Hessabah's burns healed and she was able to start doing more including helping White Deer and Rowena with the injuries and illnesses that befell those in the community.

After her capture and near execution, she'd decided to erase the memories of all of those who'd done her, Samuel and George such great harm.

No longer was she willing to live with anything unacceptable to her. Instead she threw off all of the things that no longer served her.

She fully embraced the old faith of her ancestors and incorporated all of it with the similar and now familiar traditions of the Abenaki people.

No more would she tolerate the dogma of the church, which was so hateful and narrow-minded.

She knew the Creator was not an angry old man ready to punish all who did not follow the rules enforced by the church.

She knew there was room for all faiths as long as there was love. In her heart she believed that everything and everyone is a reflection of the Creator. Harming the earth or another person, in her mind, was akin to harming the Creator.

As the spring turned to summer, Blue Sky Eyes shared the happy news that she and Grey Eagle were going to have their first baby.

"This is a gift," White Deer said.

She, Night Spirit and Grey Eagle watched over Blue Sky Eyes ensuring she ate well and rested when she needed to. The months passed quickly and the tiny woman's belly swelled. Grey Eagle smiled as his hand felt the baby kick.

"It's a boy," he said with a certainty.

"Why is it that you think that my love?"

"This baby is strong and mighty."

Night Spirit and White Deer laughed.

"I am strong and mighty. So are Night Spirit and Blue Sky Eyes. This baby will be a mighty medicine woman or medicine man like her or his mother and grandmothers," White Deer said.

Blue Sky Eyes, nodded.

"Yes, my love. Our child will be strong and mighty whether it's a boy or a girl. If the love between a child's parents makes him or her strong, then there shall be no other with the strength of this new one that's coming to us soon,' she said as she touched her adoring husband's face.

Early one morning, as the snow fell in mid-winter, Blue Sky Eyes woke her husband.

"It is time my love. Please go get your mother and Night Spirit," she said.

Grey Eagle, now fully awake, searched for something to put on but was unable to see the clothing that was folded nearby.

"Relax, my love. The baby isn't coming this second."

Quickly Grey Eagle dressed and ran to his mother's wigwam. She was still sleeping in her wigwam.

"Wake up Mother. The baby is coming!"

Next, he went to tell Night Spirit she was needed.

She promised she would be there as quickly as she could. She dressed and gathered what she needed for the baby's delivery.

When she arrived White Deer was already attending to her daughter-in-law. Many women in the Abenaki community preferred to be alone during the delivery but, for Blue Sky Eyes and Night Spirit, whose Celtic ways included being surrounded by female tribal members, so it was the case with the birth of this baby.

She laboured for 10 hours before she cried out with force. Then the sounds of a newborn could be heard crying and taking his or her first breath.

Night Spirit poked her head outside the wigwam just long enough to tell him he would see his wife and baby as soon as she was finished caring for them both.

Grey Eagle could stand it no more.

"Is Blue Sky Eyes okay?"

"She is doing very well."

"And the baby? Healthy?"

"Yes. She is strong and healthy."

"I have a girl? I HAVE A GIRL!"

Grey Eagle ran throughout the village sharing his happy news, which was met with great excitement by all.

"Her name is Willow," he said proudly.

As winter turned to spring, and spring to summer, the routines of the seasons continued. Crops were planted. Berries, roots and other wild edibles were gathered. Game was hunted and fish were caught.

White Deer and Night Spirit made medicines.

There were weddings and more babies born. Just when it looked as though all was well the great sickness, which had killed many of the people before, had returned to claim more victims.

The day after baby Willow took her first steps she came down with a fever. The toddler wailed in pain and she vomited.

Then there was the telltale rash which covered her body in pustules. It was the pox. Several of the older children complained of headaches. This was followed by a high fever, chills, severe back pain, stomach pain, vomiting and a rash a few days later.

By the end of the week nearly half of the village was sick. The smallpox virus had already killed so many Abenaki people and other first nations' tribal members. It seemed there was no stopping it as it took hold.

Night Spirit was unprepared for the magnitude of the work that would soon be required to treat the afflicted and prepare the dead for burial. By the end of the second week Willow and five other children were dead.

She and White Deer could not give in to their grief. They were exhausted but knew they had to keep doing what they could to ease the people's suffering. Despite their best efforts many succumbed.

Some who got sick managed to survive but were left with deep scars on their skin where the lesions had been.

Everywhere throughout the village the death cry was sung as those who remained were left to bury their loved ones.

Night Spirit helped prepare many bodies for burial. They were wrapped in birch bark and then placed in the burial ground high on a hill overlooking the river nearby.

All who were not sick gathered in a long house to comfort one another in their collective grief.

The song for the dead was sung. It was a time of tears and great sorrow. Everything stopped except only what was necessary to stay alive.

With the death of the chief and many tribal council members, White Deer had to perform most of the funeral ceremonies.

"I ask the ancestors to accept the remains of our loved one back into the womb of Mother Earth to complete the circle of life's journey," she said as a smudge of sweet grass, cedar, mushroom, sweet fern, and tobacco was burned.

Songs for the ancestors were sung and the prayer pipe was lit. All of those who were there took a hand-full of soil and placed it on top of a body before the grave was filled completely and then leaves were placed on top of the grave to conceal it.

A final death prayer was said. "Great Spirit watch over me and when I am old and weak give me guidance as I leave the earth."

To the beat of the tom-tom they sang.

"We give thanks to our ancestors. They came here and gave help to us. We thank all of our relations for help but first we must thank the Great Spirit."

With each funeral Hessabah watched and listened, becoming too familiar with the Abenaki funeral rites, songs and prayers.

And when White Deer became ill, it fell to Hessabah and Rowena to provide her with medicine and care.

No more pitiful sight had these women, adopted by the Abenaki people, seen. They, having immunity to the virus, watched in horror as she suffered as so many in the village already had.

In the first days of the sickness, she lay on the floor of her wigwam unable to keep any of the broth or medicines down.

Weak from fever and dehydrated from vomiting, she said in a whisper: "It shall not be long for me now. Soon I shall see my beloved once again. We shall walk along the river as we did when our love was young."

Hessabah, Rowena and Grey Eagle sat nearby. Hessabah held her hand as tears flowed unchecked down her face.

"Please don't leave me White Deer. You must stay. There is much to do. I need you. Grey Eagle and Blue Sky Eyes will have more children and they will need their wise grandmother to teach them," Hessabah said.

White Deer looked up at Hessabah and smiled weakly.

"You will teach them Night Spirit. For you know the ways of the people. You were one of us long before we met you. You are a good woman and my spirit sister. I will miss you my friend."

White Deer looked at her son and daughter-in-law.

"Be good to one another. Be strong. You will need to be in the days that lay ahead," White Deer squeezed her son's hand and then stared silently at the ceiling of the wigwam as her spirit lifted from her body.

Hessabah closed White Deer's eyelids. She had known many people who'd died and was saddened by all of those losses but, with the exception of Samuel's passing, she felt no greater loss than that of White Deer.

Once more a funeral ceremony was held. Hessabah, now able to sing the death song and pray the prayers for the dead, lead the service and helped lay her friend's body in the ground.

"Goodbye my sister-friend. You will always be with me no matter how far it is from this world to the one you are going to now," Hessabah said.

Grey Eagle tried to stop the tears, wanting to be strong for everyone else. He felt a grief unlike he'd ever known before. He was a boy of 13 when his father died in the hunting accident. With his mother gone he was now an orphan.

He stood close to Rowena, so grateful the Creator had brought her into his life and allowed her to be his spouse.

Once their tribe numbered in the hundreds but the smallpox and other illnesses, brought by the newcomers, had decimated their community. Now, they were a fraction of what they once were.

The cold grip of death had not given up its hold on the people. As the weeks passed even more people died including Rowena. So broken from Willow's passing, she didn't have the will to fight her way through the ravages of the disease.

117

As she too laid shivering and sweating from the intense fever she looked at her husband who wept silently as he knelt before her begging the Creator to spare her life.

First his father, then his baby and mother and now his beloved was being taken from him. He didn't blame the Creator. He blamed the newcomers and the diseases they brought with them. His beautiful, golden-haired wife, with the sky-colored eyes, was leaving him too.

As she drew her last breath he kissed her lips. He hoped the sickness would take him too for h no longer wanted to remain in this place without those he loved.

Grey Eagle, didn't get his wish. Instead, he remained healthy in body but his spirit had been crushed with the heavy pain in his heart over the loss of the three people he cherished the most.

Those who remained decided it was time to move to a new place far away from the English settlers and far away from the sickness they brought with them.

They would move north to where there were no newcomers and where the hunting and fishing were plentiful. With them they would take all of the provisions they would need to see them through the fall and winter months.

It would be a new start in a new place. Hessabah knew that no matter where the people went she would follow. Her people were this tribe.

But there would be no move for this Celtic woman who'd come to be called Night Spirit by the first people of this land.

As she was gathering water from a babbling stream she did not hear the person who crept up from behind. Reverend Ezra Ward, who'd run off with the others as the settlement burned, had lived a wretched existence with some of the other settlers over the past year. Dwelling in caves, most of the settlers had either starved or froze to death.

Somehow he managed to survive out of white-hot rage he felt and the obsession over his plan to make Hessabah Parsons pay.

He dreamed of the time when he would get his revenge and kill this witch. Now he had his chance. There was no one around that could stop him this time. He held her head beneath the water. If she didn't drown she was indeed a witch and he would stab her in her evil heart. If she died, then she paid the price for the evil deeds she had done, including dabbling in matters that were not a woman's place.

Hessabah was unprepared for the assault and inhaled as her head was plunged beneath the stream. Her lungs burned as they filled with water. She struggled to break free but couldn't.

His hand was tightly gripping her long hair. She kicked and thrashed to no avail. Slowly the life drained from her body. When there was no further movement from her, Reverend Ward let go and left her lying in the pool that was flowing over large rocks.

"Another witch dead; praise God!"

He stood above her body and watched her long red hair floating on the surface of the water surrounding her limp, wet body.

He turned around and came face-to-face with an enraged Grey Eagle. The man, whose soul was crushed from the heartache of so much grief, managed to summon an otherworldly strength at the sight of Night Spirit's body and was fully prepared to kill the man who'd just taken her life.

"Niona Aho Wobenakiak Kizos Posiwaganogan. We are the children of the Dawn people. Gia wobigid Sanoba Magigwogan. You are white man's wickedness. Gia dalina bamegizegak. You die today!"

Reverend Ward's eyes bulged and a stream of urine ran down his legs as Grey Eagle grabbed him by the throat and strangled him. The reverend fought to get free. He kicked and clawed but he was no match for the much larger, much younger and stronger Grey

119

Eagle who continued his strangle-hold until the reverend turned purple and lost consciousness.

As his body lay on the ground it appeared there was no life remaining in his body. Grey Eagle, who wanted to be certain this villain would not survive, plunged his hunting knife into the reverend's chest piercing his heart.

Grey Eagle then pulled Night Spirit's body from the water and carried her back to the village. The sight of her dripping remains compounded their already unthinkable grief. They delayed their journey so they could honor the woman who had become one of the people; a friend, a sister, an elder and medicine woman.

In their language and in the language she had taught them that was spoken on her island home far across the water, the people prayed to the Creator that she have a safe journey home and walk among her ancestors and theirs who they knew were all together in the afterlife.

"May there be a beautiful welcome for you in the home you are going to. You are not going somewhere strange. You are going back to the home that you never left; May your going be sheltered and your welcome assured. May your soul smile in the embrace of the Creator."

When she had made the journey home, she was greeted by many familiar faces. Hannah, Samuel, White Deer, Rowena, Willow and the many others she'd known and loved but lost along the way were all there to greet her.

"Welcome home," a familiar comforting voice said as she arrived.

"It's good to be back. Am I staying long?"

"For a while, but you have not finished all the lessons you wished to learn in that lifetime. You'll be going back. Your soul contract asked to understand repression, injustice and cruelty. There will be many more opportunities with your next lifetime..."

10

April 20, 2018

A shroud of thick fog enveloped the coastal tourist town but she knew the way home.

She'd spent a lifetime here. Well, in truth, she'd spent many lifetimes here.

In this latest incarnation Beth Williams was much the same as all of the others; smart, self-assured, loyal, loving, and outspoken.

She'd lived many lifetimes before but remembered none of them.

And, as in all of her previous lives, she had a strong desire to help, to heal and to harbor the weak and weary. It was both her calling and her curse.

How many times had she found herself at odds with those who deemed her a misfit, a malcontent and mischief-maker?

At best, throughout her lifetimes, she was an oddity. At worst, she was in league with the devil and needed to be purged from the community like some dreaded disease before she infected the minds of others.

She was a naturopathic healer who relied on what Mother Earth provided to heal those who came to her for help. And, as in lifetimes past, in this incarnation, she always encountered the weak and wounded who were both physically and emotionally harmed by others.

Healing came to her as naturally as breathing.

While other girls made plans for sleepovers, she thought about which plants she would grow come spring in her parents' garden.

She was never invited to the gatherings of the girls who would stare and whisper to one another and then laugh as they passed her in the school halls. "Soon I will leave this place," she would tell herself.

As soon as she'd graduated high school she left the conservative coastal town. With tears in their eyes, her parents waved goodbye knowing this place was too small to contain a person meant to live a much larger life.

Over the next 20 years Beth only returned for brief visits. She'd made a life many would call successful. She'd met and married John Williams. He was also a naturopath. Together, they'd travelled the world working with charity organizations helping the sick and impoverished in developing countries.

It was a wonderful life, which continued until John became suddenly ill while they were working in Botswana.

Within a few days he was gravely ill. Beth did her best to keep him comfortable but within 48 hours he, like many in the community, had succumbed to a yet undiagnosed virus that left its victims in a delirious fever and a whole host of issues including internal bleeding.

Beth was heartbroken. John was the only person who truly understood her. Alone, she was unsure of what she would do next.

"Come home," her mother urged. Widowed the year before, she knew the pain of losing one's other half.

Beth realized her mother was lonely and was getting to the point where she needed help at home.

"Okay mom. Maybe for a little while," she said.

Before she'd arrived, her mother had died too. Now Beth was grieving the two she cherished the most. She would return to her childhood home and prepare for her mother's funeral. She would take time to grieve and when she was ready, she would figure out what to do with the rest of her life.

Beth had been going on her nerves over the past three days since she'd left the African nation. She hadn't seen a bed since she'd left Botswana and, as soon as she'd had a hot shower, that's where she wanted to be.

She put on a cotton nightgown and slipped under the sheets of the bed in her childhood bedroom.

Beth was asleep within minutes but it was far from restful. She was dreaming. These were the same disturbing and familiar scenes, which played repeatedly in her dream state.

For as long as she could recall she was taken to a time when she was murdered by the zealot minister who was convinced she was a bride of Satan.

The witch trials of Salem, other areas of New England and Europe, had long held a fascination for Beth.

If a woman was strong willed, thinking outside the norm, she was labelled a witch.

Society was so rigid, and religion so strict, anyone who didn't conform, was labelled evil.

Although she recalled none of her previous incarnations, she was drawn to the ways of her Celtic ancestors.

These healers and helpers, who'd been harmed in so many ways by so many people, were resilient despite the best efforts of others to end them all.

By the tens of thousands they'd been tortured and then burned, hanged, drowned or murdered in many other sadistic ways.

In fear of capture these women had gathered in secret around sacred fires to honor the gods and goddesses, pay tribute to their ancestors and celebrate the change of seasons during the summer and winter solstices.

As in her many previous lives, this life was about understanding and fighting for those who faced repression and domination.

Like walking through the fog she'd encountered on her drive from the airport, her dreams were misty recollections of these lives past. Somehow they made sense while she was sleeping but were confusing to her or entirely forgotten when she woke.

With her return to her childhood home, these subconscious dream scenes intensified over the next several months. So intense was the violence done to her and others she was left with a sense of urgency and despair.

"I am losing my mind," she said. She'd not had nightmares like this for years and now that she'd returned they'd started again.

Her mother's funeral was small. There were no relatives left in town and very few of her parent's friends were still alive.

In the weeks after the funeral she spent many hours working in her mother's garden. The passion of growing plants and making herbal supplements and lotions from them, which her mother had taught her, was something she loved.

She could feel her mother's presence while her hands worked the soil. It was comforting. It was calming.

She and John had spent most of their time working for non-profit relief agencies so their incomes had been modest. While she had some savings, along with a small inheritance, she needed a job.

Even if she'd had more money, Beth wouldn't have wanted to be idle. She was a woman who needed to serve others.

So when she saw a help wanted sign that hung in a strange little shop on the town's main street that hugged the harbor in the New England ocean side community, she thought it might be worth checking out.

The tinkle of a bell in the doorway signalled when anyone had arrived but it was unnecessary for the shop owner could feel their presence even when she could not see them.

Preshea Circe had renamed herself as a teen. It spoke to her unlike Susan Connors, which she had been named at birth.

She'd come to this community with her husband and children more than 20 years earlier. Divorced, she needed an income. With some of the money she'd received as part of her divorce settlement and income savings, she opened Circe's Closet.

The tiny shop sold candles, incense, crystals, essential oils, tarot cards and more.

She was an oddity among the people of the town. Some called her a hippie. Others thought she was a witch. Fundamentalist church leaders preached entire sermons on the evils of this place and its owner.

Pastor William Blackmore was one of the most vocal critics of Preshea Circe and her store.

"Brothers and sisters, Satan has used witchcraft to prevent people from finding holy spirituality in God alone for centuries. He uses mediums, horoscopes, and games to entice people away from God with a promise of self-enlightenment. The Bible speaks often of the consequences of following false idols," he warned the congregation of the First Pentecostal Church the first Sunday after the shop had opened three years earlier.

The shop had nearly no local customers. Most feared what they did not understand or they valued appearance over substance.

The bulk of her trade came from those who were willing to take a risk, like the many curious and rebellious teens in town as well as the thousands of tourists who came in for the entertainment of having their tarot cards read or to buy a souvenir or two.

Pastor Blackmore and the church's elders appeared before the town council looking for a way to force the shop to close. The mayor and council knew it was a draw for tourists so they refused to interfere, which frustrated the church leaders.

Pastor Blackmore continued his fiery sermons attacking Preshea and her business.

"I tell you brothers and sisters in the book of Micah chapter five verses ten and eleven it says, 'I will tear down your walls and demolish your defenses. I will put an end to all witchcraft, and there will be no more fortune-tellers.' And again, in chapter three verse seven we read: 'Seers will be put to shame. Those who practice witchcraft will be disgraced. All of them will cover their faces, because God won't answer them.'

Brothers and sisters beware of the danger. Don't enter that evil place. No good shall come from it; I warn you," he said to those seated in the church sanctuary.

Donald and Susan Eldridge sat at the front of the church along with their twins Randall and Rose. The 14-year-olds knew their father expected perfect behavior throughout the service or they would suffer the consequences once home.

Donald nodded at the words of warning encouraging his pastor friend.

"Amen! Preach it brother!"

Pastor Blackmore looked down from the pulpit and pointed directly at Randall and Rose.

"I am speaking to you teens. Do not be lured by the wicked ways of the devil's deception. Like Eve in the garden, he will tempt you. He will make you think there is no harm in trying the things that woman is offering. She is a witch and she can cast spells on you making you defy your parents, go against the word of God and be lost for all eternity!"

"Brothers and sisters, I ask you now to bow your heads so we may have a word of prayer.

Lord, I ask you bind that woman. I pray you send a legion of your angels down to destroy that wicked place. Lord, please help our young people to be strong and avoid the temptation that is offered in the mysteries of that pit. I ask this in your name. Amen."

"Amen."

On the other side of town Beth walked the few blocks from her parents' home to Preshea's Closet. She neither knew nor cared about the preacher's warnings or prayers.

Beth entered the store and was filled with a sense of awe. Everything about the place was familiar even though she'd never been here before.

It appealed to all of her senses. She recognized the ylang ylang, orange, tangerine, patchouli, and blue tansy among the large selection of essential oils and other natural healing herbal remedies to her delight. Ethereal harp music, Celtic voices and the beat of bodhran drumming called to the ancient place within her heart.

In one corner was a reading nook filled with books on all things mystical. An entire wall was devoted to healing crystals and stones. Each had an explanation of its purpose. It was here Preshea found the newcomer.

This woman, Preshea believed, was about her age, had a great sadness about her. She's suffered a great loss and was in need of comfort, Preshea sensed.

"This one is the right stone for you," Preshea said as she placed an amethyst in Beth's hand.

"It's a powerful and protective stone and helps to calm, heal and cleanse. Emotionally, it relieves stress, and soothes sadness. It is a good crystal in healing personal losses, grief, and helping to bring peace, happiness, and contentment during transitional periods. You place this under your pillow and it will help you to sleep and better understand your dreams," she explained.

Beth had never seen this woman before and yet she knew of her sadness and her nightmares.

Preshea smiled.

"Don't freak out but I'm known in this town as the resident witch. I prefer to say I am in touch with nature and have a reverence for the old ways of my ancestors."

For the first time in this town Beth didn't feel like an oddity. In fact, being here and with his woman, it felt like home. She felt as though she was with someone she'd known.

"Yeah, you feel that too? We've known one another before. No doubt about it. Hi. I'm Preshea Circe," she said extending her hand in welcome.

"Beth Williams. Your shop is fantastic."

"Thanks. Can I help you find something?"

"Actually I am here to help you," pointing to the help wanted sign.

"Come have a cup of tea and let's get to know one another to see if it's a good fit."

Preshea already knew she'd found the person she was looking for but it was nice to spend time with someone who wasn't acting like a scared rabbit around her.

All afternoon they sat sipping tea and talking. There was a natural ease between them. With few customers in the shop they were undisturbed.

"Tell me about you," Preshea asked.

Beth explained she'd grown up in the town but had left soon after high school to go to college where she met John.

"We had 20 wonderful years together. I lost him six months ago."

"You?"

"I moved here 20 years ago with my ex-husband and kids. They grew up and moved away and he traded me in for a younger model and left town."

"I'm sorry."

"I'm not. Getting rid of that man was like losing 200 pounds. I feel so much lighter. I am more in tune with who I am and what I am meant to do. I opened this shop three years ago with the money from the divorce settlement."

"It's a fabulous shop."

"It is, isn't it? I have put everything of myself into it. The locals don't like it much but the tourists more than make up for it. That's why I need someone to help. There's simply too much to do from May until October for me to handle it all on my own. So when can you start?"

"You're hiring me?"

"Oh yes. I knew the minute I saw you that you were meant to be here."

"Funny you say that. The minute I walked into the shop I felt the same way."

They agreed she would start working on the holiday weekend, which was the start of the tourist season.

Beth reached out to shake Preshea's hand.

"Handshakes are for strangers. Hugs are for those who are familiar and getting reacquainted. We are connected. Far back, I think. Many lifetimes, don't you?"

She hugged Beth tightly. It felt natural. It felt like a homecoming from a time she couldn't recall.

"Maybe. I believe in reincarnation but don't know much about it," Beth said.

"If you want we can do a little research into who you were before."

"How do you do that?"

"Have you heard of past-life regression therapy?"

"Yes I've heard of it but don't know much about it."

"Do you want to try it some time?"

"How would I do that?"

"With some help. I can introduce you to a man I know who is both a clinical psychologist, hypnotherapist and a priest," Preshea explained.

"A priest? You mean a Roman Catholic priest? Reincarnation isn't part of the church's doctrine," Beth was certain.

"It used to be. About 500 A.D. it was removed from the church doctrine. Father Ryan can explain it better. Anyway, he can help you, like he's helped so many others, to understand what's misunderstood by most people."

"I find it hard to believe the church allows this priest to talk about reincarnation."

"He's persona non grata in the mainstream religious circles. He's a Catholic priest in the order of the St. Patrick Fathers of Ireland, but is considered a heretic by his diocese. He's not allowed to preach or say mass in any Catholic church but he refuses to be silenced and continues to share his calling.

The church is infuriated people are filling meeting halls by the hundreds because his messages are so inspiring and make complete sense to a growing number of people who are tired of church dogma and others who have been damaged in one way or another by the doctrine and some of the church leadership."

"I'd like to meet him."

"Well, you're in luck. He does a non-denominational service in the town on Saturday nights. You can come with me if you want."

"I'd like that. Maybe it will help me understand why I keep having dreams about being killed," Beth mused.

"These dreams are a roadmap to the past. If you want we can take the journey together. I always tell people that they are in complete control. You decide what happens and will only be hypnotized if you wish to be."

They planned to meet after the shop closed on Saturday and Beth would go with Preshea to one of Father Ryan's services.

Beth had no idea how much meeting this rebel priest was about to change her life and take her down the winding pathway that lead to her many lives over thousands of years.

How many lifetimes had she lived and how were these women connected through the past? Both she and Preshea felt their souls were connected. With the help of Father Ryan, they were about to discover how.

Coven of the Soul Sisters / Laverne Stewart

11

At 7 p.m. Beth arrived at Circe's Closet to find Preshea locking the shop's front door.

They drove about 15 minutes when they came to a large stone building that looked centuries old.

"We're here," Preshea said as she nodded to the building and the sign above the door, which read *Friends Along the Way*.

"Let's go. The meeting is about to start."

In a large hall Beth saw nearly every seat had been taken with the exception of a few at the back of the room.

They took their seats as a tall, thin man with shoulder length silver hair and a neatly trimmed grey beard stood from where he was seated.

With bright eyes and a beautiful smile he opened his arms widely, welcoming everyone.

There was a warmth and familiarity about this man. His Irish accent was a delight to the ears as he eased into the evening's meeting.

"There's a saying in Gaelic, 'Céad míle fáilte.' Its literal translation is *'One hundred thousand welcomes'*, or *'You are* welcome, *a* thousand *times, wherever you come from, whosoever you be.*' So I say to you all *Céad míle fáilte.* My name is Father Ryan. Like you, I am on a spiritual journey seeking to know God better and, in more than 46 years since I have worn these robes, I have been challenged and changed by the spiritual experiences I have had along the way.

For those of you who are joining us for the first time I will share with you just a wee bit about who we are. *Friends on the Journey* is a spiritual community in search of the divine in all of us.

When we look beyond our own beliefs and get to know other religions and spiritual beliefs, we can come to understand our interconnectedness. There is unity through diversity. When we are willing to look beyond ourselves and are willing to see the hearts and minds of others we can become more inclusive. This is a place where you will find support as you continue along your spiritual journey no matter what form it takes."

Beth was impressed by this man's ability to speak with ease, sharing his understanding of spirituality which he made so easy to understand through his stories.

"I believe we are spiritual beings on an earthly journey exploring what it is to be incarnate. We are in this body, which I like to call a spacesuit made of skin, and bone and blood. It allows us to survive for a time in this place but this body isn't who we truly are. In my times of meditation I have asked God many questions.

When I was a boy in Cork, Ireland in the 1950s, I had no understanding of speaking directly to God nor would I have considered the possibility that I could have that kind of personal relationship with Source.

It was understood the parish priest would serve as an intermediary and speak to God for me and then tell me what I must and must not do to please God.

One of the first things people want to know is who is God? I asked and this is what I heard clearly in my mind and spirit.

"I am the wind. I am the water. I am the earth and the sky. I am in you and around you. I am above you and below. I always was. I always will be. Some seek me in churches and temples. Others commune with me in the sacred spaces of their own humanity. However and wherever you choose to be with me it is good. All is well. I am pleased to be with you; I always am. We are one. I am a part of you. That's right dear one. I have created you in my image. I breathed life into your body. Your spirit is divine because you are my child."

Throughout my life and in getting to know other faiths, I have come to realize God's loving and compassionate and lives in all of us. We are all able to find God within our minds, spirits and bodies. Tonight I want to share with you a short presentation on the subject of reincarnation."

Over the next hour Beth and all who were listening to Father Ryan's homily were transfixed. The room was silent as no one wanted to miss a word of the message.

"Throughout the world there are people of many different faiths who all believe souls belong to groups and all of those who you know as family, friends, and even enemies, are part of the same soul group which return from one life time to another in some form or fashion.

Your ancestors return to earth when new generations are born. Did you know that in some cultures when someone is about to die a mark is placed somewhere on the body. When an elder, who is familiar with the family's genealogy, is brought in to examine the baby and sees this same mark on the newborn, it is understood this is a reincarnated ancestor.

All of the shamanistic cultures in Africa and Asia and throughout North and South America believe in reincarnation. Ancient

135

Egyptians, the Norse peoples, the Celtics did too. Even 25 percent of Christians in America believe in reincarnation so it's alive and well today.

Every soul makes an agreement with God before they're born regarding things they wish to experience in human form. And, from these experiences, there are lessons are learned. If one requires more experiences to fully learn these lessons then they will return time and time again. We are part of the same soul group living many lifetimes together.

Now the mainstream Christian church will tell you there is no such thing as reincarnation but if we look back at its history, we can see that it was part of the Roman Catholic doctrine until about 553 years AD. In fact reincarnation was promoted by the Catholic Church and then a strange thing happened between 550 and 553 AD.

There was an emperor in Constantinople at the time called Justinian. He was married to a woman named Theadora. She was not satisfied with being the wife of an emperor. She knew many of the Caesars were viewed as demi-gods. The only problem was the matter of reincarnation.

If you believe in this then you know you come back again and again. Sometimes you are poor, sometimes you are rich and even sometimes you return as a dog or other kinds of animals. So she convinced her husband to call a church council to ban reincarnation. The Pope refused to ban the doctrine so they imprisoned him and went ahead with the council but removing all of the bishops who refused to go along with the plan. So that's how reincarnation was thrown out of the church's doctrine. The scriptures were edited to take out all references to it.

You might be asking why we don't remember these past lives if reincarnation is real. Do you remember everything from the time you were born? No. How many memories can you recall from the first four years of your life? Of the countless experiences you have over more than 12,000 days, how many memories can you recall? Even though you don't remember much, doesn't mean you didn't benefit from it.

Who we are in this lifetime is a result of who we were in past lifetimes. Those things we experienced become part of our cellular memory. What makes a past life memory real? It's likely to be real if a memory changes us and brings us in closer alignment with God.

If I realize in past lives I was all genders, all ethnicities, all religions throughout history; how can I possibly be prejudiced against anybody or anything?

As a young priest I knew of the concept of reincarnation from other faiths like Buddhism and Hinduism but I didn't really take it seriously until I had my own experiences with it through past-life regression about 38 years ago while I was at a spiritual training seminar.

At that time, through past-life regression hypnosis, I recalled, in the 18th century, I was a teenaged girl giving birth to my first child. It was so real for three days after the hypnosis I could hardly walk.

Through other sessions I have reconnected with many other of my lifetimes including being persecuted for running afoul of the church. It's funny that I am having a similar experience in this life. God is trying to teach me something. Don't you think?

What's the point of this life and all of the others we experience as incarnate beings? These, I believe, are opportunities to grow in enlightenment while we struggle with the idea of being separated from God, from one another and from nature.

In each lifetime there are opportunities to learn and grow. Moving from self-concern to compassion and love for others is the whole objective."

Before she arrived at this meeting Beth had no idea what to expect. The past hour was transformative. She had a real desire to meet this man.

She followed Preshea to the front of the hall after the meeting was over.

"Father Ryan, I'd like you to meet Beth Williams. She's just returned home from Botswana where she and her late husband were working with relief agencies. Beth, this is Father Ryan."

As they shook hands Beth felt a shiver run through her spine. She wasn't sure where or how but something within her told her they'd known one another before.

She was right and soon, with his help, she would find out how they were connected.

12

Beth lay on the sofa in a room at the back of Preshea's store.

It was here she had her first past-life regression experience with Preshea and Father Ryan who explained how it worked.

"Each session takes about an hour. Relax and settle in so you are completely comfortable. Take a few moments to find a comfortable position. Remember all hypnosis is self-hypnosis. I am simply a guide. You are in complete control of what happens and in charge of your own experiences. Cool?"

"Cool. Let's do this," she said.

"Okay, pick a spot on the ceiling and focus on it. Notice as your eyes start to blink and are beginning to get heavier. With each blink you are becoming drowsier. When I count down from three to one you will fall into a deep and pleasant relaxation.

Three, you are getting sleepy. Two, you are falling into a deep relaxation. One, you are deep into a state of relaxation. You are going deeper and deeper down until all of your body is relaxed and ready to go back in time.

Every breath you take brings you into a full state of hypnosis. All of the muscles in your body are loose and relaxed. You are going back to a time of your past lives. You are calm and welcoming of this journey. Your body feels comfortable. You are completely at ease. When I count back from three, you will be back in another time. And three, two, one. We shall begin? What is your name?"

"I am Feidlimid. I am with my tribal sisters. We are the wise women. We are the healers."

"Where are you?"

"We are at the springs of Sulis."

"What are you doing there?"

"We are bathing in the healing pools and worshiping the goddess waiting for the visions she bestows upon us."

"What are the visions you see?"

"The things yet to come."

"Are you safe?

"We are now but soon it will not be so."

"Why?"

"Soon they shall come for us. Soon they shall kill us."

"What will you do?"

"We shall fight them with our mother."

"Who is your mother?"

"Queen Boudica."

"When will they come for you?"

"It won't be long."

"What's happening?"

"We are surrounded. We cannot fight them. There are too many."

Beth screamed in pain.

"What's happening?"

"I have been stabbed in the stomach. I am lying on the ground and I see the Roman soldier holding the sword, soaked and dripping with my blood. It is coming toward my neck."

Beth said no more.

"She was decapitated," Presesha said.

"Beth, what's happening now?"

"I have returned to heaven."

"Do you remain there?"

"No. I choose to return to earth."

"Where are you?"

"I am once again with my tribal sisters."

"What's happening to you?"

"I have been captured. I am in a dark place. I am struggling to breathe in this place. I have been here for days in this dungeon. The sea is near and the frigid waters are filling this hole. I am freezing. The water, with the rising tides, reaches my waist. I am screaming for pity. I am begging to be freed."

"Does someone come for you?"

"Yes."

"Are you rescued?"

"No."

"What are they doing to you?"

"They are questioning me about my tribal sisterhood and our faith. We are the worshipers of Mother Earth. We pray for a good harvest and we thank the goddesses for the abundances provided to us. I will not share the wisdom of the ages with those who are unable to hear and whose eyes refuse to see."

"What is happening now?"

"They are attempting to pry confessions of witchcraft from my mouth."

"How are they doing this?"

"They are pulling the nails from my fingers and toes. Make them stop please! Please help me!"

"Move on from here. Where are you now?"

"I am back in the dungeon. The water is now up to my chest. I know I am about to die but I am not sure whether it will be here or elsewhere. They are back again. I am to be taken from this place."

"What is happening to you now?"

"They are shaving my head and pubic area."

"Why?"

"They are examining me for the marks of Satan."

"What have they found?"

"They have discovered a dark mole on my back. They say it is all the proof they need."

"What are they doing to you now?'

"They have brought me to the center of the village. They have tied me to a post. They are throwing stones at me."

Beth started to scream.

"Please! No. Stop!"

"Do you wish to continue?"

"Yes."

"Are you in great pain?"

"Yes. I can't see. Blood is now running into my eyes."

Beth screamed in agony.

"Do you wish to continue?"

"Yes. I am in such pain. Soon I shall die."

"Move on now to another place and time. Where are you now?"

"I am on my island home. It is nearing the time of Samhain in 1689. We are preparing for the festival."

"Who is with you?"

"All of the sisterhood."

"What are you doing now?"

"We are lighting the fire. We are celebrating the feast of the dead. We are saying prayers to the goddess:

'May the earth rise up to meet you. May the wind be at your back. May the sun shine forth upon your face; and the rain fall soft upon your fields and until we meet again, may the goddess hold you in the safety of her arms.'

"Do you meet again?"

"Not all of us."

"Why?"

"One of us has been taken."

"By whom?"

"By those who wish to stop us and our faith."

"What is happening to this one?"

"They are burning her."

She was shaking and crying. Father Ryan knew she must return to the present from her hypnotic state.

"It is time to come back now Beth. You are not in pain. You are safe. Your friends are not in pain. You will wake up feeling relaxed but you will remember these past lives. When I count down from three you will be back with me in three, two and one. Wake up Beth."

She opened her eyes remembering everything and yet no longer in distress.

"I remember four lifetimes."

In all four lives, I believe, you resided in Celtic lands. In the first life I believe you lived in a pre-Christian time in Ireland where the people worshipped nature and goddesses.

For example, Cailleach is the goddess of the land and the weather. She is the embodiment of the dark mother, the harvest goddess, the hag or crone entity. She appears in the late fall, as the earth is dying, and is known as a bringer of storms.

The gods were the archetypes of humanity and culture. In Celtic culture, nature and culture live in harmony rather than being enemies of one another like we so often see in western culture.

"First you said you were at the pools of Sulis. This would have been before the Roman invasion of the British Isles in 55 BC.

Next, you fought the Roman army, which was invading your home along with your mother Queen Boudica.

Next, you were held hostage in a dungeon near an ocean before you were stoned to death.

Finally, you were recalling a lifetime in 1689 when you witnessed the murder of your friend.

In this lifetime you and your people would have believed in three worlds. The heavens were where the gods and goddesses lived, the earth was where humans and animals lived and the underworld was the residence of spirits and the ancestors, but in this belief system all three worlds were intertwined. Much of your experiences with the old faith would have involved ceremonies, rites and rituals honoring all three worlds.

Much of the faith surrounded nature. It is mother. It is also the gateway to the metaphysical and it was revered. And the veil between the mystical and the mundane was very thin and could be accessed through nature in such things as stones and waterfalls or even your own imagination.

Next you were fighting Roman soldiers with your mother, Queen Boudica, and your sisters. You died in battle.

Your third lifetime appears to have been after Christianity arrived in Ireland.

After this time, there was a blending of both faiths. For centuries people clung to aspects of the old faith which the church used to gain more acceptance. You spoke of no longer being able to practice the ancient religion openly," Father Ryan explained.

"They stoned me to death in that life," Beth was recalling the visions she'd just had.

"Yes. They did."

"How many more lifetimes have I lived, I wonder?"

"We shall find out at some point but you've had enough for now."

She looked at Preshea. "Do you think we knew one another before?"

"I know we have," Preshea answered.

"How can you be so sure? Do you remember your first life and death?"

"Yes, I do. I was one of your sisters. Our mother was Queen Boudica. Like you, I died on the battlefield."

A shiver went down Beth's spine. How many other lifetimes have we been connected she wondered. They all did.

Coven of the Soul Sisters / Laverne Stewart

13

The long weekend in May was the unofficial start of summer. With it came the hundreds of tourists to the seaside town. As in past summers, the shop was busy with customers looking for essential oils, books, tarot card readings and souvenirs. Beth and Preshea worked well together getting into a rhythm of movement so as not to be in one another's way.

Late in the afternoon two teens arrived. Both dressed in black and looking curious but frightened. Preshea was used to this. Many teens, having been warned by their parents and preachers not to enter her store, came out of curiosity or rebellion.

"May I help you," she asked.

"No. We're just looking, thanks," the boy answered.

"Okay. Let me know if you need anything"

The pair, who looked very similar to one another, whispered and kept looking at Preshea.

Beth saw them staring and asked: "What's up with those kids?"

"They want something and are trying to work up the courage to ask for it."

"What do you suppose it is?"

"Not sure. Most of these kids come in to look around and leave with nothing but a story to tell their friends about visiting the witch's store. These two are really looking for something. Maybe one of them will have the guts to ask for it."

About 10 minutes later the girl, who looked to be about 14 years old, approached the counter and looked around to be sure nobody was watching and then cleared her throat and said:

"Do you have stuff here for spells?"

"Spells?"

"Yeah, spells."

"What kind of spells?"

"Let's say somebody is hurting someone and you want them to stop what they're doing. Do you have a spell that can make them or can you make them disappear so the person they're harming will be safe?"

"You're talking about binding."

"Yeah, that's it."

"Magic isn't something you fool with. You must know what you are doing and come to it through the right intention or you can suffer great harm."

"How do we learn this?"

"I will teach you but you must trust or it will not work and the person who is doing the harm will continue doing it."

"When can you teach us?"

"Come back tomorrow just before the shop closes at 7 p.m. and tell no one."

"We will," she said.

The teens left the shop.

"What was all that about?"

Preshea had seen these kids around town but had never spoken to them. She knew they were Randall and Rose Eldridge and the fraternal twins of Susan and Donald Eldridge who was a board member at the First Pentecostal Church.

The couple, along with others, under the leadership of Pastor Blackmore, tried to get the town council to enforce a bylaw that would shut her business down.

"Those two were asking for a binding spell that would keep someone from doing harm to others."

"Why would they think you could help them?"

"Like I said, many in this town think I am a witch and have certain powers. I have invited them back tomorrow because I want to find out more about who is harming someone. If these kids are being harmed I need to do something to help them."

"How will you do that?"

"I'm not sure but first I need to get these kids to trust me so they will open up."

The following evening, just before closing time, the pair returned. Preshea and Beth were counting the day's sales and putting out new inventory that had arrived earlier in the afternoon.

"You're back," Preshea said, unsure that they would show.

"Yup. So what do we do?"

"Introductions first; I am Preshea and this is Beth. And you are?"

"Randall and Rose but we prefer to be called Rowan and Raven."

"Okay, well it's nice to meet you both. Before I can teach you, I need to know more about who is being harmed and what's being done to them."

Rowan and Raven looked at one another.

"Nope. Can't do it. Too risky," Rowan said.

"Okay how about you tell me what's being done but keep names out of it."

Raven looked at Rowan and nodded.

"It's okay. Tell her."

"Someone we know is being hurt. We need a spell to make it stop."

"This is very serious. What you are talking about is a crime and the police have to be notified," Beth said.

"No! They can't. He'll kill her and then they'll separate us and put us in foster care."

"Who will kill whom Rowan?"

Rowan covered his mouth with his hand but it was too late. He'd already disclosed and Preshea knew she needed to convince the pair they needed to tell the authorities.

She needed to settle their raw emotions. A cleansing smudge would perhaps help.

"Are you familiar with smudging?"

"Nope," they both said.

"It helps to clear away negativity. We will smudge now and I will also show you how to protect yourselves by what's known as grounding and shielding. Have you heard of that?"

"Nope."

"It helps protect you from negative energies. Okay first take off your shoes and socks."

The teens looked at her but didn't move.

"Grounding can only be done in bare feet. You need to be able to connect with the earth's energies and you can't do that with rubber soled sneakers. Now take off your shoes and socks," she explained.

Once their feet were bare she said: "Turn off your cell phones and all other electronics. Next close your eyes and imagine that there are roots growing from your feet deep into the earth. Next place your tongue against the roof of your mouth and hold it there as you take in several deep, cleansing breaths. This will help you remain calm and centered. Let's try it."

The teens closed their eyes and breathed deeply while pressing their tongues against their palates.

"Breathe deeply. Inhale and think white light and protection. Breathe out and think 'Remove all negativity'. You can do this several times per day. It helps when you are feeling stressed. Understand?"

"Yup," the teens said.

"Next we will move on to shielding. I want you to close your eyes and imagine you are in a bubble of white light. I want you to say to yourself 'Holy Mother Mary, saints, guides, angels and the ancestors I ask that you surround me with your protection and keep all harm from me.' Now you try."

The teens closed their eyes and repeated the prayer after Preshea.

"Okay, next we are moving on to throwing. Ever heard of this?"

"Nope."

"Bring your hands together close to one another but not touching. Can you feel the heat and a kind of slight electrical charge?"

"Yup."

"Okay now I want you to close your eyes and think of making a ball of energy like you are making a snowball."

"Okay," they said with their eyes closed and their hands in front of them rolling the invisible energy ball.

"Now, whenever you want to throw energy to keep someone away from you, do this."

"Will it work?"

"Maybe, if you concentrate hard enough and your intentions are in the right place. Or, if you want to be certain that the person doing harm is stopped, I can get involved."

Rowan and Raven walked to the far end of the store to talk in private.

Beth, who'd been watching, asked: "Is this stuff real?"

"Absolutely I've been doing it for years. It helps you to relax and release anxiety and those with negative energy will stay clear of someone who's protected with grounding, shielding and throwing energy. However, if these kids are dealing with domestic violence, they need far more help than these relaxation exercises and prayers."

"So what do you do to help stop it?"

"I believe I have their trust now. I hope they will open up and tell me exactly what's happening. Then maybe we can try to speak to their mother and tell her that we can help her find a safe place for her and the kids to go. If they disclose and give me their permission, I will alert the authorities. There's no emergency shelter in this town and I know their mother doesn't work. They'll have to stay with me."

"You'd do that?"

"No question."

"You are already taking heat from the church. You want more trouble."

"Bring it on. These kids and their mother need our help."

Rowan and Raven decided to allow Preshea's intervention. Long into the evening they sat in the store's back office with her and Beth sharing the abuses they'd suffered.

"Our dad can get really mean. He loses his temper and he beats mom," Rowan said quietly and Raven started to cry.

Beth held the girl allowing her to release the emotions she'd kept in for so long.

"Last week, I heard him yelling at her and calling her bad names. I tried to stop him. He threw me against the wall," he said as he hung his head.

"I tried to stop him. I always try to stop him but he's too strong."

"Rowan can you show me your back?"

The boy turned around and lifted his T-shirt. There was a large black bruise from his shoulder blade to his tailbone.

"Rowan, Raven I can help you. Do you trust me?"

They nodded.

"I need to contact some friends of mine who can help you and your mom. I can ask them if you and your mom can come to stay with me. I have helped others who were in trouble in this way before. Would you agree to this?"

The brother and sister looked at one another and nodded. They knew they needed help and they were sure it would be okay with the help of these two women.

"Stay here with Beth. I am going to call my friends. You won't be going home tonight. Trust me, when we are done, your father will be bound so tightly he won't ever be able to hurt you, your mom or anyone else again."

14

Father Ryan was a clinical psychologist who'd worked many times with Preshea and other state social workers on family violence cases.

Within an hour of receiving Preshea's call, he arrived at Circe's Closet along with an on-call emergency state social worker who they knew would do right by the children as soon as she saw the bruising on Rowan's back and heard the teens' disclosure of their father's abusive behavior.

He often used hypnosis as part of the treatment of abuse victims. It helped to get to the heart of the abuses they'd repressed for their emotional safety.

Like a festering thorn in the body, the mind needed to expel repressed memories so their emotional wounds could begin to heal.

"Rowan and Raven, I want you to meet a couple of friends of mine. This is Father Ryan and this is Meg. They are both here to help you and make sure your father doesn't do anything more to hurt you or your mom."

As soon as the teens and their mother were in a safe place, and only after they'd agreed to be treated, he knew he could help them. He had counselled so many who were caught in the cycle of violence. Some of them appeared to be from stable homes with loving families. Some were part of a larger church community, which failed to acknowledge the abuses and even aided in the cover-up of those crimes.

Rather than answering for their crimes and getting the psychological help that was needed to break the cycle of abuse, many church leaders opted to sweep the dirty deeds of the perpetrators under proverbial rugs hoping they would remain hidden. Some didn't want the light shone into the corners or under rugs where the filth had been hidden. Some of the clergy were involved in abuses too. Preachers and priests were sent away from the places where they were accused only to resurface in another area to perpetrate their crimes on new and unsuspecting victims.

With one look at their body language he could see fear, anxiety and pain. Their breathing was shallow and from their chest rather than deep relaxed breathing that came from the belly.

He approached the teens gently and carefully so the small crack Preshea had managed to open in their thick walls of self-protection wouldn't close once again.

He prayed God would speak through him to reach them at their deepest, most vulnerable level so they understood they were loved and safe.

"Rowan and Raven have you ever heard of channelling?"

"Nope," Rowan said as he crossed his arms over his chest.

Raven, who was sitting very close to her brother, was silent and kept her head down.

"You know these bodies we are in are simply spacesuits to contain who we really are. We are souls living in human bodies. When we arrive our guides join us. There are those in spirit who have lived many times like us but who have learned all of the lessons they want to know and have returned to spirit, but who wish to help other souls who want to continue to experience life in human form. You both have spirit guides. Would you like to meet them? I believe they, the angels and God, have things to say to you."

Raven, now more curious than scared, lifted her head.

"We have been in church all our lives and have never heard of spirit guides," Rowan said, his arms still crossed over his chest.

"Well you might never have heard of it because some have no knowledge of this. But just because someone doesn't know doesn't make it untrue. Knowledge about spirit guides is what you now have because I have shared it with you. Soon you will have wisdom about the guides because you will have personally experienced them. Shall we begin?"

Raven nodded and Rowan simply shrugged.

Father Ryan closed his eyes, took a deep breath and said "God, Holy Mother Mary, Christ, angels and Archangel Michael, I ask that you surround Rowan and Raven and wrap them in your loving arms of protection. I ask their guides to come forward."

With his eyes remaining closed his body and face appeared different. It was him but in a different form like he was serving as the physical vessel for those in spirit.

"Dear Ones we have seen your pain. We have watched the harm that has been done to you by the person who was called to be your protector on earth. We have sent this man and these others to help you. You will no longer be harmed. You shall be taken to a safe place and you shall see that there are so many good things in store for you. You will heal from the wounds you have suffered; you will be set free both physically and emotionally and we will use this time of trouble to help you to help others to become free from abuse. Your path, until now, has been difficult but soon the journey will become easier and you shall see the joy that can and will be. Do not hold on to bitterness and anger for it will not help you to move forward. Rather, we would ask that you replace it with love and forgiveness. Not for the one who has harmed you, rather we ask that you allow love and forgiveness to enter your hearts for your own sakes. It is when you can do this that the light can drive out the darkness and the wounds you suffer from may start to heal."

Something special had happened in this room. It was a holy moment. Everyone was quiet, not wanting the moment to end.

While no words could describe what had just happened, everyone could feel the presence of God, the saints, angels and guides.

Father Ryan opened his eyes and looked at Rowan and Raven. The boy who'd been suspicious and defensive was now weeping and being held by Preshea.

Raven, who'd been crying before, was now smiling like she'd just received a gift and indeed she had. For time spent among the heavenly realm is precious.

Rowan wiped his eyes and with a new sense of security wanted to know what would happen next.

The social worker said she would need to see his bruises and photograph them as evidence. She also needed to hear what their father had done to them so she could document it.

After two hours of listening to the brother and sister's recollections of everything that had happened to them and their mother, Meg, who was an expert on abuse victimization, knew their body language and unwavering and detailed accounts, was evidence of their victimization.

"You'll not have to go home tonight," she said.

"Where are we going?"

"You'll be taken to an emergency home tonight. The police will go to your house and your father will be taken into custody," she explained.

"Tomorrow Beth and I'll visit your mother and will speak to her about finding a safe place to go," Preshea added.

"You and your mom can come live with me if you want," Preshea said.

Rowan and Raven asked to have a minute to discuss it. In a short while they returned to say they would like to live with Preshea.

"Hey, you're pretty cool. You aren't at all evil," Rowan said.

"Sometimes it's best to get to know somebody on your own to make your own observations rather than listening to others," she said and smiled.

Having a couple of teens around the house would help liven up the place, which was too quiet since her own kids were grown and it was just her and her cat, Boudica, there these past few years, she thought.

"What's going to happen to our dad," Rowan asked.

Often abuse victims feel guilty for disclosing especially when it's a parent who is the abuser. The social worker asked:

"You need to know Rowan what you and your sister did here tonight was very brave. You wouldn't want any other kids or their parent to go through what you have. If you knew one of your friends was being harmed what would you tell him?"

"I would say 'Go tell someone you trust," he said.

"This is what you've done. You and your sister are helping yourselves and, in the long run, you'll be helping your dad. Often abusers were, at some point, victims. Now, because you have told us what's happened, we can ensure you are safe and he gets the help he needs. In the long run, he'll thank you for it. As hard as this is to believe, he likely hates what he's doing and he hates himself even more," Preshea said.

The boy nodded and smiled slightly. Raven, who was quiet throughout most of the session, asked when they were leaving.

"We can go now if you'd like," Meg said.

"Yeah, let's go," Rowan said to his sister.

The teens hugged Preshea, Beth and Father Ryan who promised he would be in touch soon.

"Okay you two, get some rest. If all goes well tomorrow I will see you at my house," Preshea said.

"Thanks," Raven said.

"My pleasure dear," Preshea said as she thought how much this boy and girl reminded her of others but she couldn't quite put her finger on who just yet. They were connected she was sure. Which lifetime ago and how she had yet to discover, but she soon would.

By now it was close to 11 o'clock. Preshea, Beth and Father Ryan waved as the car they got into with the social worker pulled away from the curb and drove down the street.

"Brave kids," Beth said.

"Indeed, that they are," Father Ryan agreed. "Well my friends, I shall say goodnight to you. Beth, if you want to undergo more past-life regression therapy why don't you call my clinic and arrange a session with my assistant. I'm happy to see you any time."

"Thank you Father Ryan. I'll do that."

"Please, call me John. I really dislike titles. They tend to put a distance between two people. Don't you think?"

"Okay, John it is."

She liked this man. He was so familiar. She was just getting to understand a little of reincarnation but, if it is true that souls experience many lives in soul groups then he and Preshea were definitely part of hers.

She wondered how many times they had known one another in past lives and which roles they played in one another's lives.

The emotional experience of the evening with the teens had left them all exhausted. They said good night and were looking for a peaceful rest. They would need it. Like a storm front moving in, an angry Pastor Blackmore was about cause havoc.

15

By midnight, when the kids hadn't returned home, their parents had started calling friends from church asking whether they were there. No one had seen them.

At 1 a.m. the couple were relieved when they heard a knock at the door thinking it was the kids who'd forgotten their keys.

As he opened the door Donald Eldridge said "You two better have a very good explanation…"

The sight of two uniformed police officers standing on the front step stopped him in mid-rant. Like a chameleon, he quickly changed his image from overbearing abuser to upstanding, kind and caring father.

"Good evening officers. I hope you have some news of our children. We are worried sick about them. They should have been home hours ago. We have called all of their friends' homes and I was just about to call the station," he said with an expression that was meant to persuade the officers that he was a loving, worried dad.

"Donald Eldridge?"

"Yes. Where are my kids?"

"They're safe," the officer replied.

"Oh, thank God," Susan Eldridge sighed in relief.

Donald demanded answers.

"Where are they?"

He was shocked to hear the police officer's response.

"Donald Eldridge we have a warrant for your arrest."

"On what grounds?!"

"Domestic violence."

The incredulous man's face turned a shade of light purple as he sputtered and fumed in his protests.

"Who is saying these horrible lies about me? Do you know I am a deacon at First Pentecostal Church? I am a respected member of this community. I will sue whoever is responsible for this!"

The arresting officers read him his rights as they placed handcuffs on him and lead him to a squad car as his crying wife protested too.

"Officers, this is a mistake. My husband is a good Christian man. Just ask people in our church. He would never hurt his own children!"

"Mrs. Eldridge your children are safe. Somebody will be in touch with you in the morning. I suggest you get some sleep."

As the officers lead Donald to their car and put him in the back he yelled "Call Pastor Blackmore and call the lawyer too' before the squad car's back door was slammed shut.

Susan did as she was told. By the time the police car was out of sight, she returned to the house where she called Pastor Blackmore.

The preacher wasted no time getting to the jail where he insisted on seeing his parishioner.

"This is ridiculous. Do you know he is a respected member of the church's board of directors? He is great with kids and his wife.

162

They're a model family. He teaches Sunday school and leads the church's youth group."

An officer sitting at the station's reception desk lifted one eyebrow and the side of his mouth twisted in incredulity. He'd seen a lot of abusers in his time and some of them were 'Good Christians'.

"Wait over there. I'll check whether you are allowed in."

Pastor Blackmore paced for nearly 30 minutes before the officer returned.

"Sorry. Only his lawyer is allowed in the holding cell with him and he's not arrived yet."

Donald Eldridge, who'd never before seen the inside of a jail cell, was frightened. He'd heard what happened behind bars. After 10 hours his lawyer had yet to arrive and he was starting to panic.

"I demand to speak to my lawyer!"

"Keep it down. He'll get here when he gets here," an on-duty officer said.

But his lawyer was still a no-show. A police officer told him he was scheduled to appear in court the next morning and, if his lawyer wasn't available, he would be represented by a state-appointed one.

Rowan and Raven had gone from the emergency shelter back to their home with Beth and Preshea. The door was locked.

They rang the bell. In a couple of minutes their mother answered. She looked terrible.

"Oh, thank God. You're safe!"

"Mom!"

The teens hugged her immediately.

"Mom, this is Beth Williams and this is…"

163

"I know who she is. What's she doing here? Why are you with her?"

"Listen mom, Pastor Blackmore is completely wrong about Preshea. She is helping us!"

"Helping you with what? Getting your father arrested?"

"Mrs. Eldridge your children came to us looking for help. They have told us your husband is violent and hurts both you and the kids."

"That's not true. Why would you say this kids?"

"We have seen the bruises on your son's back Mrs. Eldridge," Beth said.

"Mom, we don't have to keep this a secret any more. Beth, Preshea and Father Ryan are going to help us to be safe.

"Father Ryan? You mean the weirdo priest who believes in reincarnation? We don't need his help or anything from these witches. We have a pastor and we have a church family who we can go to for help if we need it. Now come on kids, come inside. I will ask you not to come anywhere near me or my kids again."

"I'm afraid that's not possible," Preshea said.

"Why not?"

The Department of Child Welfare is now involved and the kids will be placed with me for the time being. We came here to invite you to join us."

"Go live at your home? Are you kidding? Pastor Blackmore has warned us about you."

"Don't believe everything you hear," Preshea said.

"Mom, she's a good person. She is trying to help us," Raven said.

"No! Stay away from my children and from me. Come on kids. Come inside. Now!"

164

"No mom. We're going and we want you to come with us. If dad gets out of jail you know what will happen," Rowan urged.

"I don't know what you're talking about. Stop lying about your dad."

"I don't want to be here mom and neither does Raven," he said.

"Raven? Who's that?"

"I meant Rose."

"Raven. So you're starting to use witch names? What else are you doing? Are you practicing black magic? What have you done to my children you hag?"

Preshea had heard it before. There was no sense arguing with this woman.

"We have to go," she said quietly.

"Mom, come on. Please change your mind and come stay with us at Preshea's house," Raven begged.

"No, I will not and neither will you. I am calling Pastor Blackmore and putting a stop to this nonsense. You belong here at home with your father and I."

"We're going to stay with Preshea and if you know what's good for you, you will move in with us. Dad doesn't have the power over you anymore unless you let him," Raven said.

The kids walked away and got into the car parked on the street in front of the house. Susan cried as she watched them drive away.

As they were sitting in the back seat listening to music on their iPhones with headphones on, Beth used the opportunity to speak with Preshea about what had just happened.

"Why is that woman in such denial about what's happening to her and her kids?"

"I've seen it many times. Spousal abuse victims often deny they're victims hoping somehow their abuser will change. Often, after violence, the abuser will beg forgiveness. They will promise to change. They might even act on their best behavior for a while. Ultimately, unless they get help for their violent behavior, they will attack their loved ones again. I have seen too many women who denied their husbands were abusing them end up dead. If we can't convince her to get out, then at least we can help these kids."

It was a 25 minute drive to Preshea's house. When they arrived she showed them to their bedrooms in the old Victorian-style home that overlooked the bay.

"Your place is sick," Rowan said.

"That's a good or bad thing?"

"Good. Most def…"

"Oh, yeah this is sweet," Raven added.

"Sick and sweet, well I am glad you think so," Preshea said.

The kids had been away from class for the past two days and were in no rush to return but Preshea insisted.

"Yeah, I know but being educated is important. You've got the rest of today to settle in but tomorrow morning you're going back to school. Got it?"

"Got it," they agreed.

Preshea had forgotten how good it felt to hear young voices in this big old house. Boudica, her ginger cat, already decided Raven was hers and settled herself at the foot of the girl's bed.

"Why do you call her Boudica?"

"Why don't I tell you over supper? Go wash up and come to the table. It's ready."

She invited Beth to join them and the four of them sat at the large kitchen table.

"Thank you for this food and for bringing Rowan and Raven safely from harm. Blessed be," Preshea said.

The teens looked at her.

"You pray?"

"Sure I do. Lots of people do but not everyone who prays does so in the same way or believes exactly the same things. My understanding of the divine might not be the same as your understanding but nevertheless it is all good."

"That's not what we've been taught."

"Well I like to think that Source gives us all our own brains to think with. I think you are old enough to find your truth on your own rather than simply taking at face value what others tell you. Don't you? Now, help yourselves to the lasagna before it gets cold."

As they ate, Preshea told them the story of how she chose Boudica's name.

"There have been many fierce and noble female warriors throughout the ages and one of them was Queen Boudica. At the time of the Roman conquest of Britain, Boudica ruled the Iceni tribe of East Anglia alongside her husband King Prasutagus.

Boudica was a beautiful woman; tall with long red hair which flowed down her back to her waist. All was well until Prasutagus, hoping to get in good with the Romans, made the Roman Emperor Nero co-heir with his daughters to his considerable kingdom and wealth in the hope the Romans wouldn't attack his kingdom.

It didn't work. After Prasutagus's death, the Roman, Suetonius Paulinus, took all of his property but even that wasn't enough.

167

Suetonius had Boudica publicly flogged and her daughters were raped by Roman slaves.

Other tribal chiefs and their families were enslaved but the Iceni, Trinobantes and others fought back.

Boudica and her allies gave no quarter in their victories and when Londinium and Verulamium, which we now know as London and St. Albans, were stormed and the towns were burned.

Suetonius decided to challenge Boudica. He assembled an army of 10,000. Boudica and her daughters went to all her tribes before the battle, encouraging them not to be afraid.

"I am the descendant of mighty men but today I fight as one of you, for we are fighting to regain our freedom. Win the battle or perish: that is what I, a woman, will do; you men can live on in slavery if that's what you want."

The Britons attacked firing several volleys. The Roman soldiers fired back throwing their javelins into the advancing Britons which caused hundreds of people to fall and die even in the first minutes of battle.

The Romans moved in for the kill, attacking in tight formation, stabbing with their short swords. The Roman cavalry then encircled the enemy and began their slaughter from the rear. Ancient records say 80,000 men, women and children, were killed. The Roman losses amounted to 400 dead with a slightly larger number wounded.

Boudica did not die in battle but opted to swallow poison instead of be taken prisoner. She is remembered to this day in the island's folklore as a heroine for her courage."

Raven, Rowan and Beth sat in awe at Preshea's story.

"Yeah! Girl power," Raven said pumping her first in the air.

Rowan, a history buff, was enthralled.

"How do you know so much about that?

"Because I was there; I was one of Boudica's daughters. So was Beth," she said taking a bite of pasta.

"Say what?"

"You heard me. We were there. We died on the battle field and our mother took poison so they would not take her captive."

"That's crazy. You're joking right? That was more than 2,000 years ago," Raven said.

Just then, Boudica entered the room and jumped up on Preshea's lap.

"Boudica and I have known one another over many lifetimes."

"How can you be so sure this cat was your mother?"

"Well I can't be certain but I believe she is. Her personality reminds me of the mother we once knew long ago."

"Why would she come back as a cat?"

"Simple. After so many lifetimes of strife and heartache, Boudica wanted to return as a cat so she could once again be the Queen of the Kingdom where she had absolute power and would be kept in the lap of luxury, if you'll pardon the pun," she said. The cat was curled into a tight ball and purred while Preshea stoked her back.

"Do you believe in reincarnation Beth?"

169

"Yes, I do. In fact, I just found out I was once Preshea's sister, as she said, and that I have had at least three more past lives. You've never heard of reincarnation?"

"Well yeah, but it's not real," Raven said.

"Who says so?"

"Pastor Blackmore told us," Raven said with certainty of what she'd been told by her church's leader.

"And do you always believe what the Pastor tells you?"

Raven lowered her eyes. "Forget it."

Preshea knew there was something important the girl wasn't sharing.

"Raven, what did the pastor tell you that you no longer believe?"

"He said he would help Rowan and I. He never did."

"You mean to tell me you went to him about your father?"

The kids nodded.

"How long ago was that?"

"Last year," he said.

Preshea and Beth looked at one another. Both felt nauseated. How could they have been left for the past year in that home after they told their pastor? They would deal with the Reverend Blackmore as soon as possible.

They didn't have to find him. He came looking for them the next day.

"Who do you think you are?!" he yelled as soon as he saw Preshea after storming into Circe's Closet.

"I could ask you the same question!"

"I know exactly who I am. I am the pastor of the First Pentecostal Church and the spiritual leader of those two children you somehow got your claws into and no doubt are busy poisoning their minds with all of your witchcraft and black magic!"

"You have no idea what you are talking about," she said coldly.

"Oh really?"

"Really! How dare you come into my place of business accusing me of harming Rowan and Raven."

"Rowan and Raven? Their names are Randall and Rose Eldridge."

"They prefer Rowan and Raven."

"Nonsense," he scoffed.

"You know what I can't understand?"

"What's that?"

"I fail to understand how a man who professes to be Christian, who says he is the spiritual leader of those two sweet kids, could ignore them when they came to you over a year ago asking for help. They told you their father was abusing them and their mother and you did nothing!"

Pastor Blackmore blanched.

"Erm, well, you see…"

"In your capacity as a church leader you have a legal obligation to go to the authorities if you have knowledge or even a suspicion there may be someone who is being violated?"

"I didn't take them seriously then and I still don't," he said with a dismissive shrug.

"Why not?"

Preshea's hands gripped the counter top. She wanted to smack that superior look off his bloated, pink face.

"I have known their father since we both were in Bible college. He is a dear friend and I have never seen him act inappropriately with his children, wife, or any of the others at the church. He's a Sunday school teacher and a youth leader. I trust him completely."

"Oh my God! That's like letting the fox be in charge of the hen house. Of course he wouldn't be violent in front of witnesses. Do you realize that the children were interviewed by a Department of Child Welfare social worker and showed all of the indicators of being abuse victims? For over a year you allowed those kids and their mother to suffer the horror of being abused. You turned your back on them. You did nothing! Well I and several others believe them and are doing what you should have done. Now get out of my store before I call the police!"

"You haven't heard the last of me!"

"Oh yeah? Well you haven't heard the last of me either. Now get out before I put a hex on you!"

Pastor Blackmore took a small pocket Bible from an inside pocket of his suit jacket and held it in front of him.

"You will burn in hell witch!"

"Ya think? Get out!"

He turned on his heel and opened the shop's front door and ran down the street to his car.

Beth, who'd been taking cardboard boxes to the recycling bin, had heard the last of the screaming match.

"Who in the world was that?"

"Oh you haven't had the displeasure of encountering Reverend Blackmore."

"Why did you tell him you were going to put a hex on him?"

"I was just messing with his pea brain."

"He already thinks you're a witch and you're just giving him more ammunition against you."

"People like that are so closed-minded there's nothing I could possibly do or say to show him that I'm not evil. Let him think whatever he wants to think. Maybe he'll be too afraid to come back. I just want those narrow-minded, self-righteous hypocrites to leave me alone. I try to live a life of kindness. I do no harm and I do not judge."

"You just called them self-righteous hypocrites."

"That's not a judgement. It's an observation," Preshea said and giggled.

"Okay, enough drama. Let's get back to work," Beth said patting her on the arm.

173

Preshea knew with a certainty that came from many lifetimes of repression, suffering, war and death it was time to prepare for battle.

"You're right, but the drama is far from over. In fact, it's only just beginning,"

16

Donald's lawyer arrived late that afternoon and prepared him for court.

"Get me out of here."

"I'll try. You have a good reputation in the community. I'm sure we can have you released on bail."

The next day he was dressed in his best suit looking like the model of civility. The judge, like most in the court, didn't see past the façade of the designer suit.

"How do you plead?"

"Not guilty, your honor!"

"Are you looking for a judge and jury trial or trial by judge alone?"

"Judge only, sir," the Eldridge's lawyer said and then asked if he could be released on bail.

The state's attorney argued against it but the judge agreed.

"Bail is set at $10,000. The trial date is set for five months from now. October 15th. Court's adjourned."

"All rise," the bailiff said as the judge got up and walked out of the courtroom.

The gallery was filled with many church members who'd come to show support for Donald and provide comfort to Susan.

At the opposite side of the court sat Beth, Preshea, Father Ryan and the children's social worker, Meg. Raven and Rowan were glad to go to school rather than have to see their father.

Donald glared at them as he joined his wife, Pastor Blackmore and other church members present.

They marched out of the courtroom with an air of distain and superiority.

Preshea was glad the kids weren't there.

That evening, as they sat at the kitchen table eating supper she tried to reassure them everything would be fine.

"Don't worry. Your father isn't allowed to come within 50 feet of you no matter where you are. You're safe."

Rowan was thinking about his mother.

"What about mom? Who's going to keep her safe?"

"We'll pray she decides it's safer here than remaining at home. During the trial, you'll have to tell the judge, under oath, what happened. Don't worry. That's not for a long while," Preshea assured them.

"Father Ryan helped me a lot after my husband left me. It helps to talk about things like pain and sadness and anger with someone who cares."

"What would we talk about?"

"Whatever you feel like talking about. It would perhaps help you to unpack all of the things you have been holding inside for so long. You both have been through so much. Releasing these emotions will help you start to heal. It's like digging out a splinter that's deep under your skin. It hurts while it's happening but the minute it comes out it feels a whole lot better. Trust me. I know."

"You know what it's like to be abused?"

"Sure do."

"When did it happen to you?"

"When I was a little older than you I ran away and ended up on the streets for a while. Then I found some help from some older women at a shelter for teens. I have gone through a lot of therapy. That's how I ended up becoming a social worker and worked in the system for about 20 years before I retired and started the shop. You remember I told you Father Ryan is a clinical psychologist? I know he can help you. You want to meet with him again?"

"Maybe."

"Okay, you let me know and I will make sure it happens."

Later that night, as Preshea went to say goodnight they both said they'd thought about it and wanted to speak to Father Ryan.

"Good. Let's see when he can meet with you. Good night."

"Goodnight Preshea."

The next day was busy. Preshea got up early to pack lunches and drive Raven and Rowan to school. Then she met Beth for breakfast before she had to go to the shop an hour before it opened at 10 a.m.

"The kids have agreed to meet with Father Ryan for counselling."

"That's great. I am sure he can help them. I have an appointment to see him this afternoon. We are going to be doing more past-life regression work. I figured since today was my day off this would be a good time to dig a little deeper into the past and see who I was before."

"I told the kids more about my past lives."

"How did they respond?"

"They still don't believe me but how could they be open to it? They've been raised to believe it's not real."

"Well, it does take experiencing it even for those who are open to the idea, so I have found." Beth said.

177

After breakfast Preshea headed to the store and Beth went home to do some laundry before her appointment with Father Ryan.

She drove to the address he'd given. It was the clinic where he worked twice a week.

Beth was shown to a waiting area by one of the clinic's receptionists. She didn't have to wait long before she was invited to follow the woman to Father Ryan's office.

The room had low lighting, two overstuffed chairs, a long sofa and large desk.

"Make yourself comfortable. Father Ryan will be with you shortly," the woman smiled reassuringly.

In a few minutes the tall, lanky man walked into the room. Wearing jeans, a pullover and sandals he didn't look much like a priest.

"How's it going?"

"Good. You?"

"Fine, fine...you ready to get started?"

"Sure."

"Pick a spot on the ceiling and focus on it. Notice as your eyes start to blink and are beginning to get heavier. With each blink you are becoming drowsier. I want you to count down from 100. You will find as you count lower and lower numbers you will become extremely relaxed."

"Ninety-nine, ninety-eight, ninety-seven...."

"You're falling into a deep and pleasant relaxation and are getting sleepy."

"Ninety-six, ninety-five, ninety-four..."

"You're going into a deep state of relaxation. You're going deeper and deeper down until all of your body is relaxed and ready to go back in time."

"Ninety-three, ninety-two, ninety-one…"

"Each breath takes you into a full state of hypnosis. All of the muscles in your body are loose and relaxed. You're going back to a time of your past lives. You're calm, comfortable and welcoming of this journey. Your body feels heavy and yet there is comforting warmth around you. When I count back from three, you'll be back to another time. We shall begin. What is your name?"

"Hessabah."

"What is the date?

"We are in the year of our Lord 1690."

"Where are you?"

"I am on a ship."

"Where are you going?"

"To the New World."

"Are you frightened?"

"A little but I am with my husband who tells me it will be Okay."

"Is it?"

"For us, but not for others."

"What's happening?"

"People are dying. There is so much sickness and death."

"Do you arrive at your destination?"

"Yes."

"Are you happy?"

"Glad to be off the ship."

"Where is your new home?"

"Near the water in the wilderness. The English Settlers have not been good neighbors. They have stolen and brought much sickness and heartache to the Abenaki people."

"Is it dangerous?"

"For some. But not for me."

"Why not?"

"I have become friends with an Abenaki medicine woman."

"Are you friends with others?"

"Yes. All of the Abenaki people are kind to me."

"What about the people in the English Settlement?"

"Some are."

"Others are not?"

"No."

"Who is not?"

"The doctor and the reverend."

"Why aren't they kind to you?"

"They hate me."

"Why?"

"Because they can't control me and that makes them afraid."

"What do you do about it?"

"I do nothing until I am forced to run."

"Why do you run?"

"Because my husband is dead and they want me to remarry."

"Who is the man?"

"The reverend."

"What is his name?"

"Ezra Ward."

"Where do you go?"

"To my friend's village."

"Are you safe there?"

"Yes. It is good there for a while."

"Then it is not?"

"No."

"What happens?"

"Smallpox. I try to help the people but I have no medicine to stop the sickness and many die."

"Who dies?"

"My friend, her daughter-in-law, her granddaughter and dozens more."

"Do you die then?"

"Not from the sickness."

"How do you die?"

"The reverend finds me as I am gathering water from a stream."

"What does he do to you?"

"He pushes my head under. My lungs fill with water. I drown."

"Everything is fine Beth. You are safe. On the count of three I will ask you to return to the present. You will feel refreshed and alert remembering this past life. Three, you are coming back, two your eyes are opening and one you are awake."

Beth opened her eyes.

"Okay, what's up with all of the murders? First I die in battle, next stoned to death and then I am drowned because they believed I was a witch."

"Beth, I have to share something with you."

"Okay."

"Do you remember in the meeting you attended when we first met that I was giving a homily about reincarnation?"

"Yes."

"Do you recall me telling you we keep reincarnating as part of a larger soul group so we can have more life experiences?"

"Yes."

"Do you remember asking me if we were connected in past lives?"

"Yes. Why?"

"I have lived many lives before this one and you, among others, have been part of all of them."

"Were you someone I knew when I came to New England?"

"Yes."

"Who?"

"Beth, I was Reverend Ezra Ward. I murdered you."

17

Beth stared at Father Ryan and then jumped up from the sofa.

"What do you mean you murdered me?"

"I didn't murder you. My soul, at that time, agreed to incarnate as Reverend Ward and behave in this horrible way; even willing to take your life, so your soul could have this experience."

"Why would I want to experience this? Why would I want to experience the pain and suffering of drowning? Why would your soul agree to do these terrible things?"

"In order to learn how to forgive there has to be something done to us by someone else which requires forgiveness. Your spirit asked to learn this lesson. My spirit agreed to help you do this. But, as often is the case, when we left heaven and returned to earth as reincarnated beings, we both forgot the plan and the purpose of why we were there. You'd forgotten you asked to be murdered and I was so much into the part of the murderer I forgot I was there as a helper in the lesson. We're all heavenly souls having earthly experiences.

I've come to understand every being is a piece of God. Everything's an emanation of Source. Why does God do this? So She can experience things through the incarnation of souls who are acting as proxies for God when they come to earth."

"You called God 'She'. Don't you mean 'He'?"

"It makes no difference what we call God. God is neither male nor female. God is everything and we're all connected as bite-sized pieces of God. New souls most often forget where they come from and are under the illusion they're separate from God, nature and others and they act out of place of ego."

"Why do we forget where we come from?"

"There's a story in the Jewish faith that says when we're born the angels pinch the place between our nose and our mouth which cause us to have amnesia so we forget coming from heaven."

"Why would that happen?"

"If we remembered who we really are then there'd be no point in reincarnating to experience life in human form. We wouldn't learn the lessons we need to learn. The greatest mission in coming from heaven to earth is to learn how to love. We get into trouble when we mistake the parts we are playing as reality. This isn't who we are. Who we are is the soul in the shell, the spacesuit that's the body.

Souls in heaven come to earth as incarnate beings many times to learn to love unconditionally. We move from lifetime to lifetime as a group of souls playing different roles, various nationalities and religions; different intellects; different genders.

I believe souls come from two groups; one is in the light and one is in shadow. Friendly souls, who love us unconditionally, and shadowy, dark souls who're the enemy who agree to do us harm so we can learn to love our enemies.

At some point these souls who are part of our soul group agreed to come to earth to play the part of our enemy because they loved us and wanted to help us to learn to love even those who do us harm.

In some lifetimes souls want to develop patience, courage, compassion and other virtues. In each of these lifetimes we invite other souls to make the journey with us so we can be tested and to ensure we learn these lessons. Does this make sense?"

"Yes, it does."

"Self-forgiveness is an important part of this lesson too. When I think of that lifetime and what I did to you; trying to burn you at the stake and then drowning you, I am very ashamed. Then I realized it was part of the agreement we'd made. In allowing me to kill you, you were also providing me with an opportunity to forgive myself. Think about it…the most difficult people in our lives are some of our most important teachers."

Beth considered this for a moment and then said: "In the first session I remembered being killed several times. Why are these lessons learned in such difficult circumstances?"

"I believe the most important lessons of love and forgiveness are learned through the most difficult times."

"Do you think Rowan, Raven, their parents and their pastor are all part of our soul group?"

"No doubt."

"Those poor kids. Their poor mother. They've been through so much."

"Yes. I have prayed a lot about this over the years. So many kids have come to me for therapy after being the victims of violence. I asked God why and it all comes back to learning lessons we asked to learn while we are in human form.

Here is what I heard. He handed her his diary. It contained many channelled writings he was inspired to write after prayer:

'Dear one

I have a great need to share with you some thoughts about who you are and why you are here. Before you were born you came to me and said, 'I want to experience life in human form.' I asked you whether you fully understood what you were asking for.

I told you that the human experience is a very difficult one. Why would a soul want to leave the place of peace, love, joy, contentment and abundance to go to earth? Life in human form, while it can be filled with laughter, love, joy, and all of the physical pleasures can also be one of great sorrow, pain and fear. But these are some of the reasons you said you wanted to experience humanity for these things and others are unknown in heaven.

You insisted that you were prepared to face those difficulties and you said you wanted everything that came to those ones who take human form. You selected those souls who were already in the world who would be your parents. For you knew that these ones would help you to have the experiences you wished to have while you are there.

On your journey you are joined by your guide. This is one that's lived in human form before and who's encountered every experience they wished before they returned to heaven to fulfil the next part of their journey. These wise ones are those I have chosen to help souls, such as you, find their way along their earthly experience. They do not live your life for you. Rather, they stand nearby watching over you and helping you along the way.

And so it is that you are here and living in this body. You may think, 'Is that all there is to this human existence?' I have not set the boundaries of your life; you have. You allow fear to get in the way of having a life with no limits.

The world is wide open to you. Be anything you wish to be. Fill your mind and body and soul with every experience you wish to have. I am always with you on your journey. There is no need to wander alone. And when you walk hand in hand with me, and your guide, you will find that this journey you are on is a very exciting one indeed.

When it is your time to come back to me I will be here, as will all of the loved ones that have come before you. We will celebrate your earthly journey and we will rejoice that you have come home to us.'

In our human experience this makes no sense. We get angry. We want to fight back. We want to retaliate. We want to inflict pain on the person who has harmed us because we have forgotten who we are and why we're here in the first place. But retaliation and vengeance is like pouring fuel on a fire. It only adds to the pain. But when we are able to forgive we're really helping ourselves. We're living these lifetimes to learn and to help others to learn the greatest lesson of them all."

"That is?"

"Love. Really, it's the only thing that matters. Love for self, love for others and love for God because we are all tiny pieces of the divine."

She wanted to believe what he was saying. Still, she questioned how anyone could harm children or anyone else. Throughout the centuries, and over many lifetimes, she now knew she'd suffered at the hands of others.

Were she and everyone else on the planet really here to learn virtues through experiences that aren't possible to have in heaven where there is no pain, no sorrows or tears? Maybe.

"How many lifetimes have we known one another?"

"Who knows? It's hard to say."

"I'd like to find out."

"Would you?"

"Yes. Is it possible?"

"Perhaps."

"Do you think it'll help these kids to recognize their past lives?"

"Yes, it may but it has to be their choice. There are many like their father and the pastor who dismiss it as misguided nonsense or even heresy."

"The kids have said they want to speak to you. Do you think you can help them?"

"I hope so."

While Beth and Father Ryan were talking about healing through forgiveness and love there were others who were making plans to cause more wounds out of spite and hatred.

18

Donald and Susan sat in Pastor Blackmore's office.

"I know better, but I have to ask is everything alright between you two," he said first looking at one and then the other.

"Of course it's fine. I don't know why the kids would tell those lies. I think it's the influence of those women and that priest," Donald said with a hiss.

Susan kept her eyes down.

Pastor Blackmore knew in every marriage couples had spats from time to time.

"Susan, you know the husband is the head of the household. A wife's duty is to provide a comfortable and calm home for her husband. Perhaps you need to try a little harder."

Susan said nothing but inside she wanted to scream.

"This is not my fault. I have tried to be a good wife. I have cooked. I have cleaned. I have been available to Donald for everything at all times and yet it isn't enough! He always finds a reason to lash out," she wanted to tell the pastor but kept it all inside as she always did.

"I don't want my kids anywhere near those people. They are being negatively influenced. We need to have them home," he said.

"That could be difficult but we will work on it. In the meantime I believe we need to expose Preshea Circe as the evil woman she is. If we can prove she is unfit then we can get them taken from her home and placed with someone in the church. Betty and I would be happy to have them stay with us until this whole sordid mess is over."

"How do we do that? We have tried to have her store closed but the town council says there are no bylaws being broken by her or her business."

"Maybe we need to put a little heat on her."

"Like what?"

"A protest both at the store and at her home. We can get dozens of congregation members to show up. No tourists would be willing to cross a picket line to buy whatever trash she's selling in there, I guarantee it."

The two men smiled in satisfaction while Susan could only think of her kids wishing she were with them.

They drove home in silence. When they'd arrived and they walked toward the house he pushed past her and went inside ahead of her.

"I'm hungry. Make me something to eat," he grunted and then went to the family room. He turned on the TV to watch a football game.

Susan knew the drill. She was to make one of his favorite meals and bring it to him on a tray where he would eat alone and watch the game.

As she stood at the stove heating chili and warming garlic bread in the oven she thought of all of the beatings she had taken over their 16 year marriage.

"Nobody deserves to be treated this way and now he is doing it to the kids. I have to leave. I have to be with them."

She was prepared to even go live with a witch if it meant she could be with them and get away from him.

She needed to find something that would make him sleep so she could leave that night. She thought of the sleeping pills she'd been prescribed by their family doctor. She crushed a few of them up and put them in his bowl of chili. The high spice would mask the taste of the pills.

"Two ought to be enough," she thought as she added the pulverized pills to the bubbling bowl of chili."

She carried the meal into the den and set it on the coffee table in front of Donald.

"It took you long enough. Move. I can't see the play."

Silently she left the room and went upstairs to her closet where she found a suitcase and packed. Next she went to the kids' rooms and packed clothes for them. She left the bags in the closet and then went to her purse to find the paper with Preshea's address and phone number.

The minutes seemed like hours as she waited for the sleeping pills to work. Within a couple of hours she could hear loud snoring coming from the den. It was now or never, she thought as she carefully went upstairs to retrieve the suitcases and her purse.

Quickly she came down stairs and found the car keys hanging on a hook by the kitchen door. She went into the garage and put the suitcases in the trunk and then opened the garage doors.

She should have waited a while longer. Donald, who was only slightly asleep, heard the sound of the garage door opening and went to see what was going on.

Susan saw him in the doorway and quickly locked the car doors.

"Susan, where do you think you are going? Get out of that car this instant!"

She put the car in gear as he ran toward the vehicle.

"Damn it, Susan. I said get out of that car now!"

He jumped on the hood as she backed out of the garage.

With one hand he held on while his fist pounded against the windshield.

"You stupid cow! I am going to beat the shit out of you!"

Susan knew he would. She put the car in drive and pressed the accelerator. Donald, who lost his grip, fell from the car and smashed his leg against the curb when he landed.

He howled in pain and he cursed.

"I know you're going where the kids are. I am coming for you bitch."

He limped back to the house. His pants were torn and there was blood running down his leg. He went to the bathroom and removed his clothing. The skin was raw from road rash and there were bits of debris embedded in the cuts.

"I am going to kill you," he thought as he cleaned his wounds.

The medication was finally taking hold as the adrenaline from chasing after Susan wore off. He slept on the sofa in the den. He was dreaming about being in pain. It was torture.

"Please, No! I beg you, please stop," Donald was looking into the eyes of his former self. But, in this life, he was a woman.

"Dougall, please stop."

Now he was dreaming of being dragged to the centre of the village and the stocks.

His dress was torn with every lash he received.

"This will teach you to conspire with a witch!"

The horror movie continued to play on the screen of Donald Eldridge's subconscious mind. He watched as the torture continued. Fingernails and toenails were ripped from this self's body. Hot pokers burned away flesh. The nightmare continued

192

until there was a confession of conspiring with witches but before this female incarnation disclosed where the witches were hiding, she was dead.

Now Donald was dreaming he'd gone to heaven. To the celestial body he asked:

"What happens next?"

"Whatever you want to happen next, the benevolent presence said."

"I would like to go back but in the next life I would like know what it feels like to deliver the pain rather than receive it."

"So you shall. You shall be as brutal as the ones who've brutalized you."

Donald woke in a cold sweat. Why did he keep having this nightmare? Always he woke confused and angry. His leg was burning from the pain but the intensity of his anger toward his wife and the other women, who he knew were sheltering them, burned far hotter.

"You will all pay," he said as he formulated a plan to get his revenge.

Susan's fear of her husband was greater than the woman who she was told practiced witchcraft. She knew Donald would kill her if he caught up with her. She needed to get the kids and run far from this place.

As she pulled into Preshea's driveway she saw a lovely Victorian home that didn't look like a place a witch would live. She got out of the car and ran up the stairs and rang the bell.

Preshea opened the door and smiled.

"Welcome. We've been hoping you would change your mind."

Susan walked into the foyer and called for Rowan and Raven.

"Kids, it's mom! Where are you?"

The teens ran down the stairs and into their mother's arms.

"Mom! You're here! We're so happy you changed your mind."

"I couldn't stand another minute without you guys," she said as she hugged them both.

Susan knew she couldn't go to any of her church friends. They would only call Donald and he would come looking for them. Still, she couldn't stay with the kids here.

Sensing her discomfort, Preshea knew she had to find a way to make this woman see she was nothing to fear and she only had her and her children's best interests at heart.

"Mrs. Eldridge please, have some tea and let's talk a moment."

"Come on mom. Preshea is really great. You will see. You just need to get to know her."

Susan was nervous but agreed to tea.

"Okay, maybe just a cup and then we will have to be going."

"No mom. It's nice here. Preshea is a great cook and she tells really cool stories," Rowan protested.

"Please mom. We don't want to leave. It's great here. You'll see," Raven added.

Susan took the cup of camomile Preshea offered her.

"I imagine you could use this. Camomile tea is what I always drink when I have had a rough day."

"You have no idea what rough is," Susan said.

"Oh mom, she does. Preshea knows what it's like to be part of a family like ours. She told us she ran away from home when she was 15 because her dad used to beat her," Raven said.

Susan looked at Preshea.

"Is this true?"

Preshea nodded.

"That was a long time ago. The bruises from being beaten will heal but the scars you carry on your heart last a lifetime. Don't you agree?"

Susan started to cry. The years of pent up emotion spilled over like water through a broken dam.

"I am so sorry kids. I kept you there when we should have left but I had no idea where to go and no job to support us even if there was a place to escape to."

"It's okay mom. We're out of there now. We're safe," Rowan said.

Susan looked at this stranger who she'd judged so harshly for years only seeing her for who she really was for the first time.

"You are so kind. Why are you being so good to us when you have been so badly treated by so many of us for so long?"

"My soul sees your soul. We are all small pieces of God so how can I possibly mistreat anyone?"

"I misjudged you. I am sorry."

"I believe Jesus said, 'Do to others as you would have them do to you.' Many faiths have the same golden rule in one form or another. I like to say, 'Do no harm and live in the light.' So now that we've got that misunderstanding cleared up, would you like to stay?"

"I would. Thank you for your kindness," a humbled and grateful Susan said.

"Preshea, can we show mom through the house?"

"Sure. Take her upstairs and show her to her bedroom. It's the one at the end of the hall on the left."

She needed so much help. Years of abuse would take a lot of therapy to recover from. Making the decision to finally leave her husband was a good start.

As the kids were upstairs helping their mother settle in, Preshea called Beth.

"Susan Eldridge showed up here about an hour ago."

"Really? That's great news."

"Yeah, she no longer believes I am going to turn her and her kids into frogs."

"Maybe she's still hoping you will do that to her husband."

"Ha! That guy deserves to be turned into a cockroach for what he's done to those kids and their mother. I am going to call Father Ryan. If he has some room in his schedule I am going to ask if he can see Susan tomorrow. She needs therapy. I know he can help her."

"Call me in the morning?"

"Sure. If Susan is willing to see Father Ryan I will need to take her there while the kids are in school. Would you mind working alone at the shop until I can get back?"

"No, not at all. It should be fine."

Beth couldn't have been more wrong. She had no idea what she would face when she went to work the next morning.

19

Beth opened the store at 10 a.m.

The morning was busy as customers browsed and bought a lot of items. Just after noon she'd been restocking store shelves when she heard yelling coming from outside the store.

A large, angry crowd had gathered on the sidewalk in front of Circe's Closet. Many held signs that read; *Witches Not Welcome* and Exodus 22:17.

Beth went to the store's computer and Googled that Bible chapter and verse.

'Do not allow a sorceress to live.'

"You've got to be kidding me! These people are nuts!"

Beth went to the store's entrance. The yelling continued until Pastor Blackmore approached and spoke to her.

"We mean you no harm. We have come for Preshea Circe."

"She's not here. I am going to have to ask you to leave or I will be forced to call the police."

Beth tried to remain calm and not allow these people to provoke her.

"That sign there is threatening to take someone's life."

"No. No! It's meant figuratively. Not literally," he said.

"Oh? So I don't have to warn Preshea that her life is in danger?"

"Her life isn't but her livelihood is. The congregation members of First Pentecostal Church will kill her business by staying here and driving away her customers. If she has no income, she will have to leave town," Pastor Blackmore pronounced.

"This is harassment. You can't do this."

"We can and we will."

Beth went back inside and called Preshea's cell number.

It rang several times and went straight to voice mail. Beth left a message.

"You're probably at Father Ryan's office now with Susan. Call me back as soon as you get this. It's urgent."

Preshea waited in the lobby while Susan sat in the counselling room with Father Ryan.

They talked about the abuses she and the children had suffered for years. Susan was immediately at peace with Father Ryan. His gentle manner and calming voice was soothing.

"I have found hypnotherapy is very useful to get at the heart of troubles and begin healing. Would you be open to that?"

"Yes, perhaps."

"Have you heard of something called past-life regression therapy?"

"Yes I have. That's where, under hypnosis, you are taken back to lives you've lived before which helps you understand the things you need to know to move forward with this life. Pastor Blackmore has told us there is no such thing as reincarnation."

"Did he tell you Jesus was a believer in reincarnation and that it was part of Christian doctrine until about 500 AD?"

"No, I've never heard of that before."

"It's true. There were lots of things removed from the Bible over time you would find surprising including many books that featured women. However those too were deleted. In fact, only references to women which showed they were chattel or weak-minded instigators of sin were kept."

Susan looked disgusted. She wasn't surprised. Before she'd met Donald, and before she was brought into the fundamentalist church, she'd been an independent woman who was on track for a career in mental health.

"You might be surprised to know that I wasn't raised in a fundamentalist home," Susan said. "I was an independent thinker. I had goals. Before I married Donald I was working on my PhD in psychology. I know, how ironic. When I joined the church Pastor Blackmore and Donald pressured me to give up my studies and become a stay-at-home wife and mother. So I destroyed my thesis. Aside from marrying an abusive monster, that is the single biggest regret of my life."

"It's not too late. You could easily return to school and pick up where you left off," Father Ryan encouraged.

"Oh, I don't know. Where would I even find a job? I am 40 and have no experience."

"Those things have a way of working out. But first, I suggest we do some work on healing the damage done to you. You can't help your kids, or anyone else for that matter, unless you do the work to help heal yourself. Are you willing to do a past-life regression session now?"

Susan knew Donald and Pastor Blackmore would be appalled. She would be in serious trouble if they found out. Somehow, the thought of defying them gave her a sense of satisfaction. She felt emboldened in a way she hadn't felt for so long, she'd forgotten she had a right to think for herself.

She was a grown woman who deserved respect rather than being treated like a simpering domestic drudge not fit for anything except pleasing the king of the castle in the kitchen and the bedroom.

"Why not? Sure. Let's do it."

"Okay Susan I am going to ask you to count down from 100. The farther down you count, the deeper you will go into a state of relaxation and hypnosis. Ready? Let's begin."

"One hundred."

"Your eyes are starting to feel heavy."

"Ninety-nine."

"You are feeling very relaxed."

"Ninety-eight."

"Your eyes are closing.'

"Ninety-seven."

"You are going deeper and deeper down into a place of total relaxation."

"Ninety-six."

"You are completely relaxed and ready to look into your past life journeys. What is your name?"

"Dougall."

"Where are you?"

"In my house."

"Are you alone?"

"No."

"Who is with you?"

"My wife and our children."

"What is happening?"

"I am angry."

"Why?"

"She has taken something which has caused her to lose the baby she was carrying."

"How do you know this?"

"I have discovered the potion."

"What are you doing now?"

"I am beating her."

"Do you beat her often?"

"Yes."

"Where are you now?"

"I have taken her to the center of the village to whip her; to shame her. She is begging me to stop but I keep whipping her."

"Who else is there?"

"Many people in the town; the doctor, the reverend."

"Does anyone try to stop you?"

"No. They take over."

"What do they do to her?"

"They take her to a hidden place and continue beating her. I can hear her screaming."

"Why are they doing this?"

"They want to find the witches who've escaped into the woods. They know she is in collusion with them."

"Do they find the answers they are looking for?"

"No. She dies before they extract the information from her."

"Are you saddened that she is dead?"

"No. She was in league with the devil. She had to die. All women must submit to the will of God and of man or they will suffer the consequences."

"Susan, it is time to return to the present. When I count backwards from three you will begin to wake. Three, you are feeling relaxed and are starting to wake up. Two, you will remember this time but you will not be upset by it. One, you are waking up now."

She opened her eyes and looked at Father Ryan.

"I was a man. I was a monster. I beat my wife. I hurt her very badly."

"It seems so."

"She died."

"Yes."

"I didn't kill her. Someone else did."

"Yes."

"Am I connected now to the person who was my wife in that lifetime?"

"Yes. I believe you and Donald reversed roles from that lifetime to this. You were an abuser then and in this lifetime, you have become the victim. Susan, I believe souls incarnate as part of soul groups. Some souls live in the light while others are what I like to call the shadow group. They are the souls who agree to come to earth to help others to learn lessons like patience, compassion and forgiveness by doing them harm."

"Who in this life would have been the person who killed me do you suppose?"

"I was."

"What do you mean, you were?"

"In the many times I have undergone past-life regression I have been both male and female. I have lived in the light but I have also lived often in darkness doing some very evil things which, when I think of them now, I am very ashamed of. In that life I was Reverend Ezra Ward. I killed many in the name of God and your former incarnation was one of those victims.

In this lifetime I am in search of justice for the downtrodden. In my faith I am devoted to serving God through kindness, gentleness and love even for those who we might not think are deserving of it. We are all small, bite-sized pieces of God; even those who are living in darkness.

So, if I profess to love God then I must love everyone as I love the Creator. Jesus said, 'You have heard that it was said, 'Love your neighbor and hate your enemy.' But I tell you, love your enemies and pray for those who persecute you, that you may be children of your Father in heaven. He causes his sun to rise on the evil and the good, and sends rain on the righteous and the unrighteous.'"

Susan was quiet for a while taking it all in.

"You know, when the twins were about three years old they told me that they had two different mommies before me."

"Rose, or Raven as she likes to be called, told me that her other mommy and daddy died while crossing the ocean. She said she went to live with a nice lady and her husband who took care of her."

"What did you think of that?"

"At the time? Not much. Children have vivid imaginations."

"And Rowan? What did he tell you about himself?"

"He said he didn't like the name Randall. He asked that we call him by an aboriginal name. He said he missed his wife and their baby.

Until they were about five years old they spoke to one another in a language I didn't understand. As they got older it stopped. There was no more talk of who they were before they were born," said Susan.

"That happens often with children. They forget their past lives the longer they have been away from that past self. By the time a child is four or five, typically any recollection of past lives is completely forgotten. When you see Preshea and Beth ask them to share with you some of the things they've discovered about their own past lives. I think you will find it interesting. Maybe it will all start to make more sense."

Preshea was still in the waiting area and had just listened to Beth's message and called her back.

"Hey Beth, it's me. What's up?"

"That pastor and some of the people from his church were here picketing in front of the store and upsetting a lot of customers."

"Did you call the police?"

"I did."

"What happened?"

"The officer told them they couldn't block the store entrance but they could stay on the sidewalk provided they had a permit for a public gathering."

"Did they have a permit?"

"No. So the officer told them they had to clear out. You should also know some of the protestors held signs with a Bible scripture that said "Do not allow a sorceress to live.""

"Oh really? That's a threat of violence. I will get a peace bond taken out which will make it illegal for any of them to come anywhere near us, our homes or the shop. If they come back they will be arrested."

"This is insane, Preshea. Who would believe that in 2018 there would be witch hunts still happening."

"Oh, it's crazy alright. They're crazy. They're so narrow minded they can't see past their own religious dogma. Not much has changed over the centuries has it? Anybody who doesn't think like them, act like them, or follow the same set of narrow rules is to be hunted down and persecuted."

Suddenly Beth had a vision of screaming women who were being tortured. Was it a flash back to a past life? She wasn't sure.

"Beth? Are you still there?"

"Yeah, sorry. My mind wandered."

"Where were you?"

"Nowhere good."

"Susan just finished her session with Father Ryan. I don't want to leave her alone so we will swing by the school and pick up the kids and then come to the store and get you. Then we can all have supper at my place. I've invited Father Ryan to join us. Sound good?"

"Sure. See you in a bit."

Beth hoped the vision she had was of the past and not prophetic.

Across the street in the alley Donald Eldridge watched her inside the store. As soon as he had all of these bitches in one place he would make his move.

20

As they ate, for the first time in longer than she could remember, Susan felt herself relax. She even joined in the laughter as Preshea and Father Ryan shared the story of how they first met.

"I came to the store looking for a bloodstone but before I could introduce myself Preshea, who saw my crucifix, thought I was about to dowse her with holy water and start casting demons out of her."

"To be fair, you are the first priest or pastor I have met who hasn't thought I needed redemption and exorcism," Preshea chuckled.

"Over the years I have become one of your most loyal customers."

"Yes, you have, and you're a loyal friend too," Preshea said.

Rowan wanted to know more about the gemstones and crystals.

"What's a bloodstone?"

"It's a deep, earthy green gem with spots of bright red. In the ancient world it was considered to be the most beautiful of the Jaspers and was called the Sun Stone, and later, Christ's Stone. The most widely known legend comes from the Middle Ages and claims the Blood Stone was formed at the crucifixion of Jesus, when the blood of his wounds fell onto the dark green earth and turned to stone," Father Ryan explained.

"I have always been interested in stones and crystals. My father was a geologist and miner back in Ireland and used to bring me little bits and pieces of stones from time to time," he explained.

"It's an excellent blood cleanser and a powerful healing stone. It heightens intuition, increases creativity, is grounding and protecting. It gives courage, assists in living in the present moment, calms and revitalizes the mind, dispels confusion and enhances decision-making. It also reduces irritability, aggressiveness and impatience," Preshea added.

"Maybe we should give one to Pastor Blackmore and others at First Pentecostal," Susan suggested.

"What stone would you suggest for me," she asked Preshea.

"Definitely carnelian, don't you think Father Ryan?"

"Yes. For sure."

Rowan and Raven were listening intently wanting to know more.

"It's an orange-colored variety of the agate Chalcedony, a mineral of the Quartz family. Its color varies from pale pinkish-orange to deep rust. Like all agates, it has protection energies against fear, envy, and anger, and dispels sorrow, negativity, and apathy and is useful for overcoming abuse of any kind. Carnelian is also a stabilizing stone that restores vitality and motivation and stimulates creativity and initiative. In ancient times, as well as today, Carnelian is believed to help the timid to become eloquent and bold. Ancient warriors wore Carnelian around their necks for courage and physical power to conquer their enemies," Preshea explained.

Rowan and Raven wanted to discuss the battles with the Roman soldiers both she and Beth fought with their mother.

"Do you think you would have worn it when you fought the Roman soldiers?"

Susan raised an eyebrow. "Fought Roman soldiers?"

"Yeah, mom. You have to hear this. Tell her Preshea. Tell her how you and Beth and your mom fought the soldiers in a past life," Raven said.

Preshea recounted the battle in which she and Beth died and their mother took poison to avoid capture.

"Queen Boudica has reincarnated as Boudica the cat," Rowan said as he stroked the ginger tabby that was now rubbing against the leg of his chair.

"Really?"

"No kidding, mom."

"Father Ryan, what do you think? Is it possible for someone to reincarnate as a cat?"

"It's funny you should ask. It reminds me of a dear friend of mine whose nickname was 'The Cat.' I went to seminary school with a fellow named Monty McMaster. He was a character if ever there was one. He was a very large lad with coal-black hair and dark brown eyes.

Now Monty came from a rough and tumble family in County Cork where my family lived. He was, as people say, from the wrong side of the tracks. Anyway, times were tough for the McMaster family. There were 10 kids and not a one of them had anything more than the clothes on their backs and empty bellies most days.

Monty, the eldest of the children, did what he had to do to help his mother feed everyone since his old dad was more often in the drink than out of it. Sometimes Monty would lift some cheese or sausage from the market when the vendors weren't watching. As he got older he got into a bad crowd and came close to dying more than once. We called him the cat because it seemed like he had nine lives. After he got caught stealing for the last time, a benevolent magistrate said he had two choices. He could either go into the seminary, and become a priest, or he could go to jail. So Monty ended up becoming a priest like me. He was a fine fellow and a Godly man, to be sure. Like me, he was a rebel priest. We shared the same views on many things which got us in trouble with the diocese."

Rowan, who loved hearing Father Ryan's stories, asked "Like what?"

"Like me, Monty believed in reincarnation. He often said that in his next lifetime I would recognize him right away."

"Did you?"

"Oh yes. About a year after he died I was at the opening of a drug and alcohol rehabilitation center. Monty had devoted much of his work to helping addicts get clean and sober and turn their lives around.

He'd spent about five years raising funds to start the center. Just before the speeches at the official opening, which was held on the center's grounds, a very large, handsome black cat showed up. It jumped up on the podium and sat there like it knew exactly what was happening. Somebody picked the cat up and put it on the ground. The cat kept jumping up on the podium and refused to leave. Everybody found this very funny. I immediately thought the cat was Monty who'd come back to make good on his nickname."

They finished the meal with happy conversation. Beth and Father Ryan walked to their cars not seeing someone hidden in the bushes across the street.

The next morning, Preshea and Susan took the kids to school. Susan, afraid Donald might find her alone at Preshea's house, asked if it would be okay for her to help out at the store for the day.

"Sure. We can always use another pair of hands."

The morning passed without incident. But, after lunch, trouble arrived when Pastor Blackmore and Donald arrived demanding to see Susan.

"Where is she?

"She's not here," Beth said quickly.

"That's I lie. I saw her arrive here earlier today with that Circe woman."

Preshea and Susan, who were in the back office, heard just enough to know Susan needed to remain out of sight. Preshea, who'd had about all she could take from these men, came back into the front of the store ready to do battle.

"Are you gentlemen looking for some tarot cards or sage for your next smudging ceremony?"

Donald demanded to know where his wife was.

"I'm not playing games lady. Tell me where she is or there will be trouble."

"Is that a threat? Or should I say is that another threat? I heard about the signs some of your congregation members were carrying yesterday when you were picketing here. That was a death threat, Pastor Blackmore. I know the Bible says to turn the other cheek but really, I have had about enough of you, him and all of the rest of you zealots. So, do yourselves a favor and get out of here now."

"Or what," Donald challenged.

"Have you ever heard of binding and banishing spells?"

Both men took a step backward looking even more uncomfortable than they were when they'd entered the store.

"You have about 10 seconds to get your butts out of this store or I will be forced to use them on you," Preshea said.

Pastor Blackmore, who pulled his pocket Bible from his suit coat once more said: "In the name of Jesus I rebuke you."

"Jesus is my friend too, Pastor, and he knows whose hearts are filled with light and love and whose aren't. I have done you no harm but you and your people have harassed me too many times.

Enough. Stop this nonsense now or face the consequences," Presehea warned.

"You're bluffing," Donald said with a sneer.

Pastor Blackmore wasn't taking any chances.

"Come on Don. Let's leave," he urged.

The men left without another word.

"They're gone Susan. You can come out now," Beth said.

Both she and Susan, who overheard everything from where she was hiding, weren't sure if Preshea was bluffing or telling the truth about casting spells.

Nervous now, Susan needed to know more about the woman she and her kids were living with. What if she could cast spells. Were they harmful? Was this black magic?

Preshea knew she needed to take some time to teach both women more about her beliefs and practices.

"Don't worry. There's nothing evil in what I believe or do. I am a Christo-pagan. Meaning I am a follower of Christ but I also practice the traditions of my ancestors who were devoted to nature.

I'd rather solve whatever problems I have peacefully. However there are certain situations when it becomes necessary to redirect the negative energies of people who would try to do us harm.

Some may call this invoking the protection of the saints, angels and spirit guides. Others say it's magic, witchcraft or even hocus-pocus. Whatever it is, it works," she said.

"What do you do first?"

"This isn't something to be taken lightly. It's important to know what you are doing, be strong in your faith and always work from a place of light and love. There is a right way to pray and there are things you can do to invite dark forces into your world that can end up causing you and others harm," Preshea cautioned.

"First, I always pray the white light surrounds me and keeps me from all evil. I say, 'Spirit of the white light, Jesus, Mother Mary, Archangel Michael, and all from the holy heavenly realm and to the ancestors, surround me and protect me.'

When I pray I know I'm safe because I'm always taken care of by spirit. I pray a prayer of thanksgiving and gratitude. I pray knowing that my highest good will be served.

I don't even need to pray out loud for the desires of my heart are already known. Spirit knows all things. Time is a human construct. My prayers are heard and I need to trust that no matter what I believe the outcome will be as it's meant to be. Source knows what's for the greatest good and it'll happen when it's meant to happen. Included in my prayer is the request the outcome is for the greater good of all. I send out love and never hate. What goes around comes around; this is a universal rule found in every faith.

Prayer is just another word for saying you're talking to Source. I never keep praying for the same thing over and over. It's like a child nagging their mother or father.

Meditation is when you hear answers. Quite often, in meditation, I will hear a voice within acknowledging my prayers and showing indescribable love.

Taking from the wisdom of the ancestors, I sometimes will use grounding, shielding, binding and banishing when I feel under attack by those who mean to do harm.

Grounding is simply connecting to the energies of the earth by walking barefoot outside. Shielding is envisioning being surrounded by protective white light.

Binding someone is the simplest form of keeping someone from harming you. I often light sage to clear my home of negativity if someone, whose energy is dark, has been in my personal space.

I sometimes create a circle and invite Source, the angels, the ancestors and the Tuatha Dé Danann in. Tuatha Dé Danann means *the people of the goddess Dana* in Gaelic. The Tuatha Dé dwell in the otherworld but interact with humans and the human world.

When binding someone who is working to harm me or others, I use a white band to absorb energy. I wrap a photo, a drawing or a personal belonging of the person who is trying to do harm. If none of these are available I simply write their name down on a piece of paper.

As I wrap the photo, object or paper in the cloth I think pure thoughts to release the negative energy and I say:

"I bind you from doing harm to others as well as to yourself."

Once the object is completely bound, I burn it before I lower it into the bowl filled with salt water and after I thank God and the ascended masters. Then I take the wet ashes and I dispose of them somewhere off my property.

Sometimes I will throw the negative energy back to the person sending it. This is called a reflection spell.

I simply refuse to accept the negative energies and reflect them away from me and back to their original source. What goes around comes around. This is not supernatural or magic. It is attached to the same laws of nature we all live by here on earth.

I also keep sacred space in my home. I have an altar where I go to pray and meditate. It has candles which I light and photos of those deities such as Jesus and Mary I pray to.

And always, I abide by the law. When someone is threatening you I always advise going to the authorities and let them handle things."

Preshea grabbed her purse and car keys.

"Where are you going," Beth asked.

"To the police station. I'm filing a restraining order against Donald, Pastor Blackmore and First Pentecostal Church. Beth, can you take Susan and pick kids up from school?"

"Sure thing. See you later."

The police officer at the desk asked: "What is the nature of the complaint?"

"Harassment."

Preshea explained what had happened outside her store as well as her first encounter with Pastor Blackmore earlier in the week and again with Donald earlier in the day.

"I don't want the church pastor, Donald Eldridge or any of the rest of the congregation to come anywhere near me, my employee or my home."

Satisfied there was cause for concern, the restraining order was written and officers delivered it to Pastor Blackmore.

They were shown to the pastor's church office. He was flabbergasted as he read the restraining order.

"You've got to be kidding me. Nobody threatened that woman," the pastor waved his hand as if trying to erase the image of him and his flock in a negative light.

"Did some of the protestors carry signs that said; *do not allow a witch to live?*"

"Well yes, but as I explained to a store employee, it's not literal."

"Literal or figurative you cannot make threats of harm against anyone," the officer explained.

"If anyone threated someone it was she who threatened me and Mr. Eldridge. She said if we didn't leave she would cast spells on us, he said.

"Come on man, get real. Spells? Seriously? You and your congregation members are to remain at least 50 feet away from Preshea Circe, her home and her business at all times. Is that clear?"

"Fine. Yes. It's clear. But, you know as well as I do, that woman doesn't belong in this town."

The officers left the church office and went back to the station.

Pastor Blackmore was livid.

"How dare she!"

He was so angry he wanted to choke her. Suddenly, he had visions of walking to the gallows, a noose was tied around his neck as a large crowd yelled, 'Die witch.'

A cold shiver ran up his back. He'd had this scene played out in his nightmares many times but never before while he was awake.

His imagination was getting the better of him. He prayed.

"God, I ask that you protect the innocent and drive the darkness from this town."

Little did Pastor Blackmore realize the darkness was coming from him and from within his own flock. Donald Eldridge was a black cloud of anger and the storm of hatred and revenge was coming to wreak havoc on those who weren't prepared for what he planned to do to them all.

If ever there was a time when Preshea Circe needed to pray for protection, this was it.

216

21

Preshea arrived home in time to find Beth, Susan and the kids all in the kitchen preparing supper and setting the table.

"This is the nicest thing that's happened all day," she said as she kicked off her shoes and sat at the large kitchen table.

"How'd it go with the police?"

"Good. The officer I saw took a statement and promised a restraining order would force all of them at First Pentecostal to keep away from all of us, this house and the store," Preshea said.

"That's a relief," Beth said.

"It's weird that the people we once spent so much time with are now the enemy," Raven said.

"They're not the enemy, honey. They're just confused and need some time and space to calm down. Sometimes, in the heat of the moment, people say and do things they otherwise wouldn't do," Preshea said.

"You're patient. After the way you've been treated, I wouldn't blame you for being angry and bitter. I have to admit, I am. I went to people in the church for help. So did the kids. People knew Donald is abusive but they did nothing about it. They pretended like it wasn't happening. I am bitter. Very bitter," Susan said.

Preshea understood how she felt. She had come from an abusive home and held on to the anger and bitterness for a long time until Father Ryan helped her to see that holding a grudge against someone is like swallowing poison and expecting the other person to die.

"Father Ryan helped me with those same feelings. You should talk to him about it."

"Maybe I will," Susan said quietly.

The five of them enjoyed a relaxing dinner. The kids did their homework and then watched TV. Susan looked at them and marvelled at how in just a few days of being here they'd been transformed. They were relaxed. They were smiling. They were acting like happy kids.

"I should have left him years ago. I would have saved them from so much sadness. They have been harmed and they bear the emotional and physical scars."

"Don't blame yourself. You are as much a victim as they are. You did the best you knew how to do under the circumstances. In my experience, victims stay even when they know they shouldn't. Some even make excuses for the abusive behavior. They tell themselves they brought it on themselves. If they'd tried harder, been nicer, more patient, less annoying they wouldn't have been beaten. Look at me Susan. It was not your fault," Preshea said and hugged the petite blond woman who looked like she was carrying the weight of the world on her shoulders.

Susan shook with emotion. "I know. It's not my fault but I can't help think it is sometimes."

"In time, with therapy, it will make more sense. You will get perspective on this."

The phone rang. Preshea answered.

"Hello?"

"Is Susan Eldridge there please?"

"Susan, it's a woman looking for you."

Susan picked up the phone. Her hands were shaking.

"Hello?"

"Susan! It's Betty Blackmore. I just want you to know my husband and I are concerned about you and the children. Why are you staying with that woman? You know you only had to come to us and we would have gladly given you a place to stay until this can be worked out between you and Donald."

That was the final straw for Susan. She unleashed anger kept in check for years.

"Oh, is that so?"

"Certainly."

"I don't think so."

"Whatever do you mean?"

"I came to you and Pastor Blackmore telling you about Donald's behavior toward me and the children. The kids also shared their fears about their father with your husband. Neither of you did anything more than ignore my kids and tell me I needed to be a more loving, patient wife. I am no longer interested in anything you or your husband have to say. As for Preshea Cierce, she has shown more love and compassion to me and my children over the past few days than you or your husband ever have. Furthermore, I no longer wish to have anything more to do with the First Pentecostal Church. I have found a new spiritual advisor and will be attending services at Friends Along the Way from now on."

The tone of Betty's voice suddenly went from syrupy to sour.

"That so-called priest and those women you're with are warping your mind. You are walking down a dangerous path Susan. I am afraid for you and your kids."

"Oh, don't worry about us. For the first time in a long time I see things clearly. We will be just fine. Please don't call here again."

Susan placed the receiver back on the cradle.

"Bravo Susan," Beth said.

Susan grinned. "I know as soon as I hung up on her she ran to tell the pastor what I said. I only hope it doesn't cause Father Ryan any trouble."

"Oh, I wouldn't worry about Father Ryan. He's quite capable of handling people like the Blackmores," Preshea said.

"He certainly is the first cleric I've met who's open to all faiths, all ways of worship."

"More than that, even though he's ordained as a Roman Catholic priest he isn't afraid to call things as he sees them. Many of his messages go against the grain of church doctrine, which is igniting a fire in the once disillusioned Catholics and people of many other faiths who also are searching for a real relationship with God. There have been so many who've left other churches to attend Friends Along the Way that many church leaders from various faiths including Catholic parish priests are jealous. They complained to the Bishop. He is no longer welcome to say mass anywhere within the diocese."

"That's awful. How could they treat him so cruelly?"

"Father Ryan says that if you aren't upsetting someone then you are living an insipid existence. He uses Christ's life as an example. Jesus was hated by the religious leaders. They rejected him because he challenged and rebuked them. They rejected his message because it went against the grain. Father Ryan reminds me very much of Jesus in this way. Until I met him I would never have considered attending church but I wouldn't miss his services now."

Preshea, Beth and Susan weren't the only ones talking about Father Ryan. On the other side of town the preacher's wife was telling her husband about her conversation with Susan.

Pastor Blackmore's face reddened with anger. He Googled the address for *Friends Along the Way* and the home of Father Ryan.

"Tomorrow morning I am going to find that man and set him straight."

The next morning, he wasted no time finding the *Friends Along the Way* hall but discovered it was locked and nobody was there. Next, he drove an hour outside of town to the address he'd found on Google for Father Ryan's residence.

He wasn't certain, even with the GPS navigation system in his Cadillac sedan, he would be able to locate the mountain ridge residence.

This was very remote country. He drove five miles off the main highway and down a dirt road. No phone, no electricity.

"How can anyone stand to live in this wilderness?" the pastor grumbled as he continued to drive.

Father Ryan preferred solitude. He gave so much of himself to others in his ministry this was his refuge. Here he was alone with God and nature. His nearest neighbors were bear, coyotes, wild turkeys, deer, and bobcat in the dense forests as well as hawks and eagles soaring overhead.

For those who had the courage to live in silence, there's much to learn from Mother Earth. He studied under the tutelage of Gaia. The four and a half billion-year-old teacher whispers the lessons only learned while spending time in nature. These classes are taught through the sounds of the breeze blowing through the leaves on the trees or water gurgling over river rocks. There were extraordinary things to be gleaned from the old woman's wisdom but few, such as Father Ryan, and those who were spiritually connected to the land, understood.

Pastor Blackmore wasn't able to appreciate Gaia or the splendor surrounding him. Sure, the place was serene but he wasn't here to relax and drink in the beauty of the landscape and the views from high atop this mountain ridge.

After several wrong turns he finally found the entrance to Father Ryan's residence. A sign over the door said: ***Chomh fada sin o bhaile, thar a bheith fada o bhaile*** which means More than *a long way from home.*

It was so fitting. For he'd been away from Ireland since as a young priest in the late 1970s, he'd gone to Africa. Some 20 years later he took up residence in the United States where he'd remained until now. But beyond his geographical location on the planet, the sign was indicative of his soul missing his heavenly home. Nobody knows the hour when our spirits will leave our bodies. He was prepared to die, whenever his time came, for he knew the body was just a shell. He understood death wasn't the end of the story but simply time for the next chapter. He could choose to remain in the spiritual realm or reincarnate again to learn more lessons learned through human birth, life and death.

Father Ryan was in the middle of his daily meditation when a pounding on the front door caused his massive Irish wolfhound to stir from where he slept. The growling sounds Pastor Blackmore heard coming from inside were almost enough to cause him to run back to his car. He remained where he was when he heard: "One moment. I just need to call off the dog. Mungan tar liom! Mungan come with me!"

Father Ryan opened the large wooden door and smiled at the unexpected visitor.

"Hello. How might I help you?"

"Father Ryan?"

"Yes?"

"I wasn't sure. You're not wearing vestments."

"No. Only when required. I like to be comfortable. Jeans and sweaters are more my style. Never could stand the bloody collar. Chafes the neck, you see... And you are?"

"Pastor Blackmore. I am the senior church leader at First Pentecostal Church."

Father Ryan knew he was viewed as a heretic rebel among Catholic Church leaders and an oddity leading others down the slippery slope to hell among fundamentalist preachers.

"I take it this isn't a social call."

"No. It's not."

"Well, come in then. Let's have this out, shall we?"

Mungan, who was sitting next to Father Ryan, never took his eyes off Pastor Blackmore and continued to emit a low and menacing growl. The dog was well trained and wouldn't do anything unless told to by his master. Still, it was amusing to see how put off the preacher was by the dog's unfriendly, suspicious manner.

"Oh, don't worry about old Mungan here. He hardly ever bites. Come into the living room."

Pastor Blackmore gave the dog a wide berth and sat at the far end of the room trying to keep as much distance between him and the giant, hairy grey beast as possible.

"How can I help you sir?"

"I'll get right to the point. One of the families in my congregation is experiencing some difficulties. The wife has left her husband and their two children are with her. Her husband is very upset and wants them to return to home. I am trying to counsel the wife so she can see her place is with her husband and the children need their father. I believe you know to whom I am referring?"

"Ah, yes. That would be Susan Eldridge and the twins Raven and Rowan."

"It's Randall and Rose. But yes, Susan and the children are now staying with that woman who runs the occult store on Main Street in town. She is a dangerous, negative influence on them."

"I am not sure…"

"Furthermore Father Ryan, Susan has informed me that you have been counselling her and, as a result of this, she has told my wife she wants nothing more to do with me or the rest of the congregation at First Pentecostal. How dare you!"

"How dare I? How dare you! You have a moral and legal duty to report any cases of abuse you're aware of and yet, I'm told by Susan and the children, even though they came to you looking for help you chose to ignore it."

"I, um well, I didn't see a need to involve the police in the private matters of a husband and wife."

"What you mean to say is that you didn't want people to know the dirty details of an abusive domestic violence case you have chosen to ignore. Furthermore, where Susan Eldridge chooses to live and worship is neither your affair nor that of her abusive husband. She told me you and your wife advised her that she needed to work harder on her marriage and that, if she would only try to please her husband more, there'd be harmony rather than discord at home."

"Well, yes. The Bible does say, 'Wives, obey your husbands as you obey the Lord. The husband is the head of the wife, just as Christ is the head of the church. The church is his body and he saved it. Wives should obey their husbands in everything, just as people should obey Christ," the preacher said with an air of superiority.

Father Ryan knew it would come down to a theological war of words with this guy. Fundamentalists loved nothing better than judging others whose beliefs were contrary to what they saw as the direct word of God.

"Doesn't the Bible also say, 'Husbands love your wives as Christ loved the church and gave himself up for her'? When a man beats his spouse he doesn't love her. He isn't following the example of Christ-like behavior. In fact, he is doing quite the opposite. Christ loved the church so much he gave himself up; he was willing to die for her. It seems to me that Donald Eldridge has forfeited all marital rights because he broke his vow to love, honor and cherish Susan."

Pastor Blackmore switched gears.

"I have heard it said that you tell people there are many pathways to God; that all faiths are valid and people have choices in how they come to God. There is only one way to salvation. John 14:6 says: *'I am the way the truth and the life. No one comes to the father but through me'.*"

Father Ryan knew this was coming. It was the go-to for all fundamentalist Christians.

"That is your understanding based on your knowledge from your study of the Bible. You are preaching a fear-based literal message," Father Ryan said gently.

"The Bible is the inspired word of God," Pastor Blackmore argued and pounded his right fist into the palm of his left hand.

The massive dog growled as he lay at Father Ryan's feet. He reached down to soothe the dog and then asked: "Do you know why you are so angry?"

"I get angry when I see people, like you, taking the holy word of God and twisting it into something it shouldn't be," the pastor snarled.

"In my experience, fear-based literalists, if not in a position of power, ridicule any new teaching; if they're in a position of power, they incarcerate or even execute the adherents of the new teaching. On the other hand, mystics immediately recognize the new teaching as true because, at the core of their being, they

225

knew it all along. In fact, the sign of great teachers is not that they bring us wisdom we didn't already have but, rather, that they create 'Aha moments' in us as they help roll back the amnesia for what we always knew at the core of our inner divinity."

The pastor scoffed. "You really believe that bull crap? No wonder the Catholic diocese has labeled you the rebel priest."

Father Ryan enjoyed going against the grain and irritating traditionalists and literalists. He wasn't upset by the pastor's criticism.

"When you truly understand who Jesus is, and what he taught, you'll be filled with wonder and compassion and love. If your understanding, instead, leads you to fear, pride or xenophobia, then my friend, you're following the wrong Jesus."

"You still haven't addressed John 14:6," the pastor taunted.

"In early 1995 I was invited to give a series of seven lectures at the Presbyterian Church. I titled the series: *Will the real Jesus please stand up?* In preparation for the lecture I'd been reading John 14:6. While I was meditating I had a powerful vision of Jesus.

I asked him, *"Did you really say that?"* He replied, *"Yes, I did. Because the only way is love; the deepest truth is love; and the whole point of life is love. Anybody who wants to find the father needs to walk only in love."* And then, without any prompting from me, he went on to say, *"And the Buddha is the way, the truth and the life. Nobody comes to the father except through the Buddha. Because the only way is compassion; the deepest truth is compassion; and the whole point of life is compassion. Anybody who wants to find the father needs to walk only in compassion."*

"You're claiming Jesus told you there are many pathways to God? That is blasphemy. How dare you!"

You say I'm not preaching the correct message but I believe church leaders, should open to constant examination of their faith and exploration of everything even if it means understanding they could have misunderstood God's message.

Fundamentalists fear and demonize the mystics who take Jesus at his word. You are sleepwalking through life and are not truly awake."

"You have a lot of nerve saying this to me. You say I am hiding in fundamentalist fear and that I am sleepwalking?"

"Another word for being awake is the Hindu notion of self-realization. The Christian equivalent is salvation. But salvation is grossly misunderstood by church teachers who see it as an action of redemption; literally buying back from the grip of Satan, occasioned by the mythical story of Adam and Eve disobeying Yahweh in the Garden of Eden."

"Mythical? You're saying Adam and Eve weren't real?! Again with your blasphemy!"

Father Ryan continued as though he hadn't been interrupted.

"You and the fundamentalist faith say the solution is to get baptized, profess Jesus as your personal savior and bingo you're saved!"

"That's exactly right. Jesus died to save us from our sins of disobedience, including Adam and Eve's original sin. And so many other sins that people commit every day."

"Sins such as?"

"Well, for one, homosexuality! We've all heard that Leviticus is where the Bible straight up says that homosexual behaviour is an abomination. And yes, it does. It also says that homosexuals should receive the death penalty!"

Father Ryan smiled and shook his head.

"It also says the same thing about eating pork or shellfish, charging interest on loans, a whole bunch of other restrictions that were a part of the Old Testament laws. Tell me Pastor Blackmore, have you ever eaten lobster or oysters? If you have then perhaps I should take you outside and throw rocks at you until you're dead."

"Don't be ridiculous!"

"Now you're getting it my friend. It's ridiculous. Just like saying homosexuals are committing a sin. What's sinful about loving another human being?"

"Same-sex relationships are sinful! It says so many times in the Old Testament."

"But for Christians, the Old Testament doesn't apply. In the New Testament Romans 10:4 says that Christ is the end of the law. In the book of Hebrews 8:13 it says, the old law is obsolete. Jesus never said anything about a person's sexual orientation. He came to show us that love for all people and all things was the way, the truth and the life. For Jesus was love incarnate.

"Jesus came to earth to die for our sins; a debt that he paid in full with his blood on the cross for mankind, all of which have fallen short of the glory of God!"

Father Ryan remained calm as the preacher's temper continued to rise.

"Nothing could be further from the truth. Jesus did not come because an irascible divinity demanded innocent blood to satisfy his anger at being disobeyed."

"If that's true then what was the point of the savior coming to earth? The key word is SAVIOR!"

"Jesus came as an avatar, accepting incarnation with all its limitations, temptations and vicissitudes, and yet never forgetting his divine nature. He was awake as he came in, awake as he lived in his human spacesuit, and alive as he committed his soul, on the cross, into the hugging embrace of his father. This is why he could say, '*It is completed*; mission accomplished; I never went to sleep; I never forgot who I am and why I came'. As far as I can tell there is only one sin – and it has nothing to do with the ten commandments of Moses – it is to never attempt to awaken to one's true, divine nature. If I opt to stay asleep, then I have two choices. If I am a religious person, I will only believe in a transcendent, punitive deity and I will serve him in fear, so that I may dodge the fires of hell. If I am an atheist or an agnostic, then I don't really care about this Superman-in-the-sky, and I will live my life by the world's values. But if I awaken at any stage of incarnation, I will immediately recognize that only God exists. I will smile and say namasté'."

"What in the world are you talking about? What is that supposed to mean nam-ass-tay?"

"Namasté means the God in me recognizes and honors the God in you to everything that I encounter, from a wave breaking on the beach, to an acorn full of the promise of growing up to be an oak tree, to the wrinkled old lady, in the back seat of the church, fingering her rosary beads."

"Sounds like a bunch of Buddhist nonsense if you ask me," the pastor said crossing his arms over his chest.

"Here's what I have come to know. The truly liberating message of Jesus is that life is a dream which the ego is having; the ego is a dream that the soul is having; the soul is a dream which the Spirit is having, and Spirit is a dream which God is having. Everything that exists is simply God-in-drag."

"Oh my goodness man, are you high? You just said God is in drag? And we are all just a part of a dream that the Almighty is having. This isn't what I know of God and Jesus; far from it in fact," the pastor said as his reddened face hinted that his blood pressure was higher than it should be.

"Knowledge is very different from wisdom. Wisdom is information that emanates from the inside. There is great wisdom to be found in Daoism. There is a saying that goes:

'Those who know don't say. Those who say don't know. Shut your mouth. Be still. Relax. Let go of your worries. Stay out of the spotlight. Be at one with the world and get right with Tao.

If you get right with Tao, you won't be worried about praise or scorn, about winning or losing, about honor or disgrace. That's the way to be'."

"Why do you keep telling me about these other faiths? They are false. I am not interested in hearing about them."

"Would you agree with me that Jesus spoke to his disciples in parables?"

"Yes; I will give you that."

"This is why it's important we don't take what's contained in the Bible literally. If we do that then we find ourselves in big trouble. Allow me to share a little story with you pastor. When I was a younger priest, in the early 1970s, I worked with the Kalenjin peoples of Kenya. Polygamy was still fairly common at the time. Each wife had her own hut, as did the husband. When a woman got pregnant, intercourse would cease until the child was weaned – typically around age two and a half years. Then, one day, the mother would send the child across the compound with a bowl of soup for his father. The little child would be so proud thinking, 'What a big boy am I; I am bringing food to my daddy!' But what mammy and daddy knew was that this was an invitation to resume conjugal activity. So you see things aren't always what they seem to be.

Jesus said a lot of things that he never meant literally. Take for example his statement, 'If your right eye causes you to sin, gouge it out and throw it away. It's better for you to lose one part of your body than for your whole body to be thrown into hell. And

230

if your right hand causes you to sin, cut it off and throw it away. It's better for you to lose one part of your body than for your whole body to depart into hell.' Take this literally and then enter a heaven which is peopled with blind amputees.

There's a symbolic level of what he's saying. Now, you've gotta dig deeper to find the meaning.

Finally, there is the mystical level. When speaking of Jesus' teaching, the literal level is mostly predicated on fear; the symbolic level on pride; and the mystical level on pure, unconditional love.

When Jesus speaks, the interpretation of his words is completely dependent upon the spiritual maturity level of the individual listener. Those raised on a diet in which God's a distant, demanding deity, will cower in fear of eternal damnation and follow a mandate of blind obedience to law.

Those who take the word of God literally I have found will keep themselves far away from the sinners, pagans, and infidels, whatever you want to call them. And if they have any compassion for these outsiders, it's to want to convert them so they can be saved from hell.

God speaks as eloquently in Celtic mythology, African folklore and Aboriginal dreamtime as He does in the Bible, Koran, Upanishads or Pitakas. In fact, God speaks as eloquently in a single flower.

Throughout history we have seen how fundamentalist religion has created fear and divided people who are prepared to launch crusades and Jihad against outsiders, and inquisitions against insiders. They're the literalists whose faith is fear based.

Compare this to the mystics who understand that nobody is excluded from the kingdom of God – ever!

Fundamentalism has identified an enemy, but mysticism says everybody is a brother and sister because it's understood we're all bite-sized pieces of God. Instead of demonising the other they recognize the divine in everything and everyone. Rather than going to war we treat everything with unconditional love."

If you really experience God it's such utterly ineffable an experience that there's nothing you can say and anything you attempt to say will cheapen the experience. People who say a lot about God mostly don't experience Source. That's the difference between the mystics and the theologians. The theologians can tell you what God had for breakfast but they've never met her. The mystics have met her but they won't talk about her because the experience is enough."

"You just called God 'Her'. God is our heavenly Father," Pastor Blackmore said and he made a face as if he'd just tasted something rotten.

"I believe God is neither male nor female but we attempt to convey the love we feel by using metaphors. Since there's been a long history of treating God as a Father figure, I use the female pronoun simply as a way to balance the equation by mixing the personal pronouns."

"I'm also told you are a believer in reincarnation," Pastor Blackmore said in a condescending tone.

"Yes. I do. So did Jesus and the disciples. Aren't you aware of that?"

"Well, I, um. That is…"

"If you look into the history of Christianity you'll see that it was accepted until around 500 AD and then it was removed from the church's doctrine. I can tell you from personal experience that it's real. I have lived many lifetimes."

"You and your beliefs are very dangerous. By telling people this you're giving them misinformation which will ultimately lead them straight to hell."

"There is no such place."

"What are you talking about? Of course there is a hell! Those who don't accept Jesus as their personal saviour will be separated from God and will be cast into hell to suffer for all eternity," Pastor Blackmore said pounding his fist on the coffee table in front of him like he was giving a fire and brimstone sermon.

Calmly, Father Ryan said: "There's no way anyone can be separated from God. Every single person is beloved of God. God is love. As far as God is concerned, She loves a slug as much as She loves Jesus Christ.

God doesn't hold more love for one than the other. The idea of hell is a totally human construct. There's no way anyone can be separated from God. It isn't possible to be separated from God any more than you can be separated from the sun."

Pastor Blackmore had all he could stand of the rebel priest. He jumped up from the sofa quickly, which caused Mungar to bare his large fangs and growl.

"I came here to try to get you to see reason but I see you are stuck in your delusions. Just remember, Susan Eldridge is my responsibility and that of her husband. I warn you to stay out of it."

"Too late; I'm deep into it now. I'll do everything I can to help Susan and the kids find their way back from the hell you and her husband have put them through. Yes, I said hell. The only possible hell that might exist is one we create interpersonally when we create it for one another or where we psychologically convince ourselves we are sinners."

"I'm warning you to back off."

"Oh, now, where's the fun in that? Would you care to see yourself out or shall I ask Mungar to show you to the door?"

The massive dog was standing with the hair raised on the ridge of his back. Pastor Blackmore didn't waste a moment. He ran from the room and out of the house not stopping until he was in his car and locked the doors. He started the car and pushed the accelerator to the floor causing the crushed rock on the driveway to fly up and hit the side of the house.

"He looked at you like you were going to eat him. And sure enough you might have. I didn't realize how late in the day it is. You must be ready for supper. Come on boy-o. Let's eat," he said as he patted his furry friend who was happily walking beside him to the kitchen.

All the way down the mountain Pastor Blackmore thought about his meeting with Father Ryan. He was no further ahead in his effort to bring Susan back to Donald and the congregation. This was one frustrated, angry shepherd who was determined to bring the runaway sheep back into the flock.

While Pastor Blackmore was trying to find the best way to retrieve his sheep, Donald Eldridge sat in his office unable to concentrate on work.

Instead he had more important things to do like working out a plan to make all three of those evil bitches pay.

As the afternoon turned to evening it came to him. They were witches. They needed to be forced to confess their crimes. He would do whatever necessary to make them admit they were in league with the devil.

22

Pastor Blackmore decided it was time to remind people of what happens when you are out of the will of God. The sermon he had planned to preach on Sunday was pushed aside for a new message he felt inspired to write. He immediately went to his study where, over the next several hours, he crafted a sermon for the next day to warn against what happens to those who are out of alignment with God.

The next morning, as usual, the pews were filled with those who'd been coming to hear this man speak for the past 10 years. Always it was a 'You must be born again to enter the kingdom of heaven' sermon with warning for those who fall out with God and the cost to those sinners who do.

"For the wages of sin is death; but the gift of God is eternal life through Jesus Christ our Lord. At its core, sin is rebellion against God. Our sin separates us from God, the creator and sustainer of life. Jesus said, 'I am the way and the truth and the life.' Life is in God. So, when we sin and become separated from God, we become separated from true life.

I tell you brothers and sisters there are those spreading a false message that it's possible to go to heaven no matter what you do because God is all loving. This is providing false hope because all have fallen short of the glory of God. All are sinners," he said pounding his fist on the pulpit in an effort to drive home the message.

When I speak of death I'm not speaking of an immediate death of the body. What I mean is a spiritual death. When we're saved in Christ, we're rescued from ultimate spiritual death and brought into ultimate spiritual life. Paul told the Romans, 'The gift of God is eternal life in Christ Jesus our Lord.'

Even believers sins will still result in a type of spiritual death. Though we are rescued from the eternal separation from God, we're not exempt from the natural consequences. We might feel disconnected from God. We act as the unrighteous rather than as the righteous. Our sin, even as believers, hurts God and grieves His Spirit. Though it doesn't sever our relationship with Him, our sin does divide us from him.

Think of your own relationship with your children. When they disobey you, you feel disappointed in them. The relationship between you is strained. You still loved them but there are corrections that need to be made and consequences to be handed out as punishment. This can be painful for both parent and child but it's necessary.

So it is with us and God. When we rebel against God's rule in our lives, we rebel against the Life, and therefore experience death. However, when we come back to God we are resurrected from spiritual death.

It's good to see brother Eldridge here this morning. I hope you will all give him your love and support as he and Susan are struggling with some personal issues right now. I encourage you to pray Susan will see the error of her ways and return to the flock. If she refuses to do so, then we all know what's in store for her.

The Bible tells us the hottest part of hell is reserved for those who know the truth and walk away from God.

Spit flew from his mouth and his face turned a deep crimson as he became so fervent in his call for action.

"I only hope it's not too late. I am sure some of you may have heard that Susan has moved into the home of the woman who owns the occult store. She's subjecting the children to that evil. It's my belief we need to take action to stop her and these other two women from murdering the spiritual lives of those two teens!" Pastor Blackmore yelled.

"Let those witches burn in the lake of fire," one of the people in the congregation called out.

Donald Eldridge knew what he had to do. He would rescue his children and send all three of those evil women on a one-way ticket to hell.

On the other side of town a very different service was happening. Preshea, Beth, Susan and the kids were seated in the *Friends along The Way* hall, which was filled to overflowing.

Father Ryan began the homily quietly.

"May the Lord be with you."

"And also with you."

"Today's message isn't one I had thought I'd give today. Then, I had an encounter with someone yesterday who inspired me to give this message instead.

I want to talk to you this morning about the God that I don't believe in. All of us were brought up with versions of God. If you haven't outgrown your understanding of God several times throughout your life, you haven't grown psychologically or spiritually.

I don't believe God is a person but, nevertheless, I have a personal relationship with Source. The highest compliment we think we can give is to make Him or Her superhuman.

I also don't believe God is a creator and, at some point, He or She says, 'I wonder what I am going to make today?' I believe things manifest from the essence of God.

I don't believe in a partisan God. Out of all of the universes God would have a love affair with this universe, the earth, a person and a particular faith more than any other is nonsense. The Japanese believe they're the prodigies of the sun god and they're beloved more than any other race on the earth. Judaism believes the Jews are God's chosen people. Christianity believes there's only one path to heaven and that's through Jesus Christ. Roman Catholicism says outside the Catholic Church, there's no salvation. The Maasai tribe in Kenya believe all of the cattle in the world were created for them. We all think we're special in the sight of God, but of course, this isn't so.

I also don't believe God is a micro-manager watching everything we say or do. I also don't believe God is a law maker and the highest judge thinking of ways to make life more difficult for us and then punishing us when we break the law.

This is a caricature of God created by fundamentalist religion which has led to all kinds of troubles over history including crusades, witch-hunts, the inquisition and the deaths of millions. And, there's also a form of science fundamentalism that's killed more people in 200 years than all of the religious wars in history. We're polluting our air, our soil, water and foods and we're leaving the planet desiccated.

I'm convinced the Source of everything doesn't interfere in human affairs. I believe souls make pre-conception contracts in heaven and move from lifetime to lifetime as part of soul groups and they create dramas allowing every one of those souls an opportunity to learn unconditional love.

God isn't planning your life or setting obstacles in your path and trials to test you.

We come here voluntarily. In heaven we can only grow to a certain extent because the things of this world like pain and grief, are unknown in heaven. Until you experience these sorts of things you'll not be stretched outside the boundaries of how you are able to love.

God's watching from a distance but not interfering. God's watching the dramas we create for and with each other.

Pain is the price of incarnation. It's the price of being born into a world where there are natural disasters and really bad people doing really bad things.

Life isn't about fairness. Life is about love. It's not about entering a world where everything is just and legal and lawful. It's about stretching through the pain and learning how to love anyway, even the enemies.

Finally, getting to the same spiritual place as Jesus, which is total love for everything and everyone; even your enemy. It's pointless to ask why all of these things are happening to me. This is the life we have pre-selected. The hand that you were dealt is the one you asked for because you knew that it was the best way for you to learn the things that would help you make the most progress.

Every one of us has a belief system driving everything we think and do, whether we are atheists or subscribe to some form of faith.

The unexamined life is meaningless. If you don't examine your life and faith or lack of faith, there is no room for growth."

As she listened to the message Susan had an epiphany. The message spoke to her soul in a way she'd never heard before. It made complete sense to her. It was exciting. It felt freeing. Now she was fortified to move forward in her life knowing that she chose these experiences to learn and grow.

Despite the trauma, she knew she loved herself enough to rise above it and she would be happy again. She loved her children enough to leave the abusive marriage and start anew as an independent person who was able to be a single parent.

Perhaps she would even get to the point where she was able to forgive Donald.

But it would take an exceptional amount of love to be able to forgive what her monstrous husband had planned to do to her as well as to Preshea and Beth.

As they left the service that morning none of them had a clue that within 24 hours they would be fighting for their lives.

23

The day started off like every other Monday. The alarm rang at 7 a.m. Preshea made coffee and Susan started packing the kids' school lunches.

Everyone had a quick breakfast before they all got into Preshea's van and dropped Raven and Rowan off at the high school.

"Have a great day kids," she said.

"See you later," they said as they waved and turned toward the school. Today was the last day of class before summer vacation started and the kids could hardly wait for the break.

Preshea, Beth and Susan were heading for the store. There was a lot to do before it opened at 10 and as the summer tourism season was heading into high gear, there was no time to sit around as customers arrived looking for trinkets and treasures for themselves and gifts for others.

The day passed quickly.

It was just before 3 p.m. Susan and Preshea were preparing to leave the store to go to the school and collect Raven and Rowan when Susan received a call on her cell phone.

The display read private number.

"Hello?"

She started to tremble as she heard her husband's voice on the other end of the telephone line.

"I have the kids."

"What do you mean you have the kids?! The court order says you are to keep away from them!"

"They're my kids. Nobody, including a judge, is going to keep me from them. Now you listen carefully. If you want to see them again you will do exactly what I tell you. You and those two bitches you're with are to head to the abandoned fish warehouse on the wharf road. Don't call the police. Come by yourselves. I will expect you here within the hour or you will never see the kids again. Do you understand Susan?"

She was shaking so violently she nearly dropped the phone.

"Yes, I understand," she said in a whisper.

The call disconnected and Susan stared wide-eyed at Beth and Preshea.

"What's happening?"

"He took them from the school. He says the three of us must go to the warehouse on the wharf road. He said not to call the police or I will never see Raven and Rowan again," she broke down sobbing. Beth gathered Susan in her arms and held her as she cried.

"It's going to be alright Susan. We'll get the kids back," Beth assured her.

They locked the shop and ran to the van.

The warehouse was 20 minutes away. Preshea drove as fast as she could without breaking the speed limit.

By 3:30 p.m. they arrived at the abandoned warehouse and found Donald's car parked close to the building.

They went inside but it was too dark to see.

Suddenly, a powerfully bright spotlight flooded the space temporarily blinding them. When their sight adjusted they saw Donald standing in front of them holding a handgun, which was pointed in their direction.

"Donald, for the love of God, what do you think you're doing?"

"Yes, Susan, it's for the love of God and my children that I've called you all here. Now sit on those chairs and place your arms behind your backs.

They complied. When they were seated he took plastic zip ties and secured their hands and feet.

"Where are the kids," Susan screamed.

"They're not here."

"Why not?"

"I didn't think it was appropriate for them to be present for the trial."

"What trial?"

"The witch trial. You and these other two hags are on trial for crimes against God and the practice of witchcraft," he snarled.

Preshea yelled, "You've got to be kidding. Are you nuts?"

"Shut your ugly face!" he ordered Preshea and then punched her in the mouth, splitting her lip open and sending blood running down her chin.

Beth and Susan screamed.

Preshea spit blood from her mouth in Donald's direction.

"This is a trial without a jury. I am the presiding judge. We'll begin with you," he pointed at Preshea. "You are the leader of the coven. You drew in these other two. The evidence against you is clear. However, I want to hear you confess your crime."

Preshea shook her head.

"I've done nothing wrong so I have nothing to confess," she said raising her chin in defiance.

"You will when I am through with you."

Again he struck her. This time the blow landing on her left eye which started to swell shut immediately.

"Confess!"

"No!"

Once more he struck her but this time with a belt buckle, which connected with her right temple and knocked her unconscious.

"Stop this Donald. Please! You're going to kill her."

Donald turned to his wife.

"Your turn."

"I want to hear you admit what you've done."

"What do you think I have done Donald?"

"You've sold your soul to the devil and you're now practicing witchcraft with these other women," he screamed.

"Donald, please. Stop!"

"Confess!'

He lashed at her with the belt with repeated blows.

Susan and Beth were screaming for help.

"Somebody help us!"

"Shut-up or I swear to God I will shoot her," he said pointing the gun at Preshea.

The inquisition continued as he went from Susan to Beth and then back to Preshea, inflicting pain and demanding confessions.

Finally, with all three women coming in and out of consciousness, he got the answer he was looking for.

"Please, Donald. I confess. I am whatever you say I am," Susan said in a whisper through lips so swollen and bloody it was almost impossible to understand what she was saying.

"The beatings will not stop until those other two also confess," he pronounced.

"Perhaps if beating won't work, burning will," he threatened.

Beth, now nearly unrecognizable from the blood that covered her swollen face, croaked in fear.

"I confess. I am a witch."

Next he turned to Preshea.

"What about you? Do you confess too?"

Just then, Pastor Blackmore rushed into the warehouse.

"Donald, in the name of Christ, stop this!"

"Pastor, I'm doing as you instructed."

"What do you think I told you to do?"

"Kill the witches. You said the wages of sin is death and the Bible says do not allow a witch to live."

"I didn't mean to actually kill them. I was talking about taking some action that would end their lives in this town; that we needed to force them to go somewhere."

"No, they must not be allowed to live. Two of them have already confessed to witchcraft and this one is soon going to admit it when she feels the flames on the soles of her feet," he said as he lit a blow torch.

Preshea, who'd come back from the black abyss of unconsciousness croaked: "I do no harm to others and I respect Mother Earth. I believe all faiths are inspired by God including those, like me, who follow the ways of my ancestors.

"How dare you speak the name of the Lord?! You are a blasphemer and a sorcerous. You're guilty!"

Preshea began to pray.

"Spirit of the white light, Jesus, Mother Mary, Archangel Michael, and all from the holy heavenly realm, protect us. I invoke the goddess Macha who battles against injustice to woman and children and warrior Queen Maeve. Stop this man and his wickedness."

Next she began chanting "Earth below, sky above. Fill the dark of night with love. The morning sun will take our pain and we will wake renewed again. Ever mind the rule of three. Three times your acts return to thee. This lesson well thou must learn. Thou only get what thee dost earn."

The chanting continued with Susan and Beth joining in.

"Ever mind the rule of three. Three times you acts return to thee."

Donald was so taken aback by the women's chanting, he didn't notice Father Ryan run into the cavernous space with Mungar.

He screamed, "In the name of God, Jesus and all of the ascended masters, stop!"

246

Donald demanded, "Who told you about the witch trial priest?"

"You may have locked your kids in a bedroom of your house but you forgot all teenagers carry smartphones. They sent me a text message. They're fine, Susan. Don't worry. I called the police and they're right behind me."

Donald screamed in rag, "You are one of them," he said as he pointed the gun at Father Ryan and squeezed the trigger. The bullet entered the priest's chest and he dropped like stone.

A mournful howl filled the warehouse. The massive hound looked at his master lying on the concrete floor quickly becoming soaked in blood. Mungar then turned back toward the man who'd fired the gun.

The hair on the ridge of the dog's back stood up and his lips were pulled back as he bared his large teeth. A menacing growl emanated from his throat and he pounced, knocking the gun from Donald's hand causing him to lose his balance and land on his back. Mungar sunk his teeth deep into Donald's left arm.

"Ahhhhhh! Make it stop. Call the dog off!"

Mungar then went for his throat, tearing his jugular open and a steady gush of blood rushed from the open wound.

A police SWAT team arrived at that moment along with several ambulances.

Preshea, Beth and Susan were freed from their bonds and placed on stretchers.

Father Ryan and Donald were also placed on stretchers as paramedics tried to stop the blood loss in both men.

Pastor Blackmore, the only one who was able to tell the police anything, was left to give a statement to the investigators.

He was taken to the police station in the back of a squad car and, over the next three hours, he was questioned.

"What's your name?"

"Pastor William Blackmore."

"What's your connection to the people who are now being treated for their injuries?"

"I am Susan and Donald Eldridge's pastor."

"You were ordered to stay away from Preshea Circe. How did you end up with her and the others at the warehouse?"

"I received a text message from Donald. He said I needed to attend a trial and I would witness the executions of those three women."

"Did you say or do anything that would incite this violence?"

"I certainly did not!"

"Were you protesting at Circe's Closet recently with members of your congregation?"

"Yes."

"Did you carry signs which said witches shouldn't be permitted to live?"

"Yes, but as I explained before, that wasn't meant to be taken literally."

The detective leaned forward.

"Let me explain the law to you preacher. The offence of inciting violence is a crime of primary liability. That means by telling your congregation something had to be done to rid the town of these women, who you said are witches, you incited Donald Eldridge to forcibly confine and torture his wife, Beth Williams and Preshea Circe, as well as shooting Father John Ryan. If any or all of these individuals die from their wounds, you will also be charged with being an accessory to murder. You have the right to remain silent. If you do or say anything it can be used against you in a court of law. You have the right to an attorney. If you cannot afford an attorney, one will be appointed for you. Do you understand?"

"Yes. I want to call my lawyer."

Five ambulances arrived at the emergency entrance of the hospital and five stretchers were wheeled into the trauma unit. The ER doctors saw the gunshot wound to Father Ryan's chest and the massive wound on Donald Eldridge's neck.

"Get these two into the O.R. stat," the head doctor yelled.

Beth, Susan and Preshea were taken to the acute care unit where they underwent cat scans and x-rays after their wounds were cleaned and bandaged. Preshea, who'd received the worst of the beatings, had a fractured skull and was in critical condition.

Susan and Beth would both require plastic surgery to repair the serious facial damage including broken jaws and noses.

Meanwhile the efforts to save the lives of both Father Ryan and Donald Eldridge were continuing in adjoining operating theatres.

Both had lost a significant amount of blood and needed multiple transfusions.

Who lives and who dies is up to God. Sometimes those who survive trauma wish they hadn't.

Donald Eldridge was one such person. The doctors managed to repair the damage done by Mungar's bites. He had many days as he recovered from those wounds to think about what was going to happen to him. No amount of prayer could save him from his fate.

As for Father Ryan, only a miracle would save him. He was outside of his body watching the surgeons and operating room nurses fight to save his life

Father Ryan had been shot at point-blank range in the center of his chest.

The gun powder had burned his shirt and skin as the bullet shattered his breastbone into countless shards of sharp shrapnel, which were propelled and fanned-out toward his heart, lungs and large blood vessels.

The tissue within a radius of several inches from where the bullet entered his chest had been burned and shredded. His heart, being so close, also ruptured, even though the bullet hadn't penetrated it.

The bullet then struck his spinal column at an angle, making an instant exit at a sharper angle after ricocheting.

As it exited his back the bullet left a huge wound including the obliteration of part of his left shoulder.

Father Ryan's soul knew it wouldn't return to the body. He heard the sound of the heart monitor as it went from a rhythmic beep, beep, beep to a high-pitched alarm as it flat-lined.

"He's in cardiac arrest. We're losing him. Defibrillator now! One, two, three clear…"

"Nothing. Again."

"One, two, three clear …"

"Absent heart sounds; absent breath sounds. No carotid pulse. No corneal reflex. No pain response. Pupils are fixed and dilated," a nurse said.

"Call it."

"Time of death: 3:33 a.m.," the chief surgeon said.

Those who undergo a sudden and traumatic end of life are often surprised and shocked.

Father Ryan's soul watched as a white sheet was pulled over his face and his remains were transferred to a gurney from the operating table.

He followed as his remains were taken to the hospital morgue.

It wasn't long before those he loved, who'd passed to the other side before him, were there to escort him home.

"I'm not ready to go yet. I have a few stops to make first," he explained to those heavenly beings.

24

Father Ryan's spirit watched as nurses treated Susan. Her face was swollen and had a purplish-black hue from the bruising.

She was heavily medicated but knew he was there.

"Father Ryan," she whispered.

One of the two nurses in the room looked at her and said.

"No, Mrs. Eldridge. There's no Father Ryan here. I'm one of your nurses. You've been through quite an ordeal but you will be alright. Just try to relax."

"She can't see me," Father Ryan explained.

"Why not?"

"I am no longer in my body."

"You died? Oh, Father Ryan!"

Susan started to cry.

The nurses looked at one another. The elder of the two explained, "It's the medication. Sometimes they have conversations with others who aren't here even when they believe they are."

The nurses finished their work and left the room.

"Susan, I am not staying long. They're waiting for me to go home. I want you to know you have the strength inside you to remain. You must, because your children need you. Your husband will survive his injuries and will be going to prison. You're more capable than you know. Promise me you will put your education to good use. There's a place for you at the clinic if you want it. I made the arrangements to hire you before I died. The other staff are expecting you if you decide to take the job. You won't remember this conversation but you will receive a letter with a job offer. Take it.

"Thank you Father Ryan."

"Don't thank me. There is much work to be done and you're the perfect person to do it. Who better to help abuse victims than someone who's experienced it?"

"I must leave you now. I have to visit Beth and Preshea and then I must go home."

"Will I see you again?"

"Oh yes, but you won't recognize me."

"Why not?"

"I won't be Father Ryan. I will be in a new spacesuit; that is to say a new body. I will be born into a new family and could either be male or female. When it's your time to leave this body you will also decide whether you remain in heaven or return to earth to experience another life in human form. It's up to you. You decide who, what, where, when, why and how your next life will be. It's all up to you. I have to go now. Peace be with you."

"Thank you Father Ryan. You have been so kind; so loving."

"Love is everything and you are completely and utterly loved. Remember this. Exhibit this in all things and you will be as close to God as one can get. You, my dear soul sister, are a bite-sized piece of God."

The man she knew vanished. While she grieved his loss she also was happy knowing there was an afterlife and their souls would meet again at another time and in another place.

Just down the hall, much of Beth's body was wrapped in gauze bandages. Like Susan, her face was nearly unrecognizable from the swelling from the beating.

Her eyes were unable to open but she could hear his voice.

"Beth. I am here with you."

"Father Ryan. I'm so glad you made it."

"Indeed, I did but not the way you think."

"I don't understand."

"I am no longer in my body. Soon I will return to heaven."

"You are dead?"

"The body I was in is no longer but I am very much alive."

She cried.

"Don't cry. Celebrate with me. It's a great day. I am going home. I've missed it."

"I don't want to be here anymore. I miss my husband so much. I miss my parents too."

"You can't leave just yet. You are needed here to help the others."

"Help others? What do you mean?"

"You are a strong woman with lots to give. There will be many coming who seek what you already know. Stay and do this work."

"We won't see you again?"

"Not like the man I was. I will be back but you won't know it's me. Somehow we will find one another again."

"I must go now."

"Goodbye Father Ryan."

"It's not goodbye. It's never goodbye. It's until we meet again and we shall."

She sensed he was gone. Beth knew he was right. She needed to remain a while longer. There were many who needed to know what she now knew thanks to him.

On the neurological intensive care unit Preshea's body was connected to many machines. A respirator ensured she continued to breathe. A heart monitor emitted a steady beep, beep, beep. The repeated blows she received to her head caused brain swelling. She was placed in a medically-induced coma to give her body a chance to heal.

Father Ryan's spirit watched as alarms sounded. Her spirit was leaving the body. She recognized him.

"Are we going together?"

"Yes, we are, but you will only be there for a short time and then you will return to this body."

"Why can't I stay?"

"You will learn more once we get there."

Together, they walked through a long, dark tunnel. There was a light shining at the end of it which illuminated a large door. They opened it and walked through.

Preshea's spirit immediately recognized it as home. Next she felt the overwhelming sense of peace and contentment. She saw her husband, her parents and others who'd gone before her.

"Why can't I stay?"

"It's not your time. Go back now. You'll understand why soon. There's a place we're sending you. It will be the place where you will remain until it is your time to return to us. You'll be joined by others who will help. It's important work. It's the work you have always done with your soul sisters."

Preshea's spirit was pulled back through the portal and through the long tunnel. She'd returned to her body.

A doctor had restarted her heart.

"We've got her. She's back," a doctor said.

The heavenly realm always celebrates when those who'd been gone return. Father Ryan's spirit was welcomed by the ancestors, the saints, the angels, and the ascended masters including Jesus, his mother, Mary, Mohammed, Sanat Kumara, Gautama Buddha, Confucius, Kwan Yin, Saint Germain, and Kuthumi, to name but a few.

"That was different. The last time the body was strangled. This time it was shot," his spirit said to everyone assembled for the reunion. He was immediately reconnected to Source and the indescribable wonder of all-encompassing love.

God asked, "Will you return once more?"

"Yes. I need to understand perseverance and patience."

"Where do you want to go?"

"Ireland."

"When do you want to make the journey?"

"Not now but soon."

"To the same time?"

"No, I think farther back."

"We shall be watching. We shall be waiting for you to return to us when you are finished the lesson. For now, stay with us and watch what happens to these soul sisters as they say yes to the calling to which they have answered over and over again throughout many lifetimes," the voice said.

25

Donald and the pastor spent six months in jail waiting for their trials.

The evidence against both of them was strong enough that juries found both of them guilty within a few hours of deliberation following their trials.

Once the foreman declared their guilty verdicts they were taken immediately to jail cells.

After the horrific things Donald had done, everybody he once knew had cut all ties with him.

As for the pastor, there were a scant few who turned out to support him. Mostly the few who were there came to the court out of morbid curiosity looking for details of the crime.

In both cases, they were taken from the courtroom in handcuffs and leg irons. Their few possessions were taken from them, logged and put in storage.

Both men waited a week for their transfers to the state's maximum security prison. This was a strange and terrifying experience. It was easy to see they were out of their element.

"Fresh fish," one heavily tattooed prisoner said and taunted 'Here fishy, fishy, fishy."

Another got up from the bench he was lying on and sidled up to Donald.

"You're pretty. What's your name sweetheart?"

Donald was too frightened to speak.

"Cat got your tongue? Don't worry. You don't have to be afraid of me. I'm real nice to the new fish. You just do as you're told and there'll be no trouble."

Donald and the pastor had no idea what was waiting for them in prison.

The inmate who'd taunted Donald earlier looked at him and said: "You ever have your asshole probed fishy? Get ready to spread them cheeks sweetheart. It will get you ready for what I'm going do to you soon."

Donald looked at the pastor. Both were terrified. These men were used to being in charge and now they were no different than anyone else waiting to be locked away for years to come.

After three hours the bus arrived at its destination. The massive stone structure was surrounded by razor-wire and electric fencing.

"Everybody out," one of the prison guards said.

The men got off the bus and headed inside the first building where they were processed.

"Take off your clothing," they were ordered.

"Bend over and spread your ass."

260

After the rectal search they were doused with a white powder.

"In case you got the crabs or lice," one of the inmates said to the pastor.

"Shut your mouth inmate," a guard ordered

"Put this on."

They were handed bright orange jumpsuits with the Department of Corrections initials on the back. Next they moved to another area where they were given a bundle of blankets.

Donald and the pastor were then taken to cell block C. It was just after supper and the inmates were back in their cells for the night.

Neither knew what to expect. The pastor was placed in a cell with a man who was reading the Koran. The pastor wasn't sure how best to approach this man.

"Pastor William Blackmore," he said extending his hand.

"Ibrahim Elnihum. I wouldn't go using any titles around here. You're just another inmate and you'll get off on the wrong foot with a lot of the guys in here if they think you are acting all high and mighty. My advice is keep your mouth shut, do as you're told and don't make eye contact with anyone. And, another thing, never let your guard down. Anything can happen around here and if you're not ready for it you could get killed."

The pastor placed his bedding on his bunk and sat down. He placed his head in his hands. He was completely overwhelmed.

"It's easy to tell this is your first time. You have no idea how anything works. You'll figure it out soon enough."

"Can I ask you a question?"

"Depends on what it is."

"You're reading the Koran. You're a man of faith? Why are you here?"

"Long story. Let's just say it's a good thing you're meeting me now rather than 10 years ago."

"Why is that?"

"I was a dangerous man back then. I went by the name of Bruce Walker. That man no longer exists. Now I'm dedicated to peace."

The pastor sighed.

"That's a relief."

"What about you? How does a pastor get sent to prison?"

"It's also a long story."

"Well I ain't got nothing better to do than to pray, read God's word and listen to your sad story for the next 15 years. So if you feel like talking…"

The pastor lay on his bunk. He closed his eyes and thought of life before this. He never understood how far he would fall because of his rigid mindset.

He'd lost so much because he refused to soften his stance against others. He recalled the afternoon he'd gone to Father Ryan's mountain ridge home. He now could understand what he refused to listen to then.

"I have literally ruined my life and the lives of others because I took the Bible literally," he said.

The image of Susan, Beth and Preshea tied to chairs dripping with blood from the whipping they'd received and the priest lying in his own blood after being shot was always in his mind when he closed his eyes.

"You were sleepwalking through life. So was I, but in a different way, until I found God here in this cell and converted to Islam."

"What do you mean sleepwalking?"

"Until we see that we come to earth to learn lessons that are impossible to learn in paradise; until we become fully awake and realize the greatest thing is love; that God is pure love and we're all tiny bits of that loving divinity, we're all asleep and will not transcend to a higher level of consciousness."

"Tell me about who you were when you were not in here?"

"I was a drug dealer. I murdered many people. I am ashamed of the man I was then. I left behind a wife and four kids who I haven't spoken to since I was arrested."

"How did you come to convert to Islam?"

"The prison library has a section on religion. I have studied all of the books in it. The Koran and the Bible both spoke to me but I felt a calling to convert to Islam. It's a beautiful faith."

"I thought it was filled with radicals who are violent and hate Christians," the pastor said.

"You have so much to learn. Saying all Muslims are violent is like saying all Christians are members of the Ku Klux Klan. That is a stereotype that's caused so much division. If you take the time to understand the Koran and its holy teachings, you will see it's a beautiful faith. Yes, it's true, there's a small fraction of those who are radical, fundamentalists who ascribe to violence but they remind me very much of fundamentalist Christians who think in terms of black and white and practice a fear-based religion."

"You're right. I am here because I preached nobody except born-again Christians will enter the Kingdom of heaven. I told my congregation several women were evil and their lives in our town needed to end. The husband of one of those women took me at my word and set out to kill them. He shot and killed a priest who was friends with them. It's my fault. I incited that violence and am partially responsible for his death. I deserve to be here."

"Well man, maybe the time you serve in here can do some good for you and others," Ibrahim said and then returned to reading the holy book.

The pastor tried not to sleep. He was afraid he would once again have the nightmare of a terrible time, which he often returned to in his sleep. Finally, as sleep overtook him late that night, he saw the priest once more. But this time he wasn't bleeding out from a gunshot wound.

Instead he was sitting on the edge of the prison cot looking young and healthy and happy.

"Hello William."

"What are you doing here?"

"I came to see how you're doing."

264

"How does it look like I am doing? I am in this tiny cell with a Muslim man in a prison filled with rapists and killers and all sorts of evil men."

"And you? Are you so different from them?"

"I suppose not. My heart was filled with hatred for those who didn't look, think, act, or worship in the same way as myself. I hated you for your beliefs and the message you shared with others. I was intolerant where you were able to see there's a better way. I was unable to see Jesus was all about tolerance and love. My refusal to live in love and acceptance of others and my instruction of others to take action against those who are different, believe different things, follow different faiths, caused your death and the terrible things that were done to Susan and those other two women. I am ashamed of myself. I have offended God and will be punished for it."

"You cannot offend God. God is love. When you understand this then you will understand the Creator cannot be offended and doesn't punish anyone for anything."

"Will you forgive me?"

"I already have."

"Thank you."

"How will you spend your life as it is now?"

"I am not sure. I will try to survive in this place. I will try to get to know God in a way I haven't known before. I will study other faiths. I will spend my time following a Christ-like life of love and tolerance."

"That's good. In doing so, perhaps you are fulfilling your mission of this lifetime."

"There are other lifetimes?"

"Yes, as I have told you before, we come back many times to learn many lessons."

"Will you return again?"

"Yes."

"Will we see one another again?"

"I believe so. We always do."

"Will the others we know be there with us?"

"Of course. They always are."

"Will I recognize them and you?"

"It's possible for some to remember their past lives; those who are old souls."

"Are we?"

"Oh yes. We have lived many lifetimes and have learned many lessons."

"In this lifetime I have learned the importance of tolerance and what happens when you refuse to accept others for who they are and what they believed," the pastor said.

"It was a lesson with a big price."

"Yes and I have the next 20 years to remember it. By the time I leave here, if I leave here, I will be an old man. When I die, whether it is inside this prison or after I am released, I hope I do remember you. I would like to be your friend."

"If that's what you ask for, that's what you shall receive. Our experiences are ours to have. We get to choose the lives we live and the lessons we learn."

"Will I see you again before then?"

"From time to time I'll return to visit you in your dreams."

"I'll look forward to the next time."

"Goodbye William."

As William Blackmore found peace in his dreams, Donald Eldridge was terrified of what would happen to him before morning at the hands of his cellmate.

His cell was empty when he first went inside. For a short time he thought he would be left alone. Then he realized his worst nightmare was becoming reality as the inmate who'd taunted him in the holding cell and on the bus was placed in the tiny space with him.

"Well, well, well. Now isn't this just great. This is gonna be real cozy, huh fishy?"

Donald had never felt so frightened. He lost control of his bladder. The orange jumpsuit darkened as urine wet the front of it and down his legs.

"Oh fuck. Look at this. Clean yourself up. I don't want to smell stale piss."

Wetting himself gave him a reprieve from the torture he was soon to experience at the hands of the man who would rape him repeatedly over the coming months.

He was experiencing hell on earth in this small cell and Satan was a 280 pound, heavily pierced and tattooed violent rapist.

Donald Eldridge couldn't stand the idea of spending the rest of his life in a cell with this rapist or another.

Six months into his sentence he made a decision that gave him more peace than he'd had in years.

After his cellmate had raped him one night and went to sleep, he took his bed sheet and fashioned it into a noose. He got on his knees and then put the twisted bed sheet around his neck. The other end was tied to a bedpost on the opposite side of the bed, with the rope spanning the width of the bed between the mattress and box spring. He leaned forward. Within a minute he lost consciousness and the life drained from his body and he continued to suffocate.

His spirit saw his limp body dangling from the bed sheet. This wasn't the death he'd expected. This wasn't the place he thought his life would end.

Despite the violence of his death, his spirit was at peace. Ending his life was the only way he would be free of the torment he'd experienced and inflicted on his wife, his children and the others.

"Hello Donald."

The spirit that was Father Ryan was standing next to the cell doors.

"Why are you here?"

"To show you the way home."

"I should be going to hell after what I have done."

"There's no such place."

"That's not what I was told."

"You were misinformed."

The hell you experienced was in this cell carried out by the evil in that man," Father Ryan said pointing to the snoring man on the cot at the other side of the room.

"You chose the life you had before you were born so you could learn lessons and help others learn the things they came to earth to understand."

"Where are we going?"

"Home."

"Will I will be welcome there?"

"Of course. All of us are. There'll be a celebration when we get there. There will also be a review of the things you have done with your lifetime here."

"Then what will happen?"

"Then you will decide whether you will remain or return here once more in a new body and have a new life with new experiences."

"If I choose to come again will you be there?"

"Yes, but you won't know me."

"Will I be a better man than I was this time?"

"That's up to you. And, you might decide to return as female. It's all your choice. Choose to return or choose to stay in heaven. It's all up to you. Come on. It's time to leave."

"I am sorry I shot you and that you died."

"Don't you remember that's the agreement we made before we came to earth this last time?"

"Oh, yes. I do remember now."

Soon they were in the tunnel walking toward the bright light and the large wooden door. They opened it and walked through.

A large group of souls were gathered waiting to welcome them home.

"That was a quite a journey you had," a benevolent voice said to Donald's spirit.

"I was a bad man then."

"Yes, but you have lived other lives when you were kind, generous and the victim of others who were evil. Have you had enough or do you wish to go back again?"

"Perhaps I will return again for another adventure but for now I want to be here with all of you. Will Susan and the children be okay?"

"Of course they will. They will continue on the journey they said they wanted to take."

Heaven knows Susan, Raven and Rowen would flourish in the years to come.

Rowan and Raven, who were taken into foster care while their mother was hospitalized, were thrilled when they were reunited with her as well as Beth and Preshea as soon as they were discharged from the hospital.

Six months after they were taken hostage, their physical wounds had healed but all of them were still grieving the loss of Father Ryan and, with everything he'd done, Susan and the kids were still traumatized by the horrors of life with the monster they'd called husband and father. They grieved. Not for him but for not experiencing the love they should have received from him.

They as well as Beth and Preshea were still working on healing their deep emotional wounds.

They took comfort in knowing Pastor Blackmore would spend the next 20 years in prison for inciting their friend's murder as well as for their forcible confinement and torture.

The horrific things done that day stayed with the members of First Pentecostal Church too. Most, disillusioned by the behavior of a church elder and their pastor, quit the church and searched for spiritual answers elsewhere. They wanted to make sense of it all.

How could men who claimed to be Godly do this? This wasn't of God. The torture of women and the murder of a priest were evil in its truest sense.

Many sought out Susan, Beth and Preshea. They wanted to see the resilience of those who'd come so close to death. Despite the cruelty of others, they were able to carry on with their lives and were starting to help others recover from their own traumatic experiences.

One morning, as they were preparing to go to the store, the phone rang. It was a lawyer. He needed to meet with them.

"I have some news that will change your lives. I think you will want to hear it as soon as possible."

Preshea hung up the phone. "I wonder what that's all about."

26

The lawyer agreed to meet them at Circe's Closet that afternoon.

When he arrived, Beth, Susan and Preshea were decorating the store for the holidays. He asked if they could sit somewhere to discuss the news he had for them.

Beth placed the closed sign in the store window and locked the door. They went into the back office and sat down. Preshea, Beth and Susan had no idea their lives were about to take another unexpected turn for the second time in six months. This time, however, it would be welcome.

The lawyer opened his briefcase.

"I won't take up too much of your time today. We will need to meet again to sort out the fine details."

"Sort out the fine details of what?"

"Your friend, Father Ryan, was my client. As you know he was the spiritual leader of *Friends Along the Way*. What you don't know is his home in the mountains has been left, in trust, to all three of you."

The three women were speechless. None of them knew how to respond to the news. Finally Preshea managed to ask: "Why would he do that?"

"Father Ryan had no heirs. In his will he describes you as his soul sisters and the only people he could think of that would be able to take the property and put it to good use."

Preshea had visited Father Ryan at his home many times and she knew how spectacular the 30 acres of pristine, mountain wilderness were.

"What would we possibly do with it?"

"I have a letter he wrote explaining his vision for it and what you could do with it if you agree to take it on."

The lawyer handed an envelope to Preshea.

She opened the letter and read it aloud. She had to stop several times to gain her composure as she read it.

My dearest soul sisters

As I have explained to all of you, we are connected and always have been from one lifetime to another. We have helped one another learn the lessons we came to earth to learn. I thank you all for the experiences I shared with you while I was with you there.

As you know, I own a large area of land in the mountains. It was my sanctuary from the business of life. It was where I experienced some of the most profound and spiritually gratifying times of my life.

I always thought that it would make a wonderful retreat for those broken, hurting souls who need respite and renewal. When the three of you came together I knew what could happen if you were willing to take on the challenge of running the place.

The three of you have all of the requirements needed to do this work. Susan you have a masters degree in psychology. I have already told my staff at the clinic I want you to work there. I suggest you do work there and also at the retreat. Beth, before you came back from Botswana, you were working with your husband in naturopathic medicine. Would you consider taking up the medical responsibilities at the retreat?

Preshea, I know you have the store but, would you consider selling it and becoming the retreat's manager?

Together my friends, you have all of the skills needed to make it a success. There are so many people desperate for emotional, physical and spiritual healing this retreat can give.

And don't worry about the money it will take to run the place. This old priest has the luck of the Irish. I never had need of much in my life. I never spent a lot of money. I invested my earnings and those investments have paid well. The money is to be left, in trust, for the running of the retreat.

So what do you say my wonderful soul sisters? Are you ready for a new adventure? Say yes. Tell Rowan and Raven I will expect them to get involved. Teen retreats would be a great idea wouldn't they?

And be sure I will be with you in spirit, cheering you all on as you continue along your journeys until we meet again. Blessings to all of you whatever you decide. May the good Lord continue to hold you gently in the palm of her hand.

Namaste,

Father Ryan

Preshea folded the letter and wiped the tears from her eyes.

"What a kind, loving and generous man. Well gals, what do you think? Are you interested in running a retreat house?"

Beth was smiling. Ever since she had returned to the states from Botswana, following the deaths of her husband and her mother, she'd felt adrift. She had enjoyed working at Circe's Closet but she knew her calling was helping heal the sick and wounded.

"I still have my naturopathic physician's licence. I miss practicing medicine."

Susan was excited at the idea of working at the clinic and also helping with counselling sessions at a retreat.

"I have never worked before. I will need to do some upgrading with some refresher classes but I am up for the challenge if you both are."

Preshea looked at Beth and Susan and smiled.

"There are no coincidences in life. I believe we were brought together for this very purpose. Let's do it!"

Preshea looked at the lawyer and asked when they would be able to begin.

"As soon as you sign the legal documents and receive the deed and keys to the property. I see no reason for anything to stop you. I'll be in touch soon."

The women said so long to the lawyer and reopened the shop. While they waited on customers they kept thinking about the future and the work ahead.

That night they celebrated over supper with the kids at Preshea's home.

Raven and Rowan were full of questions.

"Where will we live? The retreat house is over an hour away."

Susan had thought about that too. She was going to start work at the clinic soon and wouldn't be able to make the commute daily. Preshea had a plan.

"What if you continue to live here? That way the kids can finish high school and you can work at the clinic and then come to the retreat on the weekends and whenever else works for your schedules? I don't want to sell the house. You would be doing me a favor by staying here while I am managing the retreat house which, I expect, will be a 24-7 thing."

Susan placed her hand on Preshea's and gave it a squeeze. After Donald had gone to prison she could have returned to their house but it had too many bad memories. Instead she rented it, which helped her and the kids financially. After he took his life she decided to sell it and most of their furnishings.

"That is a great idea," she said trying hard not to start crying. So much had changed in such a short time. She was no longer the abused woman living under the fist of the monster she'd married or the woman who was held hostage by the manacles of a religion that considered women second-class souls.

They celebrated the holidays together in Preshea's old Victorian home. By March all of the legal requirements for the retreat had been fulfilled and the lawyer handed them the deed and the keys. The next weekend Preshea, Beth, Susan and the kids made the drive up into the mountains for their first overnight stay at their new place.

Rowan saw the sign over the door.

"Hey what does ***Chomh fada sin o bhaile, thar a bheith fada o bhaile*** mean?"

Preshea looked up at the sign that was swinging back and forth in the wind.

277

"Father Ryan told me once. Let me think. Ah, yes. It means something like *Such a long way from home*."

They all stood in awe of the view from their elevation. It was breathtaking. With 30 acres of forested trails and a babbling brook some 500 feet below, there was no question this was a perfect place for people to come to find peace in an otherwise chaotic world.

The lawyer had explained the property had been cared for over the past six months by a local man who'd known Father Ryan since he'd first arrived 30 years earlier when he'd moved from Kenya.

The caretaker arrived later that afternoon to introduce himself to everyone.

"I'm Mark Cullen. I knew Father Ryan most of my life. I must have been about your age when he first arrived here. He was a friend and a mentor. I miss him."

"Yes, it's not the same for any of us now that he's gone," Preshea acknowledged.

"I'm Preshea. This is Susan and her son and daughter Rowan and Raven. And this is Beth Williams."

Beth and Mark stared at one another as they shook hands.

They both felt the warm surge of energy between them and a deep-seeded sense they had known one another many times before. Beth blushed and removed her hand from his. Why did his eyes stir up so much emotion?

He felt the same. Father Ryan had taught him about past lives and the connections people have with one another from one lifetime to the next. He had gone through past-life regression hypnosis.

He knew once he was a blacksmith who'd died after an accident. Maybe someday he would work up the nerve to ask if she knew about reincarnation. Whatever their relationship, in another lifetime, he felt an attraction to this woman he hoped was mutual.

A loud and deep bark brought him out of his daydreaming about Beth Williams.

"Oh, I forgot about Mungar; just a second. I have to let the dog out of the truck."

The teens followed and laughed as they saw the large hairy grey dog bounding from the truck and wagging his large tail.

"Mungar! You're here!"

"You know this fella?"

"Oh yeah. Father Ryan used to bring him to town with him sometimes. Mungar's great," Rowan said as he threw a large stick.

"Fetch boy!"

Beth had a vague memory of the day they'd been taken hostage and beaten. Father Ryan and Mungar had run into the warehouse to rescue them.

"Mungar came to live with me after Father Ryan died. The police said that even though he'd attacked the shooter he was not euthanized because he was acting in defence of his owner. Mungar is a lovely, loyal dog. I believe he misses Father Ryan as much as we do."

"Mungar is a strange name. Do you know what it means?"

Mark scratched Mungar's back, which caused his big tail to swish back and forth.

"It's Gaelic and it means *Beloved* and you are, aren't you fella? Mungar is a great friend who keeps me company up here where the nearest neighbors are bobcats and bears."

Preshea, who'd gone into the retreat house to have a quick look around, was back and starting to unload their suitcases.

Mark helped carry in their bags.

"It sure is nice to have you all here. It's been lonely since Father Ryan's been gone."

Preshea looked at the tall man with the dark hair and blue eyes who was staring at Beth. She was blushing like a schoolgirl. '*You two won't likely be lonely for long,* she thought but said nothing about the sparks that were obviously flying between the two.

In the weeks and months to come Mark and Beth discovered the truth about their soul connection as they gave in to the attraction they felt for each other.

By May the first guests arrived. The main house housed six guests and, with Mark's help, six guest cottages had been built on the property overlooking the valley below.

"Welcome everyone to the first *Friends Along the Way* retreat," Preshea said as she introduced herself, Beth, Susan, the twins and Mark.

"This weekend you will experience many things. The first rule here is there are no rules. All we ask is that you relax and simply be yourself while others do the same.

This is a place where there are no judgements or criticisms. It's a place where all faiths are welcomed and where you're free to reconnect with your spiritual selves.

Feel free to walk the nature trails or sit in silent meditation. Supper will be served at 5:30.

If you feel like joining us, we'll be having a celebration of Beltane in honor of our ancestor beginning at sunset.

After a large meal, prepared by Preshea, Beth and Susan, everyone gathered outside around a large fire Mark had lit in the courtyard.

Preshea raised her arms and said, "We celebrate this ancient Celtic fire festival which is also a time of abundant fertility and the start of the summer growing season."

The assembled walked around the flames. They danced around the flames.

Then, they jumped over the embers all in prayer for the planet, for peace and for the refreshment of their souls in a world which drains positive energy with its darkness.

Holding hands, those who stood in the circle recited blessings. Preshea led the prayers:

"Blessed be the longing that brought you here and quickens your heart and soul with wonder and merriment. May you have the courage to answer the call of the longing within you; may you seek and find the answers to the question 'Who am I?' May your soul be free and open to accept the calling of your gifts. May you have the courage to follow your path. May your outer dignity reflect your inner strength. May you see the miracle of each day as a gift; may the light of your soul guide you and may the spirit of the white light protect you from darkness. Blessed be."

"Blessed be," the circle of women replied.

Epilogue

The spirit that had lived many lifetimes both as a man and a woman, as a fighter and a person of peace, knew it was time to return to earth to learn the lessons that could only come through mortality.

The spirit formerly known as Father John Ryan, among many other incarnations, wanted to come back to earth once more. This time the spirit reincarnated as a baby boy born to a Catholic family in 1505 in Northern Ireland to the start of the time when there would be much violence, repression and heartache all in the name of God.

"It will be a violent existence. You will suffer greatly," a benevolent voice said.

"Yes."

"Why to this time? What do you want to learn?"

"I want to understand feeling of domination, repression and the fight for freedom."

"You won't be in the body long."

"No. But in the time there is I shall come to know what there is to be gained."

"You will understand what it is to feel hunger, cold, pain; things unknown by us."

"Yes."

"Are you ready to go now?"

"Yes."

"Have you chosen the mother that will carry you?"

"Yes. Her name is Sorcha Fitzgerald who is wed to Tomas Giolla Dhubh."

"What will they call you?"

"Fergus Mac Giolla Dhubh."

"They are farmers who are devoted to their faith. Like their clansmen, they will fight the invaders with everything they have. You'll stand next to your father and brothers in battle. It will be a life of suffering but you have experienced this in the both giving and receiving of pain many times before."

"Yes."

"Are you ready to go?"

"I am."

"We will be here to welcome you on your return as we always are."

"Thank you. Despite the difficulties, I am looking forward to this experience. I wish to remember everything from my past lives."

"You shall but it will cause you no end of troubles."

"I am prepared for it."

"You will need to be," the benevolent voice said.

To be continued...

You've read the story, now have the experience.

Rediscover your divine feminine self and connect with your tribe of soul sisters at a Coven of the Soul Sisters event lead by best-selling author Laverne Stewart and her tribe of soul sisters as they share their wisdom with healing herbs, stones and crystals, meditation and more.

To book a Coven of the Soul Sisters event, or to order Coven of the Soul Sisters merchandise, please go to www.covenofthesoulsistersbook.com Ms. Stewart can be contacted by email at lavernestewartauthor@gmail.com or Covenofthesoulssisters@gmail.com

Coming soon... *Father of the Soul Sisters.*

This is the second in the Coven of the Soul Sisters series. Travel back in time to the 1500s when the reincarnated versions of the soul sisters and Father Ryan once again find themselves struggling under religious persecution, trials and executions during the reformation of the church as King Henry VIII imposes his will and the Protestant faith in 1537.

Will they manage to survive? Or will they perish like thousands of their Celtic sisters and brothers as they hold fast to ancient ways struggling to exist as religion and politics create rivers of blood, misery and death?

About The Author:

Laverne Stewart, critically acclaimed best-selling author of non-fiction books *Angels and the Afterlife*, and, *Healing After Homicide – The Jackie Clark Story* (Manor House), captivated readers with the release of her remarkable first fiction offering – *Haunted Heart* (Manor House), a gripping novel of tragic romance and ghostly encounters. Now she's released her second novel, the critically acclaimed *Coven of the Soul Sisters*.

Very much at home in both fiction and non-fiction genres, Laverne Stewart has continued her exploration of the supernatural with coven. It's all a natural progression for Laverne Stewart, who has been putting thoughts to paper as long as she's been able to hold a pencil. She knew in high school that a writing career was her life's ambition.

Laverne Stewart is also a 30-year journalism veteran. After a year as a radio news anchor she made the move to television. She spent 11 years with CTV as a news magazine investigative reporter before she made the leap to print journalism before retiring to devote her time to writing books. She's an award-winning journalist and author. *Coven* is her fourth book (and her third published by Manor House).

When she's not writing about the gritty reality of life in this world she is making contact with those in the afterlife. Her first book, *Angels and the Afterlife*, opened the door to *Healing After Homicide*, and gave inspiration to *Haunted Heart* and *Coven*.

Laverne Stewart loves spending time with her husband, their two children, and the family's dog and cat at their lakeside New Brunswick home.

Coven of the Soul Sisters / Laverne Stewart

Manor House

905-648-2193